MICHELLE LYNN ROSS

Small Town Famous

FAWN
CREEK
PRESS

To the people in my hometown. Thanks for always being there to support me.
I hope you love this story as much as the last.

Acknowledgments

Well, I can't believe I managed to finish another book.

First off, thank you to my husband and kids for your patience while I wrote and rewrote this story fifty 'leven times.

I want to thank Jones Novel Editing for her help with bringing this story to life.

And a huge thank you to my community. The outpouring of support for me and my silly little stories still blows me away. Small towns really are better than they get credit for.

And lastly, thank you to you, the readers, for reading my stories! I hope you love Avery's story as much as I do!

Chapter 1

I stand under the wooden arbor and watch as my best friend makes her way down the aisle towards us. I don't believe I've seen her more beautiful. Not because of the dress or the makeup or the hair, but because of the genuine look of happiness spread across her face. I've waited for what seems like a lifetime to see her genuinely happy, and it fills my heart with joy to finally witness it.

Tyler and I have been best friends since kindergarten and I've seen her through it all. Not once, however, do I recall there ever being a time in the last twenty-three years that I've ever seen her this at peace with her life. For years, it appeared she was constantly searching for the right place or person to make her life complete. Today, as she makes her way down the aisle to Andrew, it's plain to see that she's finally found the one she's been searching for all this time. And I'm so thankful that I get to be here watching her vow to spend the rest of her life with her soulmate. There's no doubt at all that Tyler has finally found her missing piece.

But even in my excitement for my dear friend, I admit that I feel a pinch of jealousy myself. Last May, Tyler moved back home to Fawn Creek after a she and her long term boyfriend broke up. Tyler left Fawn Creek just after high school graduation and for ten years, she stayed gone. Sure, we still talked on the phone weekly and visited one another when possible, but I missed her. So, when she told me she was moving back, I was ecstatic. For the first time since we were teenagers we would have a summer together. A summer when we were both single and our only responsibilities were our jobs and my baby. However, as always, summer came to an end. Autumn came in and brought a new life for Tyler. A life with her new husband and her new business.

And now, here I am, on the sidelines, still right where I've always been. I'm still working fifty hours a week at a job that would replace me in an instant. I'm raising my daughter, mostly alone, unless of course you count my ex future mother-in-law. And my love life? Non-existent, thanks to my overbearing and controlling ex-fiance. I couldn't even consider getting into a relationship as long as he's around. I truly believe that Cory lives to make my life miserable. So instead, here I remain in concrete shoes, watching as the rest of the world moves forward.

"I now pronounce you man and wife. Andrew, you may kiss your bride." Cassidy's words break through my thoughts and snap me back to reality. I watch as my best friend leans in to kiss her husband and they make their way back up the aisle.

I quickly swallow down the ache building in my chest. This is no time for a pity party, instead I need to make myself useful. I make my way towards Lisa, Tyler's Mom, who is busily setting up the buffet area for dinner. She has no problem immediately assigning me a task of my own. I'm so focused on making sure all the condiments are perfectly arranged that I don't notice Tyler approach me until she's wrapped me in a hug.

"We did it." She says triumphantly. "I still can't believe we were able to pull off such a perfect day in such a small amount of time. Thank you for all your help."

Just six weeks ago, Tyler and Andrew got engaged, right here on the site of their future home. Even though they only planned to have an intimate family wedding, I knew pulling off the type of event she deserved would be quite a task. Somehow, however, we nailed it. Mostly thanks to the people of Fawn Creek. The community really came together to make Tyler's vision a reality. Even though they knew they wouldn't be invited to enjoy the event, because it was simply a family affair, that didn't stop the outpouring of support. The church was happy to lend out tables and chairs. The bakery had no problem squeezing in a request for a last-minute cake. Even the local flower shop gave her a great deal on the bouquets. Not to mention, our sweet coffee shop owner, Cassidy, was happy to come and officiate the ceremony. As usual, our tiny town came together to save the day.

"It really was perfect." I agree. "And you look beautiful. I'm so happy for you, Ty. No one in the world deserves this more than you do."

Just then, Lisa interrupts our moment. "Hey Avery. Would you mind going into the camper and grabbing the paper plates and napkins? I forgot to bring them out with me."

"Sure! Be right back." I say before turning on my heel and quickly making my way around the side of Andrew and Tyler's future home. Within seconds, I'm entering Andrew's tiny camper that's parked alongside the house. I eyeball the mismatched brown metal panels and rickety wood steps as I approach the trailer. I still find it hard to believe Andrew was living in this place at one time. He bought this old camper from a friend and parked it on this property after he and his brother

3

Cody purchased the land. His plan was to live in it until he could build his future home.

Thankfully, after he and Tyler got engaged, she encouraged him to move into her house instead while they wait for their house to be built. Just in the nick of time, too, winter weather is fast approaching. Thankfully, today we have the perfect weather for an outdoor wedding, but it won't last for long. A cold and bitter Kansas winter is surely just around the corner.

I carefully step inside the trailer and turn on an overhead light before beginning the hunt for the needed tableware. Since no one has been living here for months now, the camper has turned into a bit of a storage unit for wedding supplies. At least it's getting some type of use, I suppose.

I open a blue plastic tote that is sitting on the dinette table and begin to dig through it. Just then, the sound of the old metal camper door creaking open causes me to jump. I turn towards the noise to find my friend Derek standing behind me.

"Hey you." I say, smiling once our eyes meet.

Derek and I have known each other for years now. We technically met in high school, but we always ran in different circles. However, once we both hit our early twenties, our circles seemed to merge into one. Suddenly, my friend group consisted of an eclectic mix of all the young adults that hung around Fawn Creek after graduation, instead of going out to search for new lives or to attend college. I took a job in the next town over at a call center. Derek opted to become a police officer right here in our hometown. Over time, we've grown closer and he is usually the first person I call when I need help.

"Hey. I just wanted to see if you need help carrying anything." He says, with what's almost a nervous expression on his face.

"You just can't help coming to my rescue, can you?" I tease

4

him as he closes the door and leans against the countertop behind him.

He chuckles and shakes his head. "Anything I can do to get away from all the parents out there asking when I'm going to finally settle down with a nice girl of my own."

"Well, it's a legitimate question, Derek. When will you?"

He chuckles softly. "I wish I knew, Avery. If only so I can tell the paparazzi out back."

I shake my head. "They sure can't help but stick their noses in everyone else's business, can they? Well, I guess if you're here, you might as well make yourself useful." I turn and hand him a wholesale sized package of paper plates. I pick up the matching package of napkins for me to carry. "We better get back out there."

I lead Derek out of the camper and back towards the party. As soon as we round the corner towards the patio, Tyler spots us and quickly rushes over in our direction.

"Hey. There you are." She says, eyeing Derek and me suspiciously, as if we were gone for hours.

"We're about to do the bouquet toss." She tells me.

I pause and look around at the wedding guests. The attendees consist of Tyler's parents, Andrew, Cody, Sierra, my mom, my daughter, and Derek. Cassidy left as soon as the ceremony was over in order to get up bright and early tomorrow morning and open her coffee shop.

"My mom and I are the only single women here." I observe with a raised brow, adding my napkins to what Derek is already carrying before turning back to Tyler. He takes the hint and continues his journey back towards Lisa.

A smirk spreads across Tyler's face. "I think you can out muscle her. She's getting kinda old."

5

I roll my eyes and sternly shake my head. "Tyler, this is silly."

She simply shrugs. "I don't care, it's tradition. Follow me." She says, turning on her heel and heading towards the center of the patio that is being used as a dance floor this evening.

I step quickly to stay close beside her. "Since when do you care about tradition?" I ask, wrapping my arm through hers.

"Since it's my wedding day." She says, stopping and turning around to face me. "Besides, it's time for you to have a happily ever after, too. We're going to do everything we can to make it happen. Now stand here and catch this damn bouquet." She commands, before turning and marching towards the edge of the patio.

The sound of my mother's high heels on the concrete as she approaches causes me to turn towards her. She stops about five feet behind me and stands dutifully, waiting for the game to begin.

I frown and send her a look before motioning for her to join me where I stand. "Don't look at me. I don't want a husband." She laughs with a shake of her head. "I don't want to even take a chance at catching that thing."

I make a big show of rolling my eyes and then turn back to face the rest of the crowd. If this was for anyone else, or anywhere else. I'd walk away right now and hide in a bathroom until this was over. However, this is for Tyler, so here I'll stand, mortified and do as she asked.

"Single Ladies" by Beyoncé begins to play through the massive outdoor speakers as I stand awkwardly in front of the rest of the wedding guests, bracing myself. Finally, Tyler turns around and hurls the bouquet right towards me. I raise a hand and catch the flowers with little to no effort. In a display of false triumph, I wave the bouquet of white lilies and sunflowers above my head before making my way towards the rest of the wedding party at our table.

As I approach, I hear Andrew let out a deep laugh as he elbows Derek in the rib. "You're next, buddy." I hear him mutter.

* * *

"Well, that was quite an evening." I say, kicking off my heels at the front door of my house while Derek follows behind me carrying a stack of leftover food containers. Tyler's wedding went off without a hitch. My best friend and her new husband are on their way to their honeymoon in Mexico, and the rest of us were sent home with the leftover food. As usual, Tyler's mom cooked for eight times as many people as Tyler invited.

"I'm going to put Juliet in bed if you want to throw that stuff in the kitchen. I'll be right back. Feel free to stay for a little while if you want to." I say, before turning to make my way up the stairs.

"I can hang out for a bit." He says, carrying the leaning tower of Styrofoam towards the kitchen.

Apparently, the night filled with dancing and eating wore my toddler out more than I expected. I barely have her changed into her footie pajamas and laid down in her crib before she's out like a light.

When I enter the living room again, Derek is waiting for me on the couch with a plate of food and two glasses of wine on the coffee table in front of him. The plate is filled with leftovers from the wedding; cheese, crackers, sausage and grapes.

"I made us a little snack." He explains. "What do they

call this? A shark coochie board?" He asks while somehow maintaining a straight face.

I groan before correcting him. "A charcuterie board."

"Whatever... it's just a fancy Lunchables." He decides with a shrug.

"Whatever you call it, it's one of my favorite meals." I admit, picking up a piece of cheese from the plate and tossing it into my mouth.

"So, tonight was interesting." Derek says, picking up a grape and biting into it.

"You can say that again. I can't believe she made me catch the bouquet. Freaking embarrassing." I say, shaking my head. I don't mention Andrew elbowing him as though to allude that the two of us are going to end up together. Derek and I have been friends for years, but it seems more often than not lately, our friends get way too much joy out of teasing me. I do, however, wonder if they do the same to him.

"It was quite the experience." Derek agrees with a laugh, downing his wine glass. "What about Tyler's dads dance moves? I thought I was going to have call EMS for him when he started the funky chicken."

"I don't know. Ever since his heart attack he has been exercising like crazy. I bet he's more in shape that I am." I say with a laugh, as I turn on the TV and settle on an old episode of *The Office*. We settle into a comfortable silence as we snack and laugh along at the workplace antics.

As the closing credits begin to scroll across the screen, Derek checks his watch. "Okay, I better head home. I have to work tomorrow and Diesel probably misses me. He hasn't seen me all day."

Diesel is Derek's German Shepherd. Derek responded to call

at the dog pound two years ago, and while he was there, he met and subsequently fell in love with the adorable puppy. As soon as his shift ended that day, he went right back to the shelter and filed the paperwork to adopt him. They've been attached at the hip ever since. I have to admit, their relationship is pretty adorable.

"Okay, thanks for helping me get everything inside and for the company. I'll see you later."

"See ya," He echoes before making his way out the door and disappearing into the night.

* * *

My cell phone vibrating on my nightstand wakes me up the morning after the wedding. Unfortunately, it's from the last person I want to hear from, Cory.

Cory: So, are you finally ready to admit you're screwing the cop? I saw that his truck was in your driveway late last night.

I read the message and roll my eyes. When Cory and I were living in Owen together, I came home to visit my mom. Before I left town, I stopped to get gas and ran into Derek at the gas station. Our meeting was innocent, of course. We hugged hello as we always do when we've been apart for a while. I spoke to him for a few minutes and then we went our separate ways. However, by the time I got home, Cory had someone report back to him that I was seen hanging all over some man at the gas station. Cory basically demanded that I avoid Derek all together because he was supposedly out to ruin our relationship. As it turned out, Cory ruined it all on his own, by becoming a

9

controlling psychopath.

Obviously, Cory is still worried about Derek and I, although he has no right to be. *Awesome.* I'm glad he can't be bothered to move on, even though the two of us split up when I was pregnant with our daughter. She is now fifteen months old and enough time has passed that we should be able to at least co-exist.

Me: Derek and I are just friends. That's all we've ever been. There is nothing wrong with me hanging out with him and honestly, it's not your business.

Cory: My daughter is there, so that makes it my business.

I roll my eyes and toss my phone onto the bed. The only time Cory wants anything to do with Juliet is when he wants to hold her over my head. Leave it to him to ruin my day before I even step out of bed.

Chapter 2

"Well, what do you have going on today?" Madison asks, as she stands in my kitchen helping me sort through leftovers from the wedding. While it was nice of Tyler's mom to send me home with all the leftover food, there is no way Juliet and I can eat all of it before it goes bad. So, I called Madison to come over and take some off my hands. Madison runs a daycare center out of her home. She started her business so she could be home with her two girls, but it was also the perfect timing for her to take on Juliet after she was born. I couldn't picture my baby with anyone else.

I shake my head. "Not sure, actually. I think I might try looking around for a part-time job. Just something I can do every other weekend when Juliet's with her dad."

Madison frowns. "You already work so much. You'd think it would be more than enough to get you by. Could you ask for more child support?"

My eyes widen, and I shake my head quickly. "Hard pass. It is not worth fighting with Cory over money. I'd rather figure it out on my own. Honestly, we are doing fine, but I want more for us than to just squeak by. Maybe if I could just do something for long enough to pay off my car and build up my savings account, I would feel a lot better. I work so hard and feel like I have nothing to show for it."

Madison frowns. "Don't be so hard on yourself, friend. You're doing a great job. Juliet is obviously very well taken care of."

I offer her a half smile. "Thanks, I just have high expectations for myself. My mom raised my brother and me all on her own and I watched her struggle for my entire life. She always worked two or three jobs at a time and still never had much extra at the end of the month. I don't want the same for myself. Working away at a job just for the paycheck for the next forty years, while I miss out on everything that counts, sounds terrible. However, being a single mom doesn't give me a lot wiggle room either."

Madison finishes cutting up the last of the grapes and closes the lid on a plastic container. "So, what kind of part-time job are you looking for?"

"I'm not sure. Maybe waitressing or seeing if Cassidy needs help at the coffee shop." I say with a shrug. "Of course, that probably won't be enough to make a difference."

Madison's eyes widen and it's almost as though a light bulb lights up over her head. "I just had a great idea. Have you ever looked into content creation?"

I scrunch my nose. "Are you suggesting I become an Influencer? You know I'm almost thirty, right?"

"No, the term is content creator." She corrects me. "But, yeah. You have a great eye for fashion and you're like the DIY queen of Fawn Creek," she says, motioning around the kitchen that I painted and wallpapered upon moving in. "Besides, you are always posting the best foods and local events around here. People love to follow you on Facebook because of it. You might as well monetize your ability to influence people."

I frown. "I don't know, Madi. That seems like a stretch."

"Not really. I happened to notice that you already have a a a decent following on Tiktok."

"A direct effect of being stuck at home during shut down. Like everyone else, I got on there when I finally got tired of making banana bread and yes, I built up a following of a few thousand people. That doesn't mean I'll be able to just pick it back up and make a career out of it, though."

She frowns. "Why couldn't you, though? That's what other people do and you are just as capable of succeeding. You have a great eye for fashion and you can craft like it's no one's business. People would eat that stuff up. Then you could share links to things like clothes and home decor. When people buy what you share, you'll earn a commission from it."

"I don't know, Madi. Is there really any money in that kind of thing?"

She nods. "You'd be surprised. There are some people I follow online that make huge amounts of money from doing this kind of thing. Like quitting their jobs and retiring their husbands. I'm not brave enough to show my face on camera or I'd try it myself. But, you? I think you'd rock it."

"I guess it wouldn't hurt to look into it." I admit.

"It sure wouldn't. Maybe you could pay off your house and your car. Then with just monthly utilities, you could maybe find a job that would give you a little more freedom to spend time with Juliet.

"That itself sounds like a dream."

* * *

"Is that yummy?" I ask Juliet as she sits next to me in a wooden high chair at our favorite Mexican restaurant in downtown Fawn Creek. It's the Wednesday following Tyler's wedding and the last several nonstop days are finally catching up with me. So after work, we opted to walk downtown for dinner.

Currently, Juliet is eating rice mixed with queso by the handful and I am just enjoying the few spare moments to think straight.

"Mmmmm" Juliet hums in response, with her tiny fist clutched full of rice.

"Ohhh rice. Can I have a bite?" A man's voice pops out of nowhere from behind me. I don't even have to turn to look at him to confirm that it's Derek.

Juliet immediately erupts into a fit of giggles and holds her fist up in his direction. He leans forward and pretends to take a bite of her hand. I watch in awe at how much my baby adores my friend.

"Nom Nom Nom." He grumbles. "Thanks. That's yummy."

Juliet giggles again, wriggling all over in her seat.

I turn to face Derek, who is on duty and wearing his full police uniform this evening. "Hey you. What are you up to?" I ask.

"Just running in to pick up my to go order. It's not quite ready yet, so I thought I'd come say hi." He pauses. "So. Hi." He says with a cheesy grin. "What are you working on?" He asks, bending down to get a closer look at the notebook in front of me on the table.

"Well." I begin, sitting up higher in my seat. "I've been thinking about getting a part-time job. Madison threw out an idea that I should look into content creation, so I'm making a list of videos I can create, if I decide to go through with it."

Derek raises a brow. "The Fawn Creek Influencer." He says

with a chuckle. "That has a nice ring to it."

I let out a heavy sigh. "First off, the word Influencer makes me uncomfy. It just sound's cringy in my opinion. Content creator is more my speed. And I'm just considering it. Did you know there's a lot of money in it?"

"I guess I knew people made money doing it, but I wasn't sure how much."

My eyes widen. "A lot. If you're good at it." I sit back and shrug. "I just don't know for sure if I'll be good at it. It's going to take a lot of time and energy, which I have to admit I don't have a ton of. But, if I could pay off my car and maybe even my house, it would sure make my life easier."

Derek's eyes soften, and he squeezes my shoulder. "Avery, here's one thing I know for sure. If you put your mind to something, you are going to rock it every single time. I think if this is something you want to try, you should just go all in."

I frown. "Even though I know people are going to make fun of me for it? Especially if I fail?"

"Who cares?" Derek shrugs. "I'm sure you won't fail. I bet you'll get the last laugh when you are making bank and they are stuck working for someone else for the rest of their lives. I say you give it a shot. What is there to lose?"

* * *

After our dinner date, Juliet and I walk back home through Fawn Creek, taking in the quiet fall evening. The weather tonight is perfect, with just a slight breeze in the air that calls for nothing more than a sweater. I'm trying my best to enjoy it while it lasts. Before long, winter will come to Kansas and soon it'll be impossible to spend any time outside without the wind cutting right through you. I park Juliet's stroller on our screened in porch and punch in the key code for our front door. As soon as I'm inside, the zen feeling I had from walking through our tiny town is officially gone. Instead, the stress of my looming to do list takes over.

"Oh, Jules." I say with a sigh, as I place her on the living room floor among her toys. "How does this house get so messy? It's just the two of us and we're pretty much never here during the week."

Juliet babbles something that I don't quite understand before moving towards the bookshelf and getting to work at throwing her toys on the floor.

"Oh, I see. Carry on, then." I say, shaking my head before making my way towards the kitchen. I unload and reload the dishwasher before making my way to the laundry room and returning with a laundry basket full of clothes. Then, I plop down on the sofa and turn on the television, looking for something to fill the silence while I fold. Finally, I settle on a cartoon, knowing it'll at least hold Juliet's attention for a bit while I attempt to catch up on housework.

As I fold clothes and put them away upstairs, I can't stop thinking about my part-time job situation. Sure, I could look into something like waiting tables, or seeing if Cassidy needs help at Drip, or if Tyler wants help at the bookstore. Still, I could really only do those jobs on the weekends while Juliet is gone. That will only give me four days a month to work on making extra money. At that rate, I could make an extra thousand dollars over the course of five years. However, if I do this content creation thing, I could work on it whenever I have spare time.

What if, just maybe, I can find a way to make this work?

* * *

"Ugh. Bless you, woman. I missed Cassidy's coffee so much." Tyler gushes, taking a long sip of the iced cold brew latte I delivered to her at work. "Thank you for this."

"Oh, I doubt you missed it that much." I wave her off. "You just spent a week drinking poolside margaritas and eating tacos. That's basically my dream life."

"I definitely had my fair share of fruity drinks, but I can't explain it." She shrugs. "Nothing compares to Cassidy's lattes. She has it down to a science. Or they are full of drugs. Either way, I'm hooked."

Tyler just got home yesterday from her honeymoon in Mexico. This morning, I wasted no time meeting her at the bookstore to catch up. I spent the entire week trying my best to avoid bothering her so she could enjoy a real vacation with her husband. Now that she's back, though, all bets are off. I need someone to discuss this whole Influencer thing with. Especially, someone who will tell me exactly what I need to hear, not just what I want to hear. That's something I can always count on my best friend for.

"Well, now that I have you sufficiently caffeinated. I need to get your advice on something."

She quickly perks up. "Is this about Derek? Are you finally going to hook up with him?"

"No!" I exclaim, quickly shaking my head. "Derek and I are just friends. That's all we've ever been. And it's all we will ever be. I wish you would find something new to obsess over."

"Meh, my money is still on the fact that you two will end up together eventually." She predicts. "You can tell by the way he looks at you he is interested in more than being just friends."

I frown. "Can we please get this back on track?"

"Yes. Go ahead."

"Anyway. I've been thinking lately that I need to pick up a part-time job. Just a little something to do on the weekends so I can bring in some extra cash."

Tyler frowns. "You would sure think that with as much as you work already, you'd be more than good."

"I make decent money, but being a single mom is harder than I ever thought it would be. It would be nice if I could get rid of my car payment. If I'm really dreaming big, I'd like to pay off my house, too. Or at least get on track to pay it off early." I confess.

"You could sell pictures of your feet." She suggests, taking another sip of her coffee. "I hear that's a legitimate thing."

"No." I shake my head. "That's just the gateway to being a porn star. Madison suggested I try content creation."

"You're going to be an Influencer? Like one of those twenty-year-olds on Instagram?" Tyler raises a brow. "I saw one of those in Mexico on our trip. She was posing in the pool in her tiny bikini, making her boyfriend take like thirty thousand pictures of her. It was... pretty cringy."

I laugh, picturing Andrew and Tyler watching this pool scene with disgusted looks on their faces. "Yes, and no. I've done some research over the past week and it turns out there are all kinds of content creators out there. Not just hot twenty-year-olds. Actually, tons of moms that are our age do this and make decent money. You just have to pick a niche and run with it."

"What would your niche be?"

18

"Fashion, thrifting, and DIY projects." I answer confidently. "And whatever else I can come up with. I'm not saying it's a guaranteed win, but it might be worth a shot. There's a lot of money to be made doing it. Like thousands of dollars a month worth if I do it right. Hell, if I could even bring in an extra five hundred dollars a month, that would be very helpful."

Tyler's eyes widen. "Well, what the heck are you waiting for, then? What do you have to lose?"

I frown. "My dignity? You know people are going to make fun of me for this and it's going to be so embarrassing if I fail. I'm a little worried that no one is going to be interested in what an almost thirty-year-old mom from Kansas has to say."

"You'll never know if you don't try. And screw what other people think. You know as well as I do that no one else's opinion of you matters. They aren't the ones paying your bills."

Chapter 3

I walk through the streets of Fawn Creek on my way home after my visit with Tyler, replaying our conversation in my mind.

Juliet is spending the weekend with her dad and her Grandma Susan. That means, for at least a couple of days, I can focus on catching my breath.

After Juliet was born, I immediately established custody and a visitation schedule, hoping I could beat Cory to the punch. Cory didn't even argue with my proposed custody agreement, which included visitation every other weekend. However, he wasn't exactly interested in taking care of a newborn all on his own, either. Truthfully, it appeared he would not exercise his parental rights at all until his mom stepped in.

It wasn't long before she approached me about taking Juliet every other weekend during Cory's scheduled parenting time. She said that Juliet could stay at her house and Cory could come spend time with her there. At first, I wasn't too excited about the idea. I mean, why should I have to share my baby? If her dad didn't want to see her, I would have been more than happy to be with her every second that I could. Especially since I work long hours during the week. However, after talking to my mom about it, she prompted me to try it out. She said that if she were in Susan's shoes, she would want the opportunity to see her grand baby, too. And it's not Susan's fault that her son is a crappy father.

Turns out, it was honestly one of the best decisions I've made as a mom. Letting Susan keep Juliet has been such a blessing for us both. Cory gets to spend time with his daughter within the walls of Susan's home. I can breathe easily while she's gone, knowing that she is being taken care of in a safe environment. And Susan gets to build a proper relationship with Juliet. It's worked out well for all of us.

At first, it wasn't easy. While Cory may not have been ecstatic to see Juliet, he used the pickup and drop-off times as a reason to see me, and more accurately, to harass me. If I had been in town doing much of anything at all, he would stand on Susan's doorstep at drop-off to rake me across the coals about it. He never missed an opportunity to tell me what a terrible mom I was every chance he got.

It happened one final time, just after we ran into each other at the downtown concert at Mayfest. He had been drinking too much, and apparently when he saw me two stepping in the street with a cowboy, he got jealous and cornered me. Tyler, Andrew, and Derek broke things up, sending Cory on his way home. However, a week later when I saw him at Susan's, all the feelings of anger he was harboring against me were waiting on the surface. As soon as Juliet was safely inside, he followed me back to my car and screamed at me about what a worthless mother I am.

Susan was able to diffuse the situation after threatening to call the police on him, but the damage was already done. She made it clear to him that day that he could no longer see me during pickup or drop-off times because it just creates too much drama. And luckily, he has listened to her. At least so far.

I'm not sure what I would do without Susan in my corner since the day Juliet was born.

I step into my front yard, just as I hear a vehicle making its way down the old brick street towards me. I turn and watch as Derek pulls into the driveway alongside my house and throws his extended cab pickup in park.

"Hey." I say, offering him a bright smile. "What's up?"

"What are you doing out and about this morning?" He asks, as he climbs from the truck cab and closes the door behind him. "I figured you'd sleep till noon since Juliet's not home."

I roll my eyes. "Tyler's home, so I walked downtown to have coffee with her and to catch up. I missed her while she was gone. Don't you work today?"

He turns and reaches into the back of his truck, pulling out a large cardboard box. "I do, but not until later. I bought you a gift, and it just got here, so I wanted to bring it over while I had a chance."

I cock my head to the side. "A gift? Is it my birthday?" I tease.

"Nope, your birthday is in February. This is a just because gift," He declares, as he follows me into the house. Once inside, he places the box down on my coffee table and proceeds to cut through the packing tape using his pocketknife.

"What is it?" I ask, peering over his shoulder as I take a seat next to him on the floor.

"This." He says, pulling the bubble wrap from the box and tossing it next to me. "Is to help you with your new side hustle."

I feel the confused expression wash across my face. "My side hustle?"

"It's a ring light. To help you become a famous Influencer." He says, proudly.

My eyes widen. "Well, this escalated quickly. Derek, I'm still not sure I can pull something like this off. I'm definitely not confident enough for you to be buying me gifts and getting your own hopes up."

Derek continues to busy himself with opening the box and assembling the gadget. "It wasn't that expensive." He assures me. "Besides, I've been doing some research and I think Madison is on to something. The moms that share DIY stuff and recipes have tons of followers. Some are making bank. You could totally do it."

"Derek, I don't have time to do this like the stay at home moms all over my feed. I still have to work fifty hours a week at my actual job and take care of Juliet. Plus, I really need to get better at housework."

Derek cuts me off, holding up a hand as though telling me to pause. "I told you, I did some research. There's this thing called batching content. What you do is you spend a day filming tons of videos. You can change clothes and do your hair differently after every handful of videos you make, then you will have plenty of stuff ready to post. Then, you just have to jump onto your social media accounts a few times a day and post them. You could batch content on the weekends when Juliet's gone and use it for the entire two weeks in between."

"Are you done?" I ask. I admit, though, I like that he has such high hopes for me. He's even more excited than I am.

"Are you convinced to give it a decent shot?"

I smirk. "Yeah. I mean, what do I have to lose?"

Derek grins. "Just don't forget me when you become famous."

* * *

"Well, here goes nothing." I say to no one in particular, as I finish making final edits to my first official piece of content. Derek left two hours ago, and I convinced myself that I have to at least try. I immediately got to work before I could talk myself out of it.

During the pandemic, I had no problem making silly lip syncing videos and posting them online. In fact, I had a lot of fun doing it and made quite a few internet friends along the way. However, now there is something vaguely terrifying about using short videos to teach others how to do things. What if no one thinks what I'm sharing is actually helpful? What if I make all of this content only to get no views? Eventually, people in town are going to find out what I'm doing. What if this never takes off and I become the laughingstock of Fawn Creek? But also, what if it works out? What if this is the key to financial stability? This could be the answer to how I will take care of myself and my daughter without having to rely on anyone else. All I can do is try.

I take a deep breath and hit the post button, sending my video off into the depths of the internet. The video I made today was an easy one. *Seven ways to wear a simple black blazer.* Of course, filming it wasn't that simple. Between planning my outfits, perfecting my lighting, and finding the right music to add to the video; a thirty-second piece of content took me nearly an hour to create. Now, I wait and see if anything happens and hope like hell that something does.

Admittedly, over the last week, while pondering this idea, I did a bit of research myself. Much to my surprise, I already had enough followers to qualify for affiliate links through Amazon. So, I seized the opportunity to create a quick free blog to share my fashion tips from. Now that I've posted my first piece of content, *Authentically Avery* is officially live.

I place my phone on the coffee table and look around my cramped living room. Weekends without Juliet are generally quite busy. There is never a lack of housework or errands I need to complete in order to play catch up while she's gone.

Today is no different, I must get to work instead of focusing on watching my view count. Otherwise, I'll drive myself crazy. I turn on a 90's hip-hop playlist, my favorite cleaning music, and get to work. With a promise to myself that I will not touch my phone until the downstairs of my house is spotless.

After an hour of cleaning, and lots of dancing to old school rap music, I plop down on the couch and reward myself by checking my notifications. First, I find a text from Madison.

Madison: You did it! I just saw you on my feed.
Me: Seriously? 😊 I just posted it a little bit ago.
Madison: You're up to 2,000 views already!

Quickly, I open the app and go directly to my profile. Not only is my video at over 2,500 views, but my follower count is steadily increasing as well. I already had three thousand followers earlier, but now my count is inching closer to five thousand. In a matter of an hour. Maybe this will work.

Madison: Please tell me you are working on more content.
Me: No, I was working on scrubbing my toilet. I guess I need to make some more content today.
Madison: Yes! Your adoring fans are waiting.

I spend the rest of my Saturday doing just that. Some videos are just of me lip syncing to trending audio. Some are more like the blazer video and another set of videos focus on business casual outfits for work.

Just as I'm finishing up a recording of my favorite black work pants, there's a knock at my door.

I run to answer and find Derek waiting on the other side, with a large Styrofoam to go cup in hand. "Hey. I just got off work. I thought you could use some caffeine. Marshmallow Dr. Pepper." He says with a grin, handing me the cup and a wrapped straw.

"My favorite. Thank you." I say, taking the cup from him. "And yes, I can always use caffeine."

"I checked your Tiktok earlier, and it looks like you are on fire."

I blush. "Well, I don't know if I would call it on fire. But, I have had a good day with views. I've been working on content for hours now. I'm actually just finishing up my last one for the night. That thing really came in handy today." I say, motioning towards the ring light. "Thank you, again."

"Good. Well, finish up and then we should go grab some burgers. I bet you haven't eaten all day."

I frown. "Guilty. I am hungry now that you mention it." My stomach growls as though to echo my sentiment.

"Okay, well, finish recording." He says, motioning towards my phone set up in front of the living room window.

I turn and make my way back towards the recording area, only to freeze when I look up to see Derek watching me. Suddenly, I can't remember what I was doing.

"What's wrong?"

"I... I can't do this in front of you." I admit.

He raises a brow. "Why not? I'm just going to see it on my

feed later."

"Yeah, I don't know. It's actually kind of embarrassing."

"Avery. You know I've held your hair for you to throw up, right? You don't have to be embarrassed around me."

"I know. That's the weirdest part." I say, shaking my head. "Can you just wait for me on the porch? I'll be done in like twenty seconds."

Derek frowns. "It's like forty degrees out there."

I deadpan. "I seriously can't do this in front of you. It's embarrassing and weird."

He huffs and places his hand on the doorknob. "Fine, but please hurry."

"I will. Oh, and Derek?"

"Yeah."

"Cover your ears. I don't want you to hear me either."

* * *

Tyler: I just bought that curling iron you shared online. I can't wait to try it.

I pick up my phone and read the message, and then read it once more to make sure I understand. It's been just a few days since I started my content creation journey and it has definitely started off strong. But, I wasn't expecting this.

Sure, I know I've had people buy things before based on my recommendations, when my friends has asked for fashion advice, but I've never been paid for it. However, over the weekend, I found I could promote items that I already own, and earn a commission from Tiktok. So, I made a quick video

27

with my favorite curling iron. When I finally got around to posting it this morning, I never assumed it would amount to anything.

Quickly, I open up the app and check my sales report. Sure enough, I've sold three.

Tyler: Now please make a video showing how to use it. I'm going to need help. Remember, I suck at being a girl.

Me: You got it. I'll let you know when it's up.

Quickly, I pull out my notebook and add the video to my list of content ideas. It looks like it'll be a long week of creating content after Juliet is in bed, but maybe it'll pay off.

By the time I'm getting off work for the day, I have checked my sales roughly 357 times. Every time I look, the number is higher. By the time I'm getting ready to pull out of the parking lot, I have sold fifteen curling irons. Surely this is just a dream, right?

I drive back to Fawn Creek and pull into Madison's driveway. Somehow, I resist the urge to check the app again before making my way up to the door to pick up Juliet.

"Hey." Madison says, holding the door open. "How was your day?"

"Wild." I say, plopping down on her sofa. Juliet spots me and immediately climbs into my lap. I tell her hello and then continue my conversation with Madison. "My head is still spinning."

"That bad, huh? Customer service is rough."

I shake my head. "No, actually, work was whatever. But I have a video blowing up."

"Oh, the curling iron! I saw that. You getting any sales?"

I pull out my phone and check the report. "Twenty. I've sold twenty since this morning."

"Well, that's crazy. How much are you making from those?"

"Ten dollars each," I say, widening my eyes, as the realization hits me.

"Hold on, so you've made two hundred dollars today off of a thirty-second video?"

"It appears so." I confirm.

"Girl! You really are going to make a killing at this!" she exclaims.

"Hopefully it's not a fluke."

"Only time will tell. But, I think you're on to something."

By the time Juliet and I make our way across Fawn Creek to our house, my phone is alerting me of more notifications. Unfortunately, this time they aren't any I want to see.

Cory: What do you think you're some big shot Influencer now?

Cory: You have to be kidding me.

Cory: You know no one cares what you have to say. You are just a mom from Kansas, Avery. You're no one.

I finish reading Cory's messages and roll my eyes. Of course, he would be the first one to rain on my parade. Part of me wants to screen shot my sales for the day and send them over to him. Or even my follower count. As of today, over ten thousand people care what I have to say. However, it's not worth it. Instead, I open every social media account I own, locate Cory's accounts, and block him.

* * *

"Man, I hate that guy," Tyler grumbles as she takes a seat on my sofa. She stopped by on her way home from work so I could show her how to use my curling iron. "I know he's Juliet's dad and I try so hard to respect him, but I can't. I want to hit him with my car. Just once."

"Believe me, you aren't the only one. There's just nothing I can do about it. I truly believe that this man lives to make my life miserable. And I'm stuck with him for the rest of my life. This is only going to get worse as Juliet gets older."

Tyler lets out a yawn. "Well, you can not let him run your life. You deserve to have everything you want in life, and you can't let him stop you."

"I have everything I want." I argue. "Honestly, I have my own house. A good job. My content creation gig is obviously doing well already. Cory isn't keeping me from anything."

"Oh, do you have a husband that you forgot to mention?"

I scowl. "No, I don't need a husband. I'm a strong, independent woman who can take care of herself."

"I never said you need someone to take care of you. However, I know you well enough to know that you don't want to be alone. You are my fun, extroverted friend who thrives off of being around other people. Being eternally single is not what you want, but thanks to Cory that's how you're living."

"Okay, maybe Cory makes that aspect of my life difficult." I confess. "But honestly, I don't need anyone else. I need to focus on myself. I'm going to work really hard to get my financial life in order, and maybe the right guy will come into my life when I'm ready."

"Or maybe he's already here." Tyler mutters.

Chapter 4

"Anyone here?" I call out as I walk through my mom's front door and make my way into the living room.

The style of my mother's house can be best described as bohemian. Every inch of her house is covered in bright crocheted quilts, plants, wicker furniture, macrame and flea market finds she has collected over the years. She swears that this style wasn't her intention. She and my father were simply too poor to buy anything new, so they built their home on hand-me-downs from friends and family. However, over time, she held onto the more bohemian touches and built her entire style around them. Especially after she and my father divorced, and she was free to decorate as she pleased. I tease my mom that she knew exactly what she was doing because deep down she is just an old hippie at heart.

"Avery, you made it." My mom sings out as she meets me in the living room and pulls me into a tight hug. "And you brought my favorite grand baby." She adds, scooping down to pick up Juliet and giving her a tight hug.

"This outfit is cute." I say, standing back to take in her look. She's wearing rust colored linen overalls with a black short-sleeve shirt. Her salt and pepper colored hair is shoulder length, and she's wearing it in loose waves. She has feather macrame earrings to complete the look.

"I'm just learning from my fashionista of a daughter." She teases. "I bought these overalls immediately after you shared them on your Instagram last week."

I blush. "Aw, thanks Mom. You look great in them." I say with a smile. I admit, I was shocked that I made an affiliate sale on the overalls, but I should have guessed it was from my mom. She is, after all, my biggest fan.

"There's my girl!" Bellows my brother, Bryan, as he enters the room.

For a second I pause, sending him a confused look until I realize he's talking about Juliet, not me. He quickly removes Juliet from my mother's arms and hugs her tightly.

"Um, hello. I'm here too." I say, furrowing my brows in a half-hearted attempt to appear angry.

"Yeah, whatever I've seen you for, like, thirty years now." Bryan says, waving me off. "I'm not impressed."

"Asshat." I mutter.

Bryan uses his hand to cover one of Juliet's ears and pulls her close to cover the other with his shoulder. "Don't cuss in front of the baby, asshole."

"That is enough of that." My mother chimes in, interrupting our sibling spat as though we are just a couple of kids. She moves towards Bryan and pulls Juliet from Bryan's embrace. "Let's go eat some Thanksgiving lunch." She tells my daughter, ignoring me and my brother.

Bryan steps towards me and pulls me into a hug, his beard scratches against my cheek, causing it to burn just a little. "Hi Sis. I guess it's good to see you, too."

"You must not have a girlfriend." I say, rubbing my cheek

33

as I pull away. "No respectable woman would put up with that crap on your face." I joke, as I lightly pull on his beard.

He strokes his beard gently and laughs. "The ladies like it just fine. Thank you very much."

"Please don't give me any details." I immediately say, holding up my hand. "I don't want to know about your sex life."

Bryan's face turns red, and he shakes his head at my remark before rolling his eyes. My brother joined the military as soon as he turned eighteen and he hasn't lived at home since. I was only eleven the day he left for Basic Training, and we have just enough of an age gap to keep us from ever having much of a real relationship. He's not quite used to my direct personality.

The most I really remember of him was the fact that he was a jerk teenager that picked on me and tried to boss me around all the time. In retrospect, I suppose I can see now that he was just trying to help mom in whatever way he could. Once our parents divorced, my dad was basically gone with the wind. He settled down somewhere in Missouri and made himself at home with a new family. Basically, he forgot all about us.

His leaving really took a toll on our mom. We tried to encourage her to get back out there and date, but she never did. At least not to the degree that it amounted to anything. So, it was just the three of us, until Bryan enlisted and left Fawn Creek.

I don't blame him for leaving. I was a dramatic preteen girl who was always looking for someone to argue with. Besides, taking care of me was not his job, and he had his own life ahead of him. I think he's done pretty well for himself, though. But, we don't really have much of a relationship due to the distance. Maybe one day, we can change that.

Besides, I'm not the spoiled kid that I once was. Looking back, I can see that I was dealing with my own abandonment issues. I had been a daddy's girl until he left, and then I was just no one's girl. Mom was constantly busy working, trying to keep a roof over our heads and food in our mouths. This left Bryan to deal with me and all my drama. That's a lot for an eighteen-year-old boy. Hell, I'm 28 and I'm not sure I could even deal with teenage me.

* * *

"Well Mom, as always, lunch was incredible." I say, placing my cloth napkin on the table and reclining in my seat. Juliet is happily chewing on some green beans in the vintage high chair next to me.

"It really was." Bryan agrees. "Of course, I have been living off of Hamburger Helper and frozen chicken strips for as long as I can remember." He chuckles.

"Ah, it's nice to see that you have the palette of a toddler." I joke.

Bryan rolls his eyes. "I bet you don't cook four course meals either. It's hard to cook for just yourself."

I nod in agreement. "That's true. Not that I know how to cook, anyway. I tend to either eat cheese and crackers, cereal or ramen these days."

"You could know how to cook if you would have allowed me to teach you." Mom says, narrowing her eyes. "I tried with both of you when you were teenagers, so you wouldn't starve as adults. But no one wanted to learn anything. Instead, you just wanted to go hang out with your friends."

"Sorry mom. But, that was enough to assure I never moved too far away. I always knew I could come over here for an actual meal if I got tired of cereal." I offer with a smile.

Mom shakes her head and sighs. "Well, too bad that didn't work on your brother." She says, turning to him and raising an eyebrow.

I look at Bryan, who is making himself comfortable on the couch with Juliet in his lap. For someone that she only sees once or twice a year, she sure is comfortable with him. In fact, it almost seems that she's bonded more with my brother than she has with her own dad.

"Hey, at least I moved closer to home." He says defensively. Bryan has lived all over the place with the military. South Carolina and Colorado have been the most recent. However, this summer he was transferred to Texas. "Now that I have less than a ten-hour drive, I promise I'll try to make it back here more often."

"Good." My mom says with a smile. "I love having both of my babies together under one roof. And Juliet seems to enjoy having you around, too."

Bryan looks down at Juliet in his arms and grins proudly. "I admit, I enjoy being here with her, too."

* * *

"My girls!" Susan calls, when she finds Juliet and me standing at her front door on Thanksgiving evening. She throws open her arms and receives my smiling fifteen-month-old. "Thank you so much for bringing her over tonight. We are going to leave early in the morning to head to my sisters and this will make it so much easier."

I wave her off. "It's no problem at all. She loves spending time with you, and it's not like we would do anything other than sit at home all night." I lean forward and kiss the side of Juliet's head. "Have fun with Dad and Grammy. I'll see you tomorrow night. Goodnight Susan. Have a safe trip." I say, before turning on my heel to head back towards my car.

Susan and Juliet tell me goodbye before retreating to the house. I'm halfway across Susan's yard when Cory calls out my name. The sound of his voice fills me with a mixture of rage and fear. What could I have done this time for him to need to confront me? And why is Susan letting him come out here? I thought we had an agreement about this.

I turn to face him, already feeling defensive. "Cory, I don't want to argue with you on Thanksgiving."

He frowns. "I don't want to argue, either. But I have news and I figured I'd better tell you in person."

My heart sinks automatically and my mind jumps to the worst conclusions. What if he met someone, and he wants her to be around my daughter? What if he wants to keep her at his house for his weekends? I can't handle this. My body is going into full blown panic mode and he hasn't even spoken yet.

"I got a new job." Cory states. "I'll be in West Texas working for an oil company. I leave Saturday."

"Oh." I say, trying to not sound too excited. "So you're moving?"

He shrugs. "It's an on the road job. I'll be gone for three months and then back for two weeks. So, I'm going to get rid of my apartment and I'll just stay with my mom when I come to visit. I figure then I can spend time with Juliet while I'm here.

37

If that's okay with you. I'm leaving this weekend, but I'll be back for Christmas for a couple of days."

I nod, still trying to hide the joy in my heart. Cory is leaving. Cory won't be in Fawn Creek, following me around and harassing me. I know it's Thanksgiving, but man, it feels like Christmas.

"Sure, let me know when you'll be here, and I'm sure we can make it work."

"Thanks Avery. Well, I better let you go," He says, with a wave as he walks back towards the house.

Now why can't we get along like that when he isn't getting ready to leave?

* * *

It's the day after Thanksgiving and I just spent a majority of the day batching content. After a few hours of making a variety of videos, I have enough drafts saved to get me through the next week at least. Derek was definitely on to something when he suggested I create a bank of content to use later. But, it is going to take me a while to build up a big collection.

I stand from the sofa and stretch, moving through my empty house. Once upon a time, before Juliet came along, I lived for long quiet days at home. I am a classic extrovert through and through, but after a long week at work there's nothing I enjoyed more than spending time at home recharging. But now, quiet weekends at home just remind me that Juliet is gone, and I can't help but miss her. I'm not sure if it'll ever get easier, but what choice do I have? The only thing I can do is keep myself busy.

Just as I refill my coffee cup and make my way back to the

couch, my phone vibrates with a text.

Madison: Hey, what are you doing tomorrow? Want to go with me to the Christmas Market? I'd like to get a jump start on my Christmas shopping.

Me: Yes, I'd love to. The more shopping I can get done in town, the better. Let me make sure mom can keep Juliet for me.

I've been scrimping and saving for months to prepare for Christmas this year. Last year, Juliet was only three months old and did little other than cry, sleep and poop on Christmas Day. This year she will actually be able to open gifts and I am itching to do some shopping for her. I fire off a text to mom and she replies immediately that she will keep Juliet.

Me: She said yes! Count me in.
Madison: Perfect. I need to get out of this house.
Me: ☺ Everything okay?
Madison: Yeah. I just need some girl time.
Me: Same. See you then.

Chapter 5

It's two days after Thanksgiving, as well as Small Business Saturday. It's also the day of Fawn Creek's annual Christmas Market and tree lighting ceremony.

Madison and I are meeting to explore the vendors in the Blackledge Event Center. First, however, I'm making a stop for coffee and checking in on Tyler. Today is her first big sales day since opening her bookstore earlier this fall and I'm sure her nerves are likely shot.

"Hey girlfriend!" Cassidy's voice rings out across Drip as soon as I make my way through the door.

"Hey! Ready for a busy day?" I call back, approaching the counter. Fawn Creek is known for its festivals and there is one every season. The surrounding communities always funnel into town and take advantage of the small town charm, which results in enormous crowds but also great sales for our small businesses.

She lefts out a dramatic breath, and simultaneously blows her bangs out from in front of her eyes. "Oh girl, I hope so. The vendors at the market have already been keeping us hopping today. Devin has been making deliveries all morning." She smiles proudly. "He's a smart kid. He walked around the entire second floor, taking coffee orders while the vendors were setting up. Then, he texted them to me and when they were ready, he delivered them before moving up to the third story to do the same. He's probably made himself enough in tips today to cover all of his Christmas shopping." She says with a laugh. "If this keeps up, it'll be a record sales day for us."

"That's actually genius. You should have him do it again around three o'clock if you can. That's when the afternoon slump will kick in and they'll all be needing refills." I suggest.

"Oh, that's a great idea." Cassidy agrees. "And that's about the time we slow down, so it'll be a perfect way to keep him busy." She quickly scribbles the idea down on an order pad. "Just in case I forget to tell him later, I swear once I hit menopause my brain stopped working and I never remember good ideas anymore."

"Oh good. Something else to look forward to in my old age." I joke.

"I promise getting older isn't all bad. Don't let us old ladies scare you too much." She assures me. "What are you up to today?"

"I'm going to meet Madison at the Maker's Market in a little while. First, I figured I'd get a coffee and one to take to Tyler. Can I get a salted caramel macchiato and a vanilla cold brew latte? Better make them both large. It'll be a long day for everyone." I add.

Cassidy and I continue chatting as she works on my drinks.

"Hey, your brother is in town, right?" She shouts over the squeal of the espresso machine.

I nod. "He is. He and my mom are actually watching Juliet for me today so I can get some shopping done."

"Aw, I love that. I bet he's a good uncle. He used to

41

take babysitting you and Tyler very seriously when he was a teenager. He loved doing it, too."

I shake my head. "I didn't know that. All this time, I just figured he wasn't given a choice in the matter."

"Bryan was the neighborhood big brother, that's for sure. He even watched Sierra for me when she was tiny. He's a good guy."

How is it possible that I grew up with this man and never knew how loved he was by other people in our community? Just another indication that I was too busy worrying about preteen drama and myself, I suppose.

Cassidy finishes our drinks and slides them across the counter, thanking me for supporting her small business. I wish her luck for a busy day, before making my way to TBR.

Even though Tyler decided to open early today to mimic the hours of the Maker's Market, I still arrive before the bookstore is unlocked.

I lean forward to look through the window, expecting to see her busily pricing items or doing inventory. Instead, I find her holding her trash can in her lap, while she sits on the floor. I knock loudly, causing her to jump just slightly. Once she spots me, she slowly stands from her spot on the floor and makes her way towards me.

As Tyler opens the door, I immediately feel her forehead with the back of my hand. She doesn't have a fever. "Um, are you okay?" I ask. The last thing she needs today is to have a stomach bug. She can't afford to be closed this soon after her grand opening.

"I... I don't know what happened. I was unpacking candles that came in yesterday and getting them ready to go on a shelf. I took the lid off one, thinking I would light it." She shrugs. "I figured it would add to the Christmas atmosphere, but.. ugh. As soon as I put my nose to it, I immediately threw up."

"Oh no. What candles? Are they not as good as the ones we chose when you ordered them a couple of months ago?" I recall when we spent an entire afternoon smelling candle samples. We sat on the floor with a jar of coffee beans, testing every single scent. I vowed I'd never smell a candle again.

"I don't know." Tyler says, pointing to a box on the counter. "They're over there. Maybe I just got a bad batch. I hope I'm not coming down with something." She groans.

I frown and make my way towards the box of scented candles sitting next to the cash register. Immediately, I spot the one in question because it's next to the box with the lid only half sealed. "Frasier Fir." I read the label out loud before removing the lid the rest of the way and cautiously taking a sniff.

"Tyler, this smells amazing." I shake my head. "It's just as great, or maybe even better than I remember." I eye her suspiciously. "Wait. You're not on birth control, are you?"

She scowls. "No, I haven't been for a long time. I didn't like what it did to my hormones." She confesses. "Wait, are you asking if I'm pregnant? You know as well as I do how irritating it is to be accused of being knocked up just because you vomit."

I roll my eyes. "Yeah, well, sometimes it's a good indication, though. Is your period late?"

She stops to think. "Maybe? I mean, it's already pretty unpredictable. Plus, I figured my cycle was probably messed up because of all the stress from the wedding and opening the store. Plus, we went on our honeymoon, so traveling probably affected it." She goes on.

I check my watch. "The pharmacy is open. Maybe you should run over there and grab a test real quick before you open." I

43

suggest. "I'd go for you, but I don't need anyone to see me buying a pregnancy test and assume it's for me. You know how word spreads around this town. You mom would have me added to the prayer list at church before lunchtime."

Tyler shakes her head. "No, I'll run over there real quick. I have a few more minutes to kill before I open anyway, and if I wait to go get a test, I won't be able to concentrate all day."

"Are you excited?" I ask, raising an eyebrow.

She smirks. "Yes! And I'm trying really hard not to be. What if it's a fluke and my hormones really are all jacked up from all the stress? Then, I'll just be disappointed."

"Okay, well, I can't go anywhere until you pee on a stick and tell me the verdict." I announce, plopping down in the chair behind the register. "Go." I command, pointing towards the door.

Without a pause, Tyler makes her way out the door. I watch as she runs across the street into the pharmacy. While I wait, I text Madison and let her know that I'm tied up at the bookstore, so we need to meet maybe fifteen minutes later. She agrees, with no hesitation.

Within what seems like seconds, Tyler's back with a white paper pharmacy bag in hand.

"The lady at the counter tried to sell me prenatal vitamins." She hisses. "Ma'am, I haven't even tested yet. Calm down."

"She could smell it on you." I say with a laugh before sending her directly to the bathroom. When she comes back, I set a timer on my phone and we try to busy ourselves for an agonizing three minutes.

"What's Andrew going to say?" I ask, raising an eyebrow. "Is he ready for this?"

"I don't know." She answers with a shrug. "I know he wants

kids. I'm just not sure if he wanted them this quickly."

"Well, you guys moved fast enough to get married." I tease her. "I bet he will be excited. He seems like the kind of guy that wants enough kids for a baseball team."

"Speaking of moving fast." Tyler smirks. "Have you decided that you're in love with Derek yet? You know he kept checking you out at my wedding, right? And with Cory leaving town, you will finally be free to date with him stalking you."

I shake my head; I knew I shouldn't have texted her and Madison yesterday with the news about Cory. Of course, it would make the teasing about Derek increase even more.

"Derek was not checking me out at the wedding. He just felt sorry for me because my best friend put me on display as the lonely single girl." I say, rolling my eyes. "I told you, we are just friends. Cory being gone won't change that."

Tyler pouts. "It just makes it even better if you are friends first. Besides, the whole friends to lovers trope is very in right now." She shrugs. "Just ask Booktok."

I attempt to ask what that even means, but I'm interrupted by the screaming alarm on my phone. "It's time to go find out your future. To the bathroom." I command, pointing the way, as if she doesn't know where it's located.

Tyler and I make our way to the bathroom. Quickly, I open the camera app on my phone so I can record her reaction, just in case she wants it for later.

Through the camera, I watch Tyler as she slowly lifts the test from the bathroom counter and lets out a loud gasp. My best friend is having a baby.

Chapter 6

"Juliet, say cheese!" I call out to her.

Juliet moves her attention away from the old man that's holding her on his lap to smile at me with a wide grin. I snap a series of photos with my phone camera before moving back towards Santa to retrieve her.

"Good job, Baby! Tell Santa thank you." I remind her, as I pluck her from his lap.

"Tank you." Juliet mimics.

"Thanks, Santa." I say, smiling at Cody, Andrew's little brother, under the big floppy Santa hat he's wearing. Historically, the volunteer fire department has always been in charge of handling the Santa photos for Fawn Creek. As one of the newest recruits, Cody got stuck with this year's job.

We get our candy cane from his elf and move out of the way so the next child can visit him. Just then, we run right into my brother.

"Hey sis. I can't believe Fawn Creek goes all out like this for the beginning of the Christmas season. It's only gotten bigger since we were kids." He says, shaking his head.

I smile and let my eyes wander down the street, taking in the surrounding festivities. "I know. Isn't it great?"

"No. It's too many people," Bryan grumbles under his breath.

"This is a freaking nightmare. I knew I should have stayed at the house."

Bryan apparently didn't get the extroverted genes that mom, and I possess. We both live for being surrounded by people, him not so much.

"Hey guys." Derek says approaching us in the crowd. He reaches over to shake Bryan's hand. I can't help but notice that when Derek's eyes land on me, they linger a little longer than normal. Are my friends on to something? No, surely not. After all of these years and nights alone hanging out at my house, he would have acted on it by now. Right?

"Hey, man. I haven't seen you in forever. You still in the service?" Derek asks Bryan.

Bryan nods. "Yep, for now, anyway. I have about a year and a half until retirement."

Derek's eyes widen. "Oh nice. Then what?"

"I'm not sure," Bryan says with a shrug. "Between you and me, I always thought I might move back here and open up a mechanic shop. I'd like to buy some land just outside of town for a house and a shop to work out of. But, so far, I'm not seeing anything for sale that's worth buying."

Derek pauses for a second to think. "I actually might know of a place. It's not on the market, but the owner has been thinking of selling off all of his property and moving to somewhere warmer now that he's getting older. There's already a shop on the property, too. Let me see what I can find out for you."

Bryan's face brightens up. "Sweet, man. Give me your number and I'll text you so you have mine."

The boys exchange numbers and Derek turns towards me just as his radio goes off. "Duty calls." He says with a slight frown. "I'll see you guys later." He adds before quickly making

47

his way away from the crowd.

"That was cute, you two exchanging numbers and all. Glad to see that after all these years, you have finally learned to be nice and make friends." I say with a snicker. "Are you really going to move home after you retire? And have you told mom about your plans?"

He shakes his head. "Not yet. Don't say anything to her about it, please? I'll tell her when I'm ready." He pauses. "If I speak too soon, she will set a countdown and then text me every day for the next eighteen months to tell me how long I have left. I'm not saying anything until it's a done deal."

I laugh. "Your secret is safe with me." I promise. "It would be nice to have you back home, though. I know Juliet would love it."

Bryan nods. "She's a lot of my motivation to come back here." He admits. "I don't want her growing up not knowing who I am."

"I'd like that, too." I agree. "Our family isn't very big. I want her to have as many of us close by as she can."

Just then, Madison approaches us, this time with her two daughters in tow. We had finished our day date and split ways after agreeing to meet back up here this evening.

"Hey, Madi." I say to my friend before turning to say hi to her kids. "Hi Kate. Hi Kenzi." I wave to the girls. "Are you going to see Santa?"

Madison nods. "Yeah, I thought we would get here early enough to beat the crowd, but I guess not. They were in no hurry to get ready and Ben is working late so I had no help." Madison looks back at the line stretching down the street with disappointment. "We're going to be in this line forever." She whispers.

"It's actually moving pretty quick." I promise. "You'll be through it in no time."

"Alright girls, let's get in line." Madison says, directing them to the end of the line. "Maybe we will see you again before dark." She adds with a chuckle. She waves goodbye to Bryan and me just as Tyler and Andrew make their way up the sidewalk to join us.

"Hi." I say to them both. I haven't talked to her since I left her store this morning after she got the results of her pregnancy test. Andrew has a huge grin plastered on his face. Obviously, she told him the news, and he was not upset about it.

"Hey buddy, long time no see," Andrew says, shaking Bryan's hand.

I almost forgot that the two of them were friends in high school.

"What's up with you?" I ask, raising an eyebrow in his direction. Although, I'm sure he knows I know, but I refuse to steal this moment of excitement from him. Bryan raises a brow in confusion to what's happening in front of him. I turn and wink as a silent indicator that he will find out soon enough.

Andrew doesn't even speak. He just pulls a ceramic Christmas ornament from his pocket and hands it to me. A wide grin spreads across his face as I read it out loud.

"Baby Hayes, Coming Soon." I read aloud before turning back towards Andrew, who looks to be nearly exploding with excitement. "Congratulations, Dad." I say, handing the ornament back to him.

"Thank you." He says, gently taking the ornament back from me. "I have to go show Santa." He replies, slapping Bryan on the back before making his way towards the line.

I shake my head. "Welp, I guess he was happy with the news."

I say to Tyler. "How did you get a custom ornament so quick, though?"

Tyler shrugs. "I ran up to the Maker's Market and found someone that was doing custom crafts on site. I got lucky honestly, but I love it and it's so perfect."

"I'm so happy for you guys." I say, pulling her into a hug. "And if my calculations are right, our babies will have birthdays around the same time, too."

"Oh, wouldn't that be so cool? I hope you're right. We can have joint parties and you can do all the work." She teases.

Suddenly, our joyful moment is interrupted by a blood-curdling scream. We turn and see that Madison's daughter Kenzi has fallen in the street and is dramatically clutching both of her knees. Bryan, Juliet and I quickly make our way towards my friend, who looks like she is about to lose her mind.

"Mommy, I need a band-aid!" Kenzi wails out, holding on to Madison.

Madison turns to look at Kate. "Hey, we've got to run to the car and get some band-aids for Sister. Let's go."

"No, Mom! Then we'll lose our place in line! I don't want to miss Santa." She argues, now with her own tears streaming down her face.

"Honey, your sister is hurt. We have to take care of her." Madison says. "That's what we do."

"But our car is too far. I want daddy." Kate pouts, crossing her arms. "Why didn't he come with us? You're mean!"

I watch Madison's face fall as those words come out of Kate's mouth. She blinks back tears and tries her best to remain calm.

"We can take Kenzi to get cleaned up. Then you guys can stay in line." I offer to Madison, stepping forward to diffuse the situation.

Madison pauses, looking back and forth between the girls as though she is trying to decide what to do and who to take care of.

Bryan, however, is apparently tired of waiting and springs into action. "Come here." He says to the little girl, still clutching her knee, reaching out for her. She immediately goes to my brother and buries her head in his shoulder. "Come with me." He commands, looking at me.

I do as he says.

"Wait, do you need my keys to get to my first aid kit out of my van?" Madison calls after us, but Bryan is already on a mission.

"Hey, Gary." He says, approaching the town pharmacist who is currently off the clock and standing in the street enjoying a hot cocoa with his wife. Gary and Bryan were in the same graduating class in high school. "Can you help us? We need a first aid kit."

"Of course." Gary says, without hesitation as he hands his drink to his wife. "Follow me."

Gary unlocks the pharmacy door and instructs Bryan to seat Kenzi on the counter. He rolls up her leggings over both knees and inspects the damage.

"Just a couple of little scrapes. You're going to be okay." Bryan says with a soft smile.

Within minutes, she is all cleaned up, medicated, bandaged, and enjoying a sucker. She even picked out a sucker for her sister and one for Juliet.

"Thank you for this." I say to Gary. "I'm sorry we interrupted you enjoying the festival."

"No problem at all." He promises. "Glad I could help."

We make our way back to the Santa line just in time for Kenzi to join her mom and be next in line for Santa.

"Perfect timing." I proclaim as Bryan hands her over to Madison.

"You saved the day." She tells him. "Thank you."

* * *

"Okay folks. Just ten more minutes until we light up the tree!" Chris, the Mayor of Fawn Creek, proclaims over the speakers set up outside the pocket park.

Juliet, Bryan and I are standing in the street, in front of the giant tree, waiting for the ceremony to take place. Juliet is almost asleep in my arms as she snuggles up against me. We watch as the local dance studio takes the stage on the sidewalk in front of the tree and begins their holiday dance routine. At this moment, I can't help but stop and count my blessings for the holiday season.

Sure, my life isn't everything I thought it would be by now. But I have so much to be thankful for. I have a good job to provide for my daughter. I have amazing friends and family to celebrate the season with. My brother is potentially moving back home and I'm making decent progress with the content creation business.

The only thing missing now is a relationship. And as much as I wish I had one, I admit, I'm terrified to try. What if it just turns out to be a disaster like it was with Cory?

Just as the dancers begin their final set, I feel someone brush up against me. I turn, assuming that it was just someone trying to walk past me in the crowd, but smile softly as I realize it's Derek standing at my side.

"Hey." He says, looking at both me and Juliet with soft eyes.

I notice what seems like his eyes landing on my lips before he quickly looks away across the crowd. His firm jaw locks into place as he stands at attention, watching over the town he loves so much.

Just then, Sierra, Santa's wife, makes her way towards us.

"Hey. Do you want to buy Juliet an ornament?" She asks, holding up a clear plastic ornament. When I only respond with a look of confusion, she goes on. "It's a new fundraiser for the Fire Department. The ornament can be purchased for a donation of five dollars. After the kids decorate them, they can bring them back and we will hang them on the tree so they will be a part of the festivities all season. It's a new thing I'm trying this year and hopefully it'll go over well."

Before Sierra even finishes speaking, Derek hands Sierra a twenty-dollar bill. "Keep the change." He says with a smile.

Sierra's face lights up as she takes the money and shoves it into her apron pocket. She hands me the ornament. "Thanks Derek. So, maybe that whole cop verses firefighter feud isn't a real thing after all." She declares with a shrug.

Derek laughs. "I wouldn't go that far. I did it for Juliet, not for the fire department." He adds, turning to wink at me.

I thank him, just as Santa takes the microphone and speaks across the crowd. "Ho, ho, ho everyone! It's time to light the tree! Let's start the countdown! 10...9...8..."

"He's really getting into character." I say, leaning over to Derek. I pause, letting my body linger close to his a little longer than usual.

"He better watch out or he will be stuck doing this every year." Derek responds with a chuckle as he gently nudges me.

Why does it suddenly take every ounce of my strength to not kiss this man?

Chapter 7

"Thanks for coming out with me at the last minute." Madison says, as I climb into the passenger seat of her minivan and close the door. "When the girls from my graduating class invited me to the bar, I really didn't want to say no. But I also hate the idea of sticking out like a sore thumb since I'm the old married woman of the group. I don't even know who they are anymore."

"Hey, no problem." I say, waving her off. "It feels like it's been ages since I've been out. Besides, mom was more than happy to keep Juliet for the night so we can have some girl time. It's a good weekend, too. With the exception of Memorial Day weekend, this is one of the best weekends to go out to Short Creek. Everyone is in town visiting their family for the weekend and usually by Saturday night they are all sick of spending time together. So naturally, they go to the bar. It's basically a high school reunion."

Madison puts her van in park in the gravel parking lot and turns to look at me. "That's what I'm afraid of. I married Ben right out of high school. While all of my friends were out at bars and away at college, I was doing laundry and baking casseroles. I feel like I don't fit in. Not that I ever did."

"I'm happy to be your buffer. If your old friends make you

uncomfortable, we will move on."

"Thank you." She says with a soft smile. "I need this more than you know."

* * *

Madison and I are just leaving the dance floor after dancing to "Copperhead Road" when the DJ's voice echoes across the building.

"Ladies and gentlemen, it's officially 1:40 am. That means this is your last call for alcohol."

"Already?" Madison asks, looking at me with wide eyes. "Last I knew, it was only eleven."

"Time flies when you're having fun, right? We're going to need a ride home. We have had too many dollar shots tonight."

"Good call, but from who? Fawn Creek doesn't have an Uber driver." Madison asks, confused.

"My own personal Uber." I pull out my phone and fire off a quick text.

Me: Hey. Do you think you can drive Madison and me home from Short Creek?
  Derek: Sure. I'll be by in a few.
  Me: Thanks.

"Derek is on the way. Let's go outside and wait. I need some air." I say, leading Madison towards the door. "I'm sweating to death."

"Derek, huh?" Madison asks with a smirk, causing me to roll my eyes.

55

"Yes, Derek. He's my friend and doesn't mind driving me home from here as needed." I reply, with a notable defensive tone in my voice.

"Avery, when are you going to finally admit that you two have chemistry?" Madison asks, raising a brow. "I've seen the way he looks at you. He likes you, and I think you might like him, too. You guys would make such a cute couple."

I cross my arms and turn to face her. "Do you really think he's into me?"

"Yes. No man is going to be at your beck and call the way he is, unless he wants to be with you. You should give it a shot."

"And what if I ruin our entire friendship by making a move that he doesn't want me to make?"

"You won't." Madison says, putting her hands on my shoulders. "Besides, what if you never try and you totally miss out on something incredible?"

I'm just about to respond when Derek's police cruiser pulls into the parking lot in front of us and parks.

"Your chariot, m'lady." I say, as I walk towards the car and open the back door for Madison. She slides into the seat and I close the door quietly, before walking around to climb into the passenger seat.

"Hey. Thanks for coming." I say with a smile as I close my door.

"Anytime." He replies with a grin. "Madison, are you good back there?"

I turn to look at my friend, who is nervously perched in the middle of the backseat. "Yeah." She assures him. "Just never been in a cop car before."

"Well, hopefully you'll never be in one against your will." He teases. "Did you girls have a good night?"

"Yes, just what I needed." I say. Madison nods in agreement.

"Good." He replies. "Madison, you still live in your little house on divorce alley?"

I turn just in time to see Madison's face immediately fall.

"What alley?" She asks. "Did you hear something about me or...?"

"Um, no," He says, shaking his head, trying to reassure her. "That's just what they used to call the little neighborhood you live in. "Why? Are you good?"

Madison lets out a heavy breath. "Yeah, no I'm fine. I've just never heard it called that before."

Derek frowns. "It was a thing in the 80's. Sorry, didn't mean to weird you out."

She shakes her head. "No, you're good. Sorry. Too many dollar shots." She says, waving him off.

Derek pulls into Madison's driveway and puts the car in park.

"Avery, I'll text you tomorrow to take me to pick up my car, if that's okay?" Madison says to me.

"Of course." I say, as Derek climbs from his seat to let Madison out of the locked backseat of the cruiser.

"Thanks again, Derek." She calls out with a wave as she makes her way towards the house and lets herself inside. Once the door is closed again, we continue our journey towards my house.

"Thanks again for coming to my rescue." I say, reaching over to squeeze Derek's hand that's resting on the center console. He lightly squeezes back before letting go and begins using both hands to steer.

"It's my pleasure, really." He assures me.

"You sound like a Chick-fil-A employee." I retort with a giggle. "But really, thank you. For everything."

57

Derek pulls his car up to the curb in front of my house and turns to face me. "And really, I mean it. I enjoy helping you, Avery. I enjoy being there for you when you need me."

I don't reply, instead I just stop and look down at my lap. Maybe everyone is right. Maybe he does have a thing for me. What would be the harm in getting into a relationship with Derek? He's sweet and takes amazing care of me. Not to mention the fact that the man is gorgeous.

"Do you need help getting inside?" Derek asks, raising a brow as he turns towards me, interrupting my train of thought.

"I wouldn't turn it down." I answer shyly. *Now's my chance.*

I'm not drunk at all. But the alcohol Madison and I drank tonight is still hanging out just enough in my body to give me the courage to make a move.

Derek laughs and opens his door before walking around to open mine. He slips his hand into mine and walks towards the house with me, side by side. On my screened-in porch, he inputs the code to unlock the door.

"I can't believe you remember my door code by heart."

"Well yeah, it's Juliet's birthday. How could I forget?" He smirks.

Of course he would remember her birthday. He's spent more time with her since she was born than her own father has.

I gave him the code after I moved in here, back when Cory was constantly harassing me. Whenever Cory would bother me, Derek would come by before I got home from work to make sure the house was safe.

Derek places his hand on the small of my back to lead me inside the house. Even though this man has touched me a million times before, tonight I feel myself melt under his touch.

Once the door closes, I turn towards him. Suddenly, I feel

braver than I ever have with him, or honestly with anyone. I close the distance between us and wrap my arms around his neck, pulling his body towards mine. Just as I lift my head to move my lips towards his, I feel him pull away.

"Okay, Drunky. Let's get you off your feet." He says, his voice turning serious, as he leads me towards the couch.

"I have a bed upstairs."

"Yep, and I don't need you falling down those stairs in an hour because you decided you want a snack. You can sleep down here." He commands before making his way to the kitchen.

I plop down on the sofa and stare down at the floor. The feeling of embarrassment is washing over me and I wish like nothing else I could turn back time. It doesn't matter what my friends say. Derek isn't into me. He doesn't want to kiss me. He doesn't want to be with me and that just proved it. And now, I've ruined our entire friendship because I tried to make a move that he didn't want me to make. Great.

I listen as Derek opens and closes cabinet doors, and then he quickly returns. "Here, take this aspirin." He says, handing me two pills and a cup of water. "You're going to feel awful in the morning, I'm afraid."

I nod and do as he says, as he goes back to the kitchen. He reappears with a loaf of bread in his hand. "And eat a slice of bread, too. We need to soak up all those dollar shots I'm sure you took," He says, handing me a slice of bread.

I take it from him and make a show of tearing off a piece to shove into my mouth.

"Are you good? Do you need anything else from me?" He asks.

I shake my head. "I'm fine. Thanks again for the ride." I say, looking down at my lap.

"Call me if you need me." He says, already stepping back-wards towards the door. "Bye Avery." He adds, before turning and leaving.

As he disappears into the night, I feel my heart break in my chest. Who knows if I'll ever see him in my front room again?

* * *

I wake up Sunday morning with a dull headache behind my eyes and ringing in my ears. It's not long after I open my eyes that the events of last night come rushing back to me.

I tried to kiss Derek. Derek turned me down and left. I'm never going to be able to look at him again. What have I done?

After a cup of coffee and another dose of aspirin, I get dressed, take Madison to get her car and go to Mom's to pick up Juliet. Bryan is loading up his weekend duffle bag into his truck when I pull up.

"Leaving so soon?" I call to him as I make my way across the yard.

"You look like hell." He replies.

I'm sure to him I look like someone that's suffering from a major hangover. Little does he know that I've spent the morning crying after ruining one of my longest friendships.

"Thanks." I answer with a huff, before moving in to hug him. "It was nice hanging out with you this weekend. See you at Christmas?"

"You betcha." He agrees before lowering his voice. "And remember, not a word to mom about me moving back here. I don't want to get her hopes up."

I nod and hold up a pinkie to his face. "Pinkie promise." I

declare.

He smirks and shakes his head before hooking his pinkie in mine. "Take care of yourself, kid. I'll see you soon."

I turn and watch as Bryan hops in his truck and backs out of mom's driveway. Once he's gone, I continue my journey into my mother's home.

I step through the front door and follow the sounds of toddler giggles that lead me to the kitchen. I stop in the doorway and watch as my daughter sits happily in the highchair, snacking away on what looks to be pieces of pancake.

"Mommy's here!" My mom declares, causing Juliet to clap enthusiastically. "Did you have a good night?" Mom asks me.

I pause, trying to decide how to answer. I had a fun night with Madison until I ruined my friendship with Derek, but I won't be getting into that with my mother. "Yeah, it was great. Thanks again for keeping her."

Mom waves me off. "She's such an easy kid. She slept all night and then woke up with a smile. I'd keep her for you any day."

I grin. "She is a pretty great kid."

"So, what are you girls doing today?" Mom asks.

I shrug. "We might decorate for Christmas and try to get some content made." I could use some Christmas cheer in my life.

* * *

It's the Monday after Thanksgiving and it's been basically one of the worst Monday's I've had in a long time. I woke up to find out I was out of coffee, and of course my hair didn't want to cooperate at all. To top it off, Juliet had a blowout in her diaper on our first attempt out the door and I'm going to be late, again.

All my life, I have yearned to be the girl that has it all together. The one that's on time and organized and has a plan for everything. Unfortunately, that is not me. I'm late more often than I am early. I suck at budgeting my time, and it's only gotten worse since Juliet arrived. Truthfully, I have the best intentions, but unfortunately, this is where I fail the most.

Since I'm already late anyway, I might as well not skip out on getting a coffee to take with me for my commute. There's no point in being both late and tired. I pull up in front of Drip and quickly hurry to the backseat to get Juliet out of her car seat. We make our way up to the door of the coffee shop. I'm just about to step inside when I notice a Fawn Creek police officer sitting at a table, enjoying a coffee and a doughnut. *Derek.*

Immediately, I freeze. I haven't spoken to Derek since he left my house Sunday morning. I'm not ready to face him yet and relive the embarrassment of him turning me down. Quickly, I spin on my heel on the sidewalk to head back towards my SUV when I hit an icy patch on the concrete. Suddenly, everything happens so quickly. My legs go out from under me and I clutch Juliet, who I'm still carrying, praying that I won't drop her. I land on my butt with a thud. Luckily, my heavy down coat covers my rear and offers a bit of a cushion when I make contact with the sidewalk. If only I could climb inside my coat and hide for the rest of my life.

"Holy crap, are you okay?" Derek asks, as he pushes open the door to the coffee shop and rushes to my side.

I let out a heavy sigh. Couldn't it have been anyone other than him to see that?

"I'm okay." I assure him as he helps me get back on my feet. "My pride just hurts a little."

"That was impressive." He says, squeezing my shoulder. "I can't believe you didn't drop Juliet in the process. Good job, mom."

"Yeah, thanks." I answer, my face growing hot with embarrassment.

"Come on, let's get you a coffee." He says, holding the door open for me.

"You know. I..." I say, looking around for an escape. "I think I'm just going to go." Without waiting for his response, I quickly book it towards my waiting car, this time paying closer attention to the ground below in case of another icy patch.

"Avery, wait!" Derek calls back after me, but I'm already committed.

"I'm running late." I shout back. Quickly, I buckle Juliet into her seat and I climb into mine without looking back at him.

So much for playing it cool.

Chapter 8

It's Tuesday. I am just finishing cleaning up the kitchen when there is a knock at the door. I turn to Juliet and frown. I'm not expecting anyone and honestly, after the last few days, I'm not dying for company.

I wipe my hands on a dishtowel and quickly make my way to see who it is. Standing on tiptoe, I check the peephole to find Derek looking back at me. *Shit.*

I let out a heavy breath and open the door to face him.

"Hey." I say with a forced smile.

"Hi. Glad to see you're not dead." He scowls, crossing his arms in front of his chest. "You know, it probably wouldn't kill you to answer a text."

I quickly press my palm to my forehead. "Sorry, I meant to reply, and then I got busy." I say, obviously lying.

Derek had messaged me both yesterday when I left the coffee shop and then again today. I didn't open either of them. I just wasn't ready to face him and my embarrassment from our last two encounters.

"What's your problem?" He asks, with a look of concern on his face. "I'm worried about you. We haven't gone this long without talking since you and Cory were together." The words are hardly out of his mouth when he frowns and asks. "You aren't talking to him again, are you?"

"No, it's nothing like that." I reply, shaking my head. "Come in. We can talk, I guess."

Derek follows me into the house and we make our way to the kitchen, passing Juliet, who is sitting on the floor looking at a pile of board books.

"Looks like Aunt Tyler's been here." He observes.

"I think she really only wanted a bookstore so she could buy books at a discount." I say with a laugh. "Juliet is going to need a full library with a floor to ceiling ladder by the time she's twelve, if Tyler has anything to say about it."

I move towards the counter and begin concentrating really hard on cleaning up my kitchen.

"So." Derek says, leaning against the fridge. "Are we going to talk, or do you just want me to watch you clean?"

I pause, waiting to find the right words. "Derek, the truth is that I'm freaking mortified, okay?" I finally admit, without removing my eyes from the small section of counter top that I'm wiping over and over.

"About what? Falling at the coffee shop?"

I turn to face him. This time I'm the one crossing my arms. "You know why. I threw myself at you like a complete idiot Saturday night."

He laughs and shakes his head. "Honestly, I wasn't sure if you remembered doing that. I just figured you were really drunk." He confesses.

"So what? You were just never going to mention it again?" I ask. "Were you just going to let me walk around looking for a moron for the rest of my life?"

He shakes his head. "Avery, you would be surprised at half of the stuff I've seen the people in this town do when they've had

65

too much to drink. I have just learned to pretend that I don't remember it until they bring it up. We all do things like that from time to time. There's no need to embarrass them all over again."

I toss the towel down on the counter. "Derek, I wasn't drunk. In fact, by the time you came to get us, I was pretty much sobered up." I admit.

"Wait. So you weren't drunk?"

"No."

"So you really wanted to kiss me? What brought that on?" He raises a brow.

I throw my hands in the air. "I don't know. For months, all of my friends have been telling me you have the hots for me and I didn't believe them. Then, after I saw you at the tree lighting, I just kind of got into my head, you know? I thought maybe we could be something after all. So, I decided to be brave and try to make a move. And you turned me down. So, now I would like to just find a rock to crawl under and die alone without ever speaking of this again."

Derek moves towards me, his eyes locked on mine. There's barely half a foot between his face and mine. "Avery, do you really think that I don't want you?"

I shrug. "Well, I feel as though you made it pretty clear you weren't interested on Saturday."

Derek shakes his head. "Avery, you could have been standing in front of me naked, begging me to sleep with you, and I would have wrapped you in a blanket and sent you to bed alone. You know why?" He asks.

"Because you're not interested?"

"Because you had been drinking." He reaches over and grabs my hand, squeezing it tightly. "Avery, of course I wanted to kiss you. Hell, that's all I've wanted for years. But not if I thought you might wake up the next day and regret it. Or if there was even a chance that you would have felt taken advantage of."

I feel my face blush once again and I stare down at my feet. Derek places a finger under my chin, raising my face so I have no other option than to look into his eyes.

He continues, lowering his voice. "I would never take the chance of letting something like that happen between us if there is any possibility that you were going to regret it in the morning. I never want you to feel taken advantage of. Avery, I respect you too much for that." He grins and moves closer to me. "I've waited a long time to kiss you. I've dreamed for years of calling you mine. The feelings I have for you are real. And I never want you to think that I wanted you only because you threw yourself at me. What I want from you runs so much deeper than that."

This time, when I reach for him, wrapping my arms around his neck and pull him close, he doesn't resist.

This is really happening, isn't it?

Slowly he lowers his mouth to mine, gently colliding our lips together.

Our first kiss is everything I imagined, and yet somehow better than I pictured it would be. We move in unison as he cradles the back of my neck and I continue to move with him. After several moments, he pulls back and smiles down at me. "Feel better, now?" He asks.

"Much."

* * *

67

"I freaking knew it." Tyler says, as she leans over the counter in TBR. I stopped in to the store after work on Wednesday to fill her in on my latest Derek saga. She's handling it about as well as I expected.

"So, are you guys, like, going steady now?" She teases.

I roll my eyes and take a sip of my coffee, hiding my grin behind my cup. "I guess you could call it that."

"I knew you guys had the hots for each other. It's about damn time the two of you did something about it." She continues to gloat. "When's the wedding?"

I groan. "Stop it. This is all still pretty new to me. Besides, after rushing into things with Cory, I am terrified that I'm going to move too quickly and screw things up. I'm going to take this one slow."

Tyler quickly shakes her head. "No, ma'am. You will screw nothing up. Besides, there's a big difference between Cory and Derek. Cory is a narcissistic asshole and Derek is not."

I take another long sip of my coffee before placing it on the table next to me. "True. Which is exactly why I'm terrified to screw this up. Not only would I be messing up the first healthy relationship I've had in years, but also, I would screw up mine and Derek's friendship."

Tyler stops what she's doing and turns to face me, looking directly into my eyes. "Nope. We're not doing this. Avery, I love you. You are one of the bravest women I know. I've never known you to be afraid of anything. I refuse to stand by and watch you let fear ruin the best thing you've ever had. If there was ever a time for you to go all in with something, it's now."

I roll my eyes slightly and then look at Tyler with a soft smile. "Man, being an old married woman has made you quite bossy."

Tyler stops sorting a pile of stickers on the counter in front of her. "Just wait until this baby gets here. I'll be a real pain." She says before changing the subject. "So tell me, what was the first kiss like? Is he a good kisser? Was it awkward?"

My face reddens, and Tyler immediately gets her answer. "That good, huh?"

I let out a heavy sigh. "So good. Like, I'm not sure I've ever kissed someone for the first time and had it go as smoothly as this kiss was. That has to mean something, right?"

"Um, like the fact that you two are meant to be and every person in this town has known it for as long as we've known the both of you? Yes. Duh." Tyler finishes the stickers in front of her and turns back to me with a smile. "Gosh, I am just so happy for you! I told you that you were next. See? The bouquet never lies!"

"You." I pause, standing from my chair. "Are insane." I say before chunking my empty cup into a nearby trash can. "I need to go pick up Juliet and head home. Thanks for being my sounding board."

Tyler moves towards me and pulls me into a hug. "I really am so happy for you, friend. I can't wait to see where this takes you."

* * *

I strap a bundled up Juliet into her stroller and cover her up with a warm blanket before we make our way towards downtown for the annual Fawn Creek Christmas parade. As I turn the corner onto Main Street, I pause to zip up my coat, tightening it against my body as the cold winter air blows all around us. At the beginning of December in Kansas, the weather for the parade can range anywhere from sunny and seventy degrees, or blistering cold. Unfortunately, this year, Mother Nature opted for the latter.

In no time, we complete the two-block trek and search for a place along Main Street to watch the parade. Quickly, I settle on a spot in front of the Blackledge Event Center. Just as I am working on fishing my phone out of my pocket so I can text Madison, I spy her making her way towards me.

"Hey girls." I say as Madison and her daughters settle in next to me on the curb. Kenzi and Kate are both wrapped warmly in puffy coats with stocking caps on their heads and gloves covering their hands. "Are you guys ready to catch a bunch of candy?" I ask the excited brunettes.

Both girls scream in excitement back to me with a resounding "Yes!" causing Juliet to join in on the screams as well.

"I'm going to get a whole bag full." Kenzi says, pulling a plastic shopping bag from her coat pocket and waving it in front of me.

"I bet you will." I assure her.

Fawn Creek's Christmas parade is one of the best in the area. Besides all the businesses in town having floats of their own, many other communities travel to town to join in. Fire departments, businesses and high school bands come from all the surrounding towns, just to walk down our tiny Main Street and throw candy to children on a Thursday night in the beginning of December. And it's worth every frozen second.

The parade begins, with a Police Cruiser making its way along the parade route, ringing its siren to alert the onlookers of the start of the event. I watch Juliet's eyes light up as she studies the car make its way past us.

"Rick!" she screams to the cruiser, waving her tiny hand at

the officer on duty. "My Rick!"

"Oh, sister, that's not Derek." I say to her. "I bet we will see him soon, though. He's around here somewhere."

"Well, that's adorable." Madison says, leaning over to talk to me. "She really likes him, doesn't she?"

I nod. "So much. She always has." I confess. "He was the first man to hold her after she was born. I'm sure it sounds weird, but I feel like that is probably why they have such a strong connection."

"I'm so glad you guys finally got together. It gives me hope for the rest of the world." She confesses. "Has it been a weird transition to go from friends to dating?"

I ponder this for a moment and then shrug. "Not really. We have always spent a lot of time hanging out. Now we just kiss a lot while we do it," I say with a chuckle. "I can't believe it's already been two weeks. It feels like so much longer than that."

"That's a good sign, Avery. That means it's meant to be." Madison says with a grin, just as our favorite on-duty police officer approaches us.

Quickly, he bends down to kiss my lips gently before Juliet demands his attention from her stroller.

"Rick!" Juliet screams, squealing in her stroller and stretching her arms towards him. "Hold you!" She demands.

Derek shakes his head and laughs, before leaning down to release her from the buckles. He holds Juliet close to his body as she cuddles against him.

As the parade marches on, Madison's girls busy themselves with catching as much candy as possible. They stop every so often to hand me a sucker for Juliet. I tuck the candy away in my pocket as I watch Juliet enjoy her time with Derek, oblivious to the candy being hurled at us. That is, until she sees Andrew's

71

truck pulling the float for TBR and making its way towards us.

The trailer is covered in a collection of wood Christmas trees. But not just any trees. The trees are constructed of rectangular blocks of wood, painted to look like various children's books. Tyler painted the sides of the blocks to represent book titles. They truly do look like big stacks of books. Then, she wrapped the trees in colorful Christmas lights and adorned the tops with bright yellow stars. The instrumental Christmas music playing over Andrew's sound system is the finishing touch.

I was so excited when Tyler told me this idea, but to see it in person is absolutely mind blowing. She and Andrew made a great team at pulling this together, as usual. On the float sits Tyler with her parents, helping throw handfuls of candy. They look frozen, but I don't think I've ever seen my best friend happier to be doing what she loves, sharing her love of literature with her community.

As the float reaches us, Tyler waves excitedly and throws extra candy towards our awaiting group of kids. The big girls scramble to grab it and fill their plastic shopping bags. Juliet even lets go of Derek long enough to pick up some of her own, allowing him the perfect opportunity to excuse himself and continue his foot patrol.

Eventually, the last float of the parade comes into view. The city's largest fire truck, with Santa Claus perched on top, waving to the children of Fawn Creek. The girls excitedly wave to Santa as he approaches, and don't stop until he is far past us.

"Alright ladies." I say, as the parade ends and the people of Fawn Creek move from their spots and fill the street. "That's enough standing in the freezing cold for me. I'm going home." I turn to Madison and pull her into a hug. "We'll see you tomorrow morning."

We say our goodbyes, and just as we make our way down the street back towards my house, I hear a voice call out behind me. "You ladies need an escort home?"

I turn and find Derek jogging to catch up with us. I don't even try to hide the smile that comes across my face as I wait for him to catch up. As he reaches us, he wraps his arm around my waist and pulls me in for a long kiss.

"This is a pretty rough neighborhood. You should probably walk us home." I agree with a giggle.

We fall into a steady stride as we make our way towards my house.

"Well, I think Juliet enjoyed herself. You didn't bring her last year, did you?" Derek asks.

I shake my head, surprised that Derek remembered at all. "Nope, she was too little, and it was even colder than this, so we sat that one out. I'm glad I waited, though. It was fun to really see the whole thing through her eyes. I think she loved it."

"Next year, she will be out there catching candy like the rest of them. I can't wait to see what her personality is like as she grows up a little more." He admits. "It's been fun to watch her grow and change."

"I imagine she will be a diva, and I will have to pick up the candy for her because she won't want to get her gloves dirty." I say with a laugh.

"Like mother like daughter." He teases as we make our way into my yard.

He helps me get myself and Juliet into the house before turning to make his way back downtown. He pauses and turns back to me. "I really enjoyed spending time with you two tonight. Thanks for letting me be a part of your life." He says, gently kissing my lips.

"Thanks for choosing to be a part of ours."

Chapter 9

"Hey! It's just me!" I call out to Tyler over the sound of the bell ringing above the door at TBR.

"Hey! What are you doing here? Need to pick up a book for the weekend?" Tyler teases. She, of all people, knows that I am the last person who's going to come in here and pick up a book for myself. I've never been much of a reader. Honestly, I just have trouble sitting down for long enough to enjoy it. It never takes me long before I get distracted and find something else to focus on.

"No, what about a movie? You have any of those?"

Tyler laughs. "Mark my words. One of these days, I'll turn you into a reader. But, no, I don't have any movies. Does this look like Aardvark video to you?" She asks, referring the video rental store in Fawn Creek when we were teenagers.

"Not really, but I'm sure I spent enough time in there as a kid that I could help you recreate it from memory. If not, I'll bring Derek in to help. He worked there through most of high school."

"Oh my gosh, I totally forgot about that! I knew I recognized him from somewhere. If I remember correctly, didn't you have a little crush on him in junior high?"

Immediately, I feel my face blush. "Maybe just a little." I

admit. "But we were never really in the same social circles back then. It's weird how things circle back around, isn't it?"

"Not weird at all. That's called destiny. You were meant to be together. I'm just glad that you finally saw it for yourself."

After my visit with Tyler, I leave TBR and head home. It's Friday, and it's Susan's weekend with Juliet. That means I have the entire weekend to play catch up.

As soon as I turn onto the old brick street and approach my house, I can already see the mountain of packages on my porch. I feel my stomach drop.

"What have I done?" I moan out loud as I put my car in park in my driveway. Because of the holiday shopping season and my follower count basically imploding overnight, I have been on the radar of apparently every company with something to sell. Every morning, I wake up to dozens of emails with requests from brands offering to send me their products in exchange for content. Apparently, I've gotten a little too overzealous with the collaborations I've accepted. So much for catching up, now I have even more to deal with.

I make my way towards the door and examine the mess waiting for me, but all I can do is shake my head. Who knew content creation would be this overwhelming?

I'm just barely inside the house when I toss my keys on the entryway table and I hear a loud, frantic squeak coming from the hall closet under the staircase.

Slowly, I make my way towards the door and gently turn the knob, trying to will myself into being brave enough to investigate. However, the little bit of bravery that I was feeling is quickly gone when the high-pitched scream continues. Shivering, I jump back from the door and fish my phone out of my purse.

"Hey." Derek answers on the first ring. "What's up? You okay?"

"Are you busy? I need help."

* * *

"Avery! It's safe to come out now!" Derek calls up the stairs.

I peek my head around the staircase to find Derek standing at the bottom of the landing, wearing his police uniform. "Are you sure? What was it? A raccoon? Sasquatch?"

"Just a mouse." He chuckles, obviously getting a kick out of my fear. "He's gone now."

"A mouse?" I slowly creep down the staircase. "I didn't know a mouse could be so loud. Was it a giant radioactive mouse?"

"I think since that closet is pretty well empty, his voice was echoing. He was stuck in a glue trap and pretty pissed off about it. But I got him out and let him loose out by the street."

I stare at him with a raised brow. "You let him loose? Isn't he going to come back?"

"I didn't really have any other options of what to do with him. Maybe since he got set free, he will count his blessings and find somewhere else to nest." He shakes his head. "The bad news is, if there is one, there are most likely more."

The thought of my house being full of mice makes my stomach turn. "Well, great. I'll have the exterminator come by, I guess. Thank you for coming to save me." I say, still standing cautiously on the step, terrified to move any further.

"Sure, anytime." He shrugs. "Call me a softy, but I hate those sticky traps. They're inhumane. Even if it is just a mouse, it makes me feel bad. Don't worry about calling anyone. I'll go grab you some real traps from the hardware store tomorrow after my workout and set them for you."

Derek mentioning his workout makes me smirk. One thing that has stayed consistent about him for as long as I've known this guy is his workout schedule. He runs twice a week, no matter what the weather is doing. Rain, snow or sleet. He is more reliable than the post office. Then three days a week, he lights weights in his home gym that he built in his spare bedroom. Come to think of it, he's probably the kind of guy that works out on vacation. As for me, the only cardio I do is running late. Maybe they're right when they say opposites attract.

I have to admit, all of his hard work pays off. There are plenty of women in this town that are known for sitting on their porch in the morning with their coffee, just to glimpse a sweaty, shirtless Derek pass by on his morning run. I can't say I blame them.

"Care to explain all that?" Derek says, breaking my concentration. He's eyeballing the mountain of boxes that are still on my porch. "Do you have a shopping addiction that we need to talk about? Do I need to organize an intervention? I've always wanted to do one of those."

I let out a heavy sigh as I move to help Derek carry the boxes inside. "No, that is simply the result of my social media going crazy." I say, shaking my head. "Companies are sending me products to make videos with. They pay me commission for sales off of those videos. I might have girl bossed a bit too close to the sun and accepted more than I can handle. So now, I have a very busy weekend ahead of me."

Derek finishes carrying the last load and closes the door before turning to look at me with pity in his eyes. "What can I do to help?" He asks. "You look overwhelmed."

"I am, and I'm not sure how to fix it. Truthfully, I may have bitten off more than I can chew." I admit. "It's going to take me all day tomorrow to open all this stuff and sort through it."

Derek's radio sounds, reminding the two of us he is still on duty.

"Shoot, I gotta get going. If you want, I can come over tomorrow and help. I'm off all day."

"And you want to spend it opening boxes with me?"

"I want it to spend it with you. I don't care what we do." He says, moving towards me. He wraps his arm and around waist and pulls me close before lightly kissing my lips. "I'll be back tomorrow morning and I'll stay for as long as you need me."

"It's probably an all-day job."

"I'll pack a bag." He says with a wink. "See you tomorrow."

* * *

"So, just out of curiosity, why are you on the phone with me instead of shaving your legs?" Tyler asks with a giggle. As soon as Derek walked out to the door, I couldn't help but call her to analyze the situation.

"How are we even sure that's what he meant?" I ask, pacing my living room. "Maybe he really is just coming over to help me open packages."

"I think he just wants to help you open HIS package." She teases.

"This. This is the awkward part of dating a guy that you have been friends with for years. I don't know if it's too soon. It's not like I just met the guy. I've literally known him for most of my life. Why does this feel so awkward?"

"Babe, you just have to rip the band-aid off. Or in this case, his pants. Rip those off."

"Pregnancy is making you feisty, Tyler. I'm not even sure to what to say. Usually I'm the inappropriate one."

"Yeah well. That's what happens when you sit around reading romance novels all day and call it work." She laughs. "Okay, I gotta go. It's time for me to lock up and head home. Let me know how tomorrow goes."

* * *

"How about a celebratory glass of wine?" I call out from the kitchen.

"Bring the whole bottle. Hell, bring two if you have it. I need one glass for every paper cut I got from opening things today." Derek calls back.

I move into the living room and hand Derek a glass before placing a bottle on the table in front of us.

"Pizza is ordered and should be here in twenty minutes." He reports back to me. "I still can not believe the amount of stuff we dealt with today. You're going to have to take a week off work in order to get videos made about everything."

"That's no lie." I groan. "But hey, thanks to you, everything is assembled and organized. Now I can just work really hard for the next fourteen days to get it all recorded and posted before I get in trouble for breaching my content agreement."

"I still can not believe they sent you furniture." Derek says, eyeballing the sixteen drawer dresser now standing in the corner of my dining room.

"Where else will I put the fifty new pieces of clothing they sent me?" I laugh. "You should see the things I turned down."

"Like what? Humor me."

I grab my phone and open my email, rapidly scrolling through my deleted folder. "For example, can you imagine me as the face of this miniature chainsaw?" I ask, holding up my phone to show him the photo. "Or perhaps this fishnet full bodysuit?"

Derek raises a brow. "The bodysuit looks interesting."

"Would it be as interesting if you were scrolling through your feed and found me modeling it on camera?" I roll my eyes. "Even I need to maintain some standards."

"Fair enough." He says with a laugh. "What else?"

"Well, there are several companies interested in me becoming the face for their colon cleanse products, and there are some very fancy Japanese knives that I have no business even thinking about touching." I turn my phone to show him a knife that looks more like a sword that a kitchen tool. "There's a lot to sift through."

"That's an understatement." Derek says with a laugh, just as a knock at the door interrupts us.

"That must be the pizza." He says, as I stand to move to answer.

"Oh my gosh, you're Authentically Avery." The young woman on my porch says excitedly. "I was wondering it that was you."

"Yep, that's me." I answer, my eyes darting to Derek. I have no idea who this girl is.

"Sorry, I follow you online. You are so pretty and so funny." She says with wide eyes. "I'm just so excited to meet you."

I smile gently. "Well, thank you for following me. I'm glad

you like my content."

Derek interrupts the awkward moment to move our way and pay for the pizza. "Keep the change." He says with a smile.

"Thank you so much." The woman says, handing him the pizza box and putting the money in her pocket. "Well, nice meeting you."

"You too." I agree and close the door before turning to look at Derek.

Derek places the pizza down on the table and takes his seat back on the sofa. "I didn't realize my girlfriend was so widely known. I'm impressed."

"As you should be." I say, joining him. "That was super weird."

"That's what happens when you're famous." He says with a chuckle. "We're going to have to hire you a security team."

"I think you will do just fine." I say, leaning into him and gently kissing his lips. "You don't mind protecting me, do you?"

"Oh Avery. I want to do a whole lot more than protect you."

"Then what are you waiting for?" I challenge.

* * *

A beam of light streams into my room through a crack in the curtain, shining directly into my face. As I roll over to hide from it, I find myself crashing right into Derek's chiseled back.

"Sorry." I mutter before wrapping an arm across him and snuggling into his back.

"Don't be sorry. You can crash into me in bed any time you want to." He mutters with a laugh before rolling over to face me.

"I might take you up on that. I slept better last night than I have in a long time. Of course, I'm sure the wine helped."

"I'm sure all the cardio we did last night helped, too." He teases.

I feel my face blush as I remember the night before. We barely made it through a slice of pizza for each of us before we found ourselves in my bed. I admit, there has been several times since Derek and I started dating that I have imagined what making love to him would be like. What I didn't expect, however, is how easy it would be. Every move, every kiss, every caress, just felt so natural. It was almost as though we've been doing this for years. Now, it's all I want to do.

The thought of his hands on my body in the darkness immediately makes my body feel heated once again. I look up into his eyes and find him looking down at me with the same curious desire. He leans down to kiss me.

"I can't even begin to tell you how badly I want to stay." He groans into my mouth. "But I can't. I have to go home and get ready for work."

Damn. That's not what I expected to hear.

"But I'm off Tuesday." He adds, wiggling his eyebrows. "I could stay over that night."

I bite my lip. "Derek. Are you going to hate me if I say I'm not really ready for sleepovers on nights that Juliet is home? I know she's still really little and won't quite understand anyway, but...."

Derek stops me by holding a finger up to my lips. "Shh.. you don't have to explain yourself. I get it. This is all still new and it will take some adjustments." He wraps his arms tightly around me and kisses my forehead. "I waited this long for you. I don't mind to waiting a couple of weeks to do it again."

"Really?"

"Yes, really. I told you, Avery, I'm in this for the long haul. You are what I want and I know Juliet is a part of that packaged deal. You know what's best for your daughter, and I'm here to support whatever those choices are. Besides, it'll be worth the wait."

Oh shit. I thought I was taking it slow, but I'm pretty sure I'm in love with this man.

Chapter 10

"Are you sure you're ready for this?" I ask Derek as we approach the front door of my mom's house, with Christmas gifts in tow. As soon as my mom found out that Derek and I were dating, she insisted I bring him to Christmas. "It's not too late to back out, you know."

Derek chuckles and rolls his eyes. "Why would I back out? I've known both your mom and your brother for ages, and they have always been nice to me."

I shrug. "I know. It's just different now that we're dating. And we've only been together for a few weeks, so I don't want you to feel obligated to get into this whole family holiday thing before you're ready."

Derek stops on the sidewalk and turns to face me. "Avery. I already told you. I've been waiting for the two of us to get together for a long time now. This is exactly what I want. I want to do life with you. The fun things and the boring things and everything in between. I'm happy to be here because I am all in. Okay?"

I take a deep breath and nod lightly. "I'm sorry, this is all just still new to me." And it is. When Cory and I were dating, I couldn't have paid him to come visit my family, even after we were engaged. I gently squeeze Derek's hand and turn back towards the house, leading Derek to the front door with Juliet in my arms.

"Merry Christmas." My mom calls out as we cross the threshold into her living room. Her vintage silver Christmas tree is scattered in colorful bulbs and there's Christmas music playing softly over her Alexa.

"Merry Christmas." I reply, placing Juliet on the ground. I watch as she immediately dashes over to see her Uncle Bryan. "How do you do that?" I ask him. "This kid has only met you a handful of times, but somehow you are like her favorite person on the planet." I shake my head and then answer my own question. "It has to be the beard or something. Madison's kids were the same way at the tree lighting ceremony."

Bryan immediately blushes at the mention of Madison.

I help Derek place the presents under the tree that he carried in for me.

Bryan shrugs. "Maybe it's just that Juliet knows I'm cooler than you." He suggests.

I scrunch my nose. "No, she probably just realizes that you both have a toddler mentality." I turn towards my mom. "Thanks for agreeing to do Christmas on Christmas Eve this year, since Juliet will be with her dad tomorrow."

"It's not a problem." Mom says, waving me off. "I'm just happy to have all of you here together. And Derek, I'm so glad you came, too."

He shrugs and smiles politely. "Thanks for the invite. I hear your cooking is pretty spectacular."

Bryan smirks. "Did Avery tell you she did not get the cooking gene from our mom?" I reach over and smack Bryan's arm, sending him a warning look.

He scoffs. "What? Shouldn't Derek be warned that a life with

86

you will be a life filled with cereal for dinner? The man deserves a warning so he can get out while he has a chance."

Just as I open my mouth to argue with my brother, Mom interrupts. "That's enough. Let's go eat before everything gets cold." She says, motioning us towards the dining room. "No more bickering, you two. It's Christmas."

After dinner, we take our seats in the living room around the Christmas tree with mugs full of hot chocolate to open gifts. It's not long before Juliet has the floor covered in a multitude of new toys.

I shake my head. "A toy tool bench?" I ask Bryan in disbelief.

"What?" He says with a chuckle. "The girl needs to know how to fix things, doesn't she?"

I smirk. "I suppose so. At least it's not slime or a karaoke machine."

"Oh, I'll add those to my list of things to buy when she gets a little older." He jokes.

I narrow my eyes at him. "Just remember, payback is a bitch." I reply. "If you ever have kids, I will buy them things ten times worse than you buy for mine."

Bryan rolls his eyes. "Avery, I'm not afraid of a little bit of a war. You just remember that." He says with a wink.

Mom looks back and forth between my brother and me before letting out a heavy breath. "I swear, you two pick on each other a lot for a couple of people that haven't lived in the same state in almost twenty years."

Just then, a sly smile spreads across Bryan's face. "Oh speaking of which, there's one more thing I forgot to give you, Mom." He says, pushing himself off the sofa to dig a folded sheet of paper out of his pocket.

She narrows her brows as he hands over the paper, and she

87

unfolds it. "What's this?" She asks, as she reads over it.

"That's my new address." Bryan says with a grin.

"New address? What do you mean?"

"Well, I still have to finish my contract, but in the meantime, I'm buying some land with a shop on the edge of town. I'm going to have a trailer put on the property and open a mechanic shop. Think Fawn Creek could use another mechanic?"

Mom's eyes fill with tears. "Wait. Please tell me you're not kidding. You're really moving back home? So I'm going to have you both here with me in Fawn Creek again?" She asks excitedly, looking back and forth between the two of us.

"Afraid so," Bryan confirms. "If you think Avery and I are annoying now, just wait until you have to put up with us every Sunday evening for family dinner."

Quickly, Mom reaches up and wipes the tears from the corners of her eyes. "I think I'll find a way to manage." She says with a chuckle. "Thank you. This is the best gift you could have gotten me."

Bryan nods and then motions to Derek. "You can thank that guy. He's the one that found me the property and put in a good word for me with the owner so I could get it for a steal of a price."

Mom turns to Derek. "Well, I guess that makes you a winner in my book." She says with a smile. "Thank you."

As if he wasn't already.

* * *

It's just before 8:00 am on Christmas morning when Derek lightly taps on my front door. As quietly as possible, I make my way to the entryway and let him in. He greets me with a kiss before he puts a pile of presents on the floor in front of the tree.

"Good morning." I swoon, looking into his eyes. "Thanks for coming over."

"Thanks for inviting me. Christmas morning is pretty lonely when you live by yourself. Especially with my parents out of town. Besides, I'm excited to watch Juliet open her gifts. I can't believe she's not up yet."

I nod. "It's a miracle when the adults wake up before a kid on Christmas morning and I'm just trying to enjoy it." I admit.

"Well, would a French toast casserole help you enjoy it a little more?" He asks, but without waiting for a response, Derek disappears out the front door, returning moments later carrying a casserole dish.

"I'm so glad you can cook." I say with a laugh. "That smells way better than the breakfast cereal I was planning to have today. How did you have time to make that? You were here pretty late last night."

Derek shrugs. "It took basically no time."

Derek and I stayed up last night to create the magic of Christmas. After filling stockings and putting together a plastic dollhouse, he practically crawled out the door after midnight after promising to return this morning to enjoy the fruits of his labor and keeping true to our agreement not to have any sleepovers while Juliet is home.

Even though we were the ones to make the magic happen last night with our Christmas prep, it still takes my breath away this morning. We settle onto the couch with the Christmas tree as the only thing illuminating the space, with our coffee and our breakfast. There is just something about enjoying the stillness of Christmas morning by the glow of twinkling lights before the chaos begins. Just as I finish my first cup of coffee, I hear a tiny voice come over the baby monitor, asking for her mama.

"Well, it was nice while it lasted." I say with a laugh as I stand from the couch. "I'll be right back."

Within minutes, Juliet is having the time of her life, ripping open sheets of wrapping paper to reveal her gifts. The pile of new toys and books grows next to her as she completes the unwrapping process.

After she finishes opening and begins to play with her toys, I plop down next to Derek, exhausted.

"Looks to me like Juliet had a pretty good Christmas," Derek says. "I hope you did, too."

"Of course, thank you for my gifts." I say, looking at the pile next to me, including a vinyl cutting machine and everything to go with it. "You outdid yourself, and I feel like I need to go get you more than a few shirts and locally brewed beer."

"Nonsense," He says, wrapping his arms around me and pulling me close. "I have everything I need here with you two girls. Besides, I know you've been eyeballing that machine for a while. You'll have a lot of fun making things for yourself and Juliet, I'm sure."

"You're too good to me." I say, slowly kissing his lips. "I hate to say it, but I need to get Juliet ready. Susan will be here soon to pick her up so she can do this all over again at her house." I say as I move from the couch and pick up Juliet. "Hey sister, it's time to go get dressed and go to Grandma's."

"Toys!" Juliet screams, reaching for her gifts scattered all over the living room floor. "I want play toys!"

I sigh. "I know. They'll be there when you get back." I

promise her. "For now, you have to get ready to go see Daddy and Grammy."

Juliet begins to cry and buries her head in my shoulder as she fights me. Realistically, I know the source of her sadness is from wanting to play with all of her cool new gifts. However, her cries are just enough to make me tear up, too. I hate having to share her. Especially on days like today.

By the time I finish getting her dressed and packing her diaper bag, the doorbell rings.

"Can you grab that?" I yell down to Derek before turning to make my way down the stairs. But, I'm stopped in my tracks when I hear two male voices in the entryway of my house.

Quietly, I finish making my way down the stairs and find myself face to face with Cory and Derek. I plaster on my best fake smile and move towards the door.

"Hey. I thought your mom was coming to pick her up." I say, handing over Juliet and then her diaper bag.

He tells Juliet hi and then nods at me. "Yeah, she was in the middle of cooking breakfast, so I told her I'd come instead. Hope that's okay."

I shrug. "Of course. Well, everything she needs is in her bag. You guys have a great day and I'll come get her at noon tomorrow."

"Sounds good." He says, turning towards the door. "Tell Mom bye." He mutters to Juliet, with an obvious tone of anger in his voice.

"Bye baby. Have a good Christmas." I say to Juliet, causing her to turn and look back at me.

She immediately sticks out her bottom lip, and it quivers. Before I can say anything else, Cory walks out the door, closing it loudly behind him. I watch as they make their way to his

91

mother's car waiting in the driveway.

"Welp, I guess if Cory didn't know about us yet, he does now." I say nervously. "I didn't mean to hard launch us like that. Just because of how big of a jerk he always is, but I suppose at least the band-aid is off."

"We'll see." Derek shrugs. "The day is still young."

* * *

Cory: I knew it.

Me: You knew what, exactly?

Cory: I knew you were messing around with the cop. Why else would he be at your house before 10 am on Christmas morning? You were cheating on me with him the entire time, weren't you? You were just waiting on me to leave town so you could do it out in the open.

Me: No. Derek and I really were just friends when I told you we were. He and I didn't start dating until recently.

Cory: I don't believe you. And by the way, nice job putting your kid last by having a sleepover with a random guy on Christmas Eve. I knew you were a whore.

Me: You don't have to believe me. Go enjoy Christmas with your daughter and quit worrying about my life.

* * *

"Of course he has a problem with you dating a guy that's actually nice to you," Tyler says, rolling her eyes. It's the day after Christmas, and I came over to visit with her while I kill time waiting to pick up Juliet. "What did he expect, that you would become a nun when you two split up?"

I shake my head. "Beats me what he was expecting, honestly. I'm more angry over the fact that he accused me of cheating on him. When we were together, he was adamant that I was coming to Fawn Creek to cheat on him with Derek, because goodness knows that I couldn't be trusted to be friends with a guy." I say, rolling my eyes.

"Well, I for one, say screw what he thinks." Tyler says, crossing her arms over her chest. "You deserve to be happy more than anyone I know, and he lost the ability to have a say in your life when he sent you to the ER when you were pregnant with Juliet."

I nod, staring down at the coffee cup in my hand, remembering very clearly that night.

I had come to Fawn Creek to visit my mom while I was pregnant because Cory and I were living in Owen. While I was at her house, my mom suggested I look into a rental house a few blocks away. She hoped we would move back to Fawn Creek to be closer to family before the baby arrived. However, Cory was watching my every move on Life360, the tracking app he convinced me to download. When he saw I had gone somewhere I hadn't told him I was going, he immediately assumed that I was seeing another man. When I got home, he was already a six-pack deep. He was drunk and ready to argue. It all happened pretty quickly. Cory had me backed into a corner, and was screaming in my face when I tried to move and get around him. When he grabbed my arm to stop me, I lost my balance and my head hit an unfinished corner of the door frame behind me. This was about the time the police arrived, because the neighbors called them. I didn't even know I was hurt until

93

I felt the back of my head grow warm. I reached behind me to feel the spot, expecting a bump, but when I pulled my hand back, it was covered in blood. Never in my life have I been able to handle blood, and this time was no different. I took one look at my hand and I fainted, right in front of the officers on duty. They called an ambulance and forced me to go get checked out because I was visibly pregnant. This resulted in a night at the hospital to be monitored. Cory ended up getting arrested, not because he hurt me but because he tried to fight the officers when they questioned him. I had a long heart to heart with both Tyler and Derek the next day. During our talk, everything I had been dealing with came to the surface, including the fact that Cory had been controlling me through lies and manipulation since the day we found out I was pregnant. Tyler made me promise not to go back. The fact that I never want my daughter to put up with what I did gave me the strength to stay gone.

Tyler leans over and squeezes my hand, breaking my concentration. "Hey. Don't let him get to you and don't let him make you feel like less of a person for finally finding happiness."

I shake my head. "Don't worry, I won't. I just can't wait for him to leave town again and for my life to get back to normal. If there is even such a thing."

* * *

I make my way up to Susan's door right at twelve o'clock on the dot to pick up Juliet. I quickly press the doorbell button and step back, bracing myself for Cory to be the one to answer and to start a fight. However, Susan is the one to come to the door.

"Hi, Avery. Come on in." She says, holding the glass storm

door open. When I hesitate, she smiles softly. "Cory already headed back to Texas this morning." She assures me.

I nod softly and follow her into the house. Juliet is sitting on the floor, playing with a box filled with a pink and purple toddler sized LEGO set. "Mommy!" She cheers as she sees me enter the room. Abandoning her mess, she runs towards me and wraps her arms around my leg.

I bend down to pick her up and squeeze her tightly. "Hi, baby. How was your Christmas?"

"I got toys!" she cheers, throwing her hands over her head. The grin across her chubby little face brings me more joy than I was expecting.

"Aw, I'm so glad you had a good day." I reply, hugging her close to me once again. "Are you ready to go home?"

Juliet nods enthusiastically and then turns to wave at Susan. "Bye Grammy!" She bellows.

I laugh and crouch to set Juliet on the floor. "No. Let's pick up your toys first and then we will go."

Juliet rushes back to pick up her mess as I stand to face Susan. Susan is busily repacking Juliet's diaper bag. "I didn't realize Cory was headed back so soon." I say.

She scowls slightly and shakes her head. "Me neither. He got up this morning and told me he was heading back to work. I imagine it has something to do with a certain someone dating a hunky Fawn Creek Police Officer." She adds with a smirk.

I frown. "I didn't mean to upset him, seriously. If I knew he was coming for Juliet, I would've brought her here myself. Derek didn't stay the night, he just came over early to do Christmas with us."

Susan zips up Juliet's bag and then moves towards me, resting her hands on my shoulders. Her eyes search mine before she speaks gently. "Avery, it's none of my son's business who you are dating, and it's not mine either. As long as whoever it is treats you and Juliet right, then his opinion is irrelevant. I don't care if he does sleep at your house. It's your house and your choice to make." She pauses for a second to look back at Juliet and then lowers her voice. "Frankly, Cory should have been a better boyfriend to you if he was so worried about you ending up with someone else. I don't know Derek personally, but from what I've seen of him around town, I know he is a good guy. My son will get over it, eventually. I just want you to know that I support you and I know you won't let anyone around Juliet that you don't trust."

I let out a heavy breath and lean forward to wrap Susan in a hug. "Thank you." I say into her hair. "Your approval means a lot to me." I confide before pulling back to look at her.

"Oh, sweet girl." She says, gently smoothing my hair against my head. "I sure wish my son had been a different man. You are the kind of daughter-in-law that mothers hope for."

Just as I feel a puddle of tears building behind my eyes, Juliet speaks up. "Mama all clean!" She announces, throwing her arms wide to show us she finished cleaning up her mess.

She and Susan say their goodbyes before we make our way to the car. I strap her into her car seat and turn back once more to look at Susan's house. Maybe we are going to be okay after all.

Chapter 11

"Well, how do I look?" I ask as I make my way down the staircase into the living room, where Derek is waiting for me. I'm wearing a black cocktail dress with a pair of my highest heels. My long hair is in loose waves and trail down my back.

He lets out a slow, steady whistle. "Baby. You look incredible." He says, as he raises himself from the sofa and makes his way towards me. He closes the space between us and wraps his arms around my waist before lightly kissing my lips. "I am so damn lucky to get to be your date tonight." He mutters into my hair.

"You don't look so bad yourself." I say, standing back to admire Derek in a suit and tie for once. He's even more dressed up tonight than he was for Andrew and Tyler's wedding in the fall. "I like this look on you." I coo. "This is a nice change from your work uniform or a Grunt Style shirt and jeans."

He grins. "Well, it takes a pretty special lady to get me into a suit and tie. Especially when I have the night off for New Year's Eve. If it wasn't for you and this party, I'd be at home in bed long before midnight."

"Sorry, old man, but I really appreciate you taking one for the team." I say, straightening up his tie. "We just have to make it until midnight to watch the fireworks and then we can make our way back home and fall into bed."

Derek tightens his grip around my waist and bends me backwards to kiss my lips. "It's a good thing I'm crazy about you, and I know you are looking forward to this. Otherwise, I'd carry you back up those stairs and we wouldn't surface again until after the new year."

"While I don't mind the sound of that at all, our friends are going to be mad if we stand them up. Rain check?"

"I suppose so. We better get going before I change my mind and whisk you up those stairs." He says with a wink.

We step into the Blackledge Event Center and take the elevator up to the third floor. The Fawn Creek Betterment Group decided that this year a New Year's Eve Gala would be a great way to bring in some money for improvements needed in the downtown area. For weeks, they have advertised the fun that awaits us this evening and as soon as we step into the event space, I know we will not be let down.

The entire room is decorated in a motif of black and gold, in the form of balloons, streamers and table decor. At one end of the room is a large balloon arch being manned by a professional photographer. It's just the beginning of the party, but there's already a long line for photos.

Along another section of wall, there are a series of tables pushed together, holding what has to be the world's largest grazing table. The first section begins with a variety of meats and cheeses, in addition to jams, crackers and nuts. As we follow along the set up, we find where the display turns to a variety of fruits. After that, it leads to the biggest collection of cookies and delicate cake samples I've ever seen. I pull out my phone and capture photos and video clips while the table is still full and pristine looking.

"Let's find our group and then I need to come back and try one of everything." I tell Derek with a grin.

Just then, Sierra's voice calls out across the crowd to get our attention. I wave back and we make our way towards the large round table where Tyler, Andrew, Sierra, Cody, Madison and Ava are all waiting for us. We sit in the two remaining empty seats.

"Hey guys. Madison, where's Ben?" I ask.

She shakes her head. "He couldn't make it. Luckily, Ava saved the day and agreed to be my date." Ava is the local real estate broker. She rents an office in Tyler's building, and she is friends with Sierra and Madison.

"This is so fancy." I say, lowering my voice before picking up the place card in front of me. My name is written in calligraphy across the front.

"I know!" Tyler agrees. "I almost feel like someone is going to realize I don't belong here and come kick me out. Sheesh, I feel out of place." She confides.

"That'd be fine by me." Snickers Andrew before taking a sip of his beer.

Tyler rolls her eyes and turns back towards me. "Ignore him. He doesn't like anything that requires him to wear jeans that aren't stained."

"Well, I think you guys look amazing. All of you. I'm so glad we did this. After all the holiday madness, I needed some time off." I admit. "Now, I need to go find a drink. Derek, wanna come?"

"Lead the way." He says with a grin.

We make our way towards the bar and naturally, my mother is the hired bartender for the evening. As she spots us, her eyes light up.

"Hey." I say with a grin as we approach her. "I'm surprised Roscoe gave you a night off tonight." Mom works part-time at the little bar on the edge of town. She has since I was a kid.

"It was a hard sell, but he has other people that can help him manage the bar." She winks. "Besides, Cassidy needed me and how could I say no?" She motions towards Cassidy, who is running around making sure the event is perfect, as usual. "Do you want to try the special? It's a blackberry champagne mule."

"Oh, fancy. Yes, please." I say before turning to Derek to ask what he would like.

"Two please." He adds, handing mom our drink tickets, as he continues to survey the room. I guess one thing about dating an officer, is that he is never really off duty. He is always on alert.

Just then, Cassidy approaches us. "Oh, I'm so glad you came!" she exclaims, pulling me into a tight hug. "And thank you for the silent auction donation. It's going to be a big hit."

Last week, Cassidy had approached me about a donation for the auction tonight. Thanks to a plethora of items companies have sent me to make content with, I was able to piece together quite the basket. I started with a large trendy silicone bag and added a fancy metal tumbler. Then, I threw in a fully stocked snacklebox, a blanket, some high end makeup, and some hair tools. Overall, I think I did a great job, if I say so myself. Plus, it helped clear out some of the surplus that's taken over my dining room. It was a win for everyone.

"I can't wait to see how much it brings in." I confess. "It was a lot of fun to put together."

"Well, I've seen a lot of women eyeballing it already." My mom says. "I think it'll do well."

We spend the evening eating a four course meal, dancing to every line dance ever invented, bidding on too many things in the silent auction and taking way too many photos at the photo booth. By 11:45, all the ladies have kicked off their shoes and the men have ditched their coats and ties.

"It's almost time for the firework show." Tyler announces as she sits down to put her shoes back on. "Do you guys want to go outside to watch them? The view will be great out there."

"Plus, then we can hop in the car and head home." Andrew adds. He looks as tired as I feel.

"Sure! I think we are heading home afterwards, too." I say, looking at Derek.

He nods in agreement. "I'm ready for bed." He says with a laugh. "Like two hours ago."

"Boo... you old people," Sierra says with a teasing laugh. "The party doesn't end until two. Are you really going home now?"

I nod. "Afraid so. When you are elderly like us, you will also find yourself going to bed at 12:03 in the morning on New Years, if not sooner. Enjoy your energy while it lasts."

"Okay, goodnight you couple of grannies." Sierra says with a chuckle, waving goodbye as she pulls Cody back to the dance floor.

We say our goodbyes to our friends before making our way downstairs. At the end of the downtown area in Fawn Creek stands a pair of grain silos that overlook the business district. The fireworks will be shot off just behind the silos, creating a grand display over the top of them. Standing in the center of downtown gives us the perfect vantage point.

As we reach our destination, the brisk winter air immediately sends a chill through my cocktail dress, and I pull my coat tighter around my body. Derek stands behind me and wraps his arms around me to help keep me warm.

Tyler and Andrew are all huddled together next to us. Tyler looks almost as though she could fall asleep on Andrew's shoulder as we wait for the show to begin.

"When will this horrible exhaustion go away?" She groans. "I swear I could sleep for twenty-two hours and still wake up wanting a nap."

I reach over and pat her shoulder. "Not much longer, friend. In another couple of months, you'll have so much energy you won't know what to do."

"I hope so," Tyler replies with a sigh, just as her eyes move towards the space above the silos. "Oh, it's starting." She announces, pointing to the horizon.

We watch as the bursts of lights fill the night sky, one by one. I snuggle in closer to Derek, who still has his arms around my waist and his head resting on my shoulder. After a couple of minutes, I tilt my head back to look at him, and lightly he kisses my lips.

"Avery." He says just above a whisper, almost so quiet I don't hear him.

"Hmm?" I answer in response, craning my neck back once again.

"I love you."

The sound of those words sends a rush of emotions through my body. I've known that I loved him ever since the day we decided to try our hand at a relationship. I could feel it deep within my core, and maybe even before. However, this is the first time either of us has vocalized it.

"I love you, too." I say, spinning around to face him and wrapping my eyes around his neck.

"Happy New Year, Baby. I can't wait to see where this year takes us." He says as he places his finger under my chin to bring my lips to his.

"Neither can I."

I think it's already off to a great start.

* * *

"Well, tell me, are you one of those resolution type people?" Derek asks over his plate of scrambled eggs. It's just after ten o'clock and we both just crawled out of bed after our late night. Thankfully, Derek is a pretty excellent cook and made us some hangover breakfast.

"Not really." I shrug, clutching my cup of coffee. "I've never been a fan of waiting for a specific day to work on something. If it's important enough to you, you should just start. Even if it's just a random Tuesday in November. I do have some goals that I'd like to accomplish before the year is over, though." I admit.

"And what are those?" He asks, resting his fork on his empty plate, giving me his full attention.

"Well, first off, I want to finish paying off my car. That will take a lot of stress off my shoulders. Then, I really want to start working to pay off my house. My ultimate goal is to only have monthly bills looming over my head. Maybe then, by the time Juliet is in school, I can find a job that will allow me to be more present with her."

Derek nods. "What do you think you want to do?"

"Honestly, I don't know. For a while I thought I'd want to open a boutique, but the more I watch Tyler with her bookstore, the more I know I don't want that."

Derek frowns, obviously confused. "Why not?"

"I already have a job that demands a lot of my time and takes me away from my daughter. If I open a physical store, I'm going to be tied to it 24/7. Basically, I'll be less available to Juliet than I already am. At the end of the day, that's not what I'm aiming for. I want something that I can build around my life, not the other way around. I don't know yet what that will be, but it'll come to me eventually. For now, I just need to focus on what's in front of me. It's just important to me to be in a good place when Juliet is older and in school." I say with a shrug. "My dad left when I was four. He just got up and walked out on us, leaving my mom to take care of both me and Bryan on her own. Most of the time, she was our sole provider. Every so often she'd get a child support payment, but my dad mostly worked under the table so he didn't have to send anything, leaving it all in my mom's hands. Of course, we never went without, though. Mom always worked at least two jobs, if not three, to ensure that." I frown, looking back into my drink. "It was a double-edged sword, though. She couldn't just take off work to come to the Halloween parade or our class parties because she had bills to pay. Looking back, I understand she did what she had to do to provide for us, but at the time, all I knew was I was the kid whose mom never showed up. It sucked and I don't want Juliet to have that same experience."

Derek reaches across the table and squeezes my hand. "Avery, you are already doing such a good job at being that mom."

I nod. "And I want to continue that. I want to be the mom that shows up, but also I want to have a career. I want Juliet to have a positive role model in her life that she can proud of. Now I just have to figure out how to make it happen, while also doing what feeds my soul." I say with a shrug, before realizing that I've been rambling on. "I'm sorry. That was a lot. I didn't mean to dump all of that trauma on you." I say with a sigh. "What about you? Do you have any goals?" I ask, trying to change the subject.

Derek smirks before reaching across the table to squeeze my hand. "Just one. To figure out how to help you reach yours."

Chapter 12

One Month Later

I step up to the counter at Drip and place my order with Cassidy just as a flier taped to the wall catches my attention.

"Valentine's Day Daddy Daughter Dance." I read to myself as I let out a sigh. Just one more reminder of what I can't offer to Juliet. And another reminder of what I never got to do as a child. I just never had anyone that could even step in for this type of thing. My grandpa lived too far away to take me. My father was missing in action and my big brother was a teenage boy with better things to do. One year, Mom offered to take me herself, but I refused to allow it. I couldn't stand the thought of showing up with my mom at a Daddy Daughter Dance. I might as well have had a sign pinned to my back reminding everyone that I was the kid without a father.

And now, Juliet is following in my footsteps.

Cassidy brings me my drink and her eyes shift over to read the flier. "Is Juliet's dad going to be in town that day?" She asks, motioning her head towards the text.

I shake my head and take a quick sip of my drink. "No, he was just here for Christmas. He isn't due to come home again until March." I sigh.

"Maybe your brother can come to town and take her."

Cassidy suggests.

Immediately, I feel my face brighten. Of course, Bryan would love to take her. "That's a good idea." I tell Cassidy. "Thank you."

I pull my phone out from my pocket and text Bryan a photo of the flier.

Me: You doing anything on Valentine's Day weekend? I was wondering if you'd like to take Juliet to this.

Bryan: Oh man. I wish I was free that night. I'd take her in a heartbeat. But I'll be out of town for training.

Me: That's okay. Thanks anyway.

Cassidy watches me frown at my phone and knows the answer I just received. "He can't make it?"

I shake my head. "Nope." I say, shoving my phone back in my pocket. "It's fine. She's too little to know what she's missing out on, anyway. Maybe Cory will be around next year."

Just then, the bell above the coffee shop entrance dings merrily as Derek and his partner, Officer Andrews, step inside.

"Hey, maybe Derek can do it." Cassidy suggests, as she turns and heads back towards the espresso machine.

As soon as the words leave her mouth, I wish I could crawl under the floorboards of the store and hide. This is the exact thing I didn't want her to have to experience. A pity date for the dance is worse than no date at all.

"Do what?" Derek asks, as he walks next to me and lightly kisses my cheek. I feel my face blush under the contact of his lips.

"The Daddy Daughter Dance." Cassidy offers, pointing at the flier. "Juliet's dad won't be here and her uncle can't make it to town."

Without a pause, Derek pulls his phone out of his pocket and checks his calendar. "I work daylights that day, so I'm free to take her that evening if you want me to." Derek offers.

I smile, but just on the side of my mouth. More than anything, I wish I could just escape this entire conversation. Derek and I have been dating for nearly two months now. Juliet is completely smitten with him, and well, I am too. Of course, I'm okay with him taking her, but is it too soon? What if I let them develop this relationship and in a couple of months, Derek and I break up? Am I setting my baby up for more heartache?

I look up at Derek and search his expression. "I just don't want you to feel obligated to take her. It's not your job as my boyfriend to do this kind of stuff."

Derek turns to face me, placing his hands on my shoulders, and looks deep into my eyes before he speaks. "Avery, who says I feel obligated? I love Juliet and even if we weren't dating, I would still take her for you. She can never have too many people in her life that love her. I think the two of us would have a great time. If you are okay with it, I'm all in."

* * *

It's just before six o'clock in the evening when the doorbell rings. "Just a second!" I call down the stairway, as I make a final adjustment to Juliet's puffy pink formal dress. She pauses to look at herself in the mirror and does a little lopsided toddler twirl.

"You look so pretty." I tell her with a wide smile. "I think Derek is here to take you to your big dance. Wanna go find out?"

She nods excitedly. "Yay Rick! I want to dance!" She stomps in place, causing her black Mary Janes to hit the floor with tiny thuds.

"Well, we better go answer the door then." I lift Juliet from the floor and we quickly make our way downstairs. I pause and check the peephole. On the other side, I find Derek waiting patiently with his hands behind his back. I stoop down and stand Juliet on the hardwood floor before grabbing my phone from my back pocket and opening the camera. Once I make sure I'm recording, I open the front door and allow Juliet to meet her date face to face.

At the sight of Derek, she throws her hands in the air. "Rick!" She screams.

"Hi sweet girl." Derek says, crouching down to get to her level. "Do you want to go to the dance with me?"

Juliet nods excitedly, starting once again to break out her dance moves.

"Wow, you're a really good dancer." Derek tells her. "Hey, I got you a flower. Let me see your arm and we will put it on you."

Juliet sticks one hand out towards Derek, and sways almost as though she suddenly became shy. Derek slides a tiny white corsage on her wrist and makes sure it's in the perfect position before pulling away.

Juliet beams at her new accessory and then brings it to her face to smell the fake flower. "Mama smell!" She demands. I lean down and also smell the flower.

"Oh, that smells so pretty." I reply, throwing a quick wink in Derek's direction.

"Are you ready to go?" Derek asks.

"Let me get just a few pictures of you guys and then you can be on your way." I promise. I pose the two of them on the sidewalk in front of the house and get a series of photos before handing Derek my car keys. We had decided ahead of time that it would be easier for him to take my car than bother with moving her car seat.

I stand on the porch and watch as my car disappears down the street, to make the three-block trek to the dance. Why do I feel like half of my heart just drove away?

* * *

I'm sitting on my porch in my rocker enjoying a hot mug of chai tea when Derek and Juliet come pulling into the driveway after the dance.

Derek climbs from the car with a grin as I move towards him. "She's out like a light." He says with a laugh. "We weren't even out of our parking spot yet."

He opens the back door and I can't help but chuckle at the sight of my tiny toddler passed out in her big poofy dress.

"Did she party too hard?" I ask, unbuckling her from her car seat and lugging my sleeping toddler into my arms.

"So hard." He confirms. "Avery, I wish you could have seen her. She was dancing with Madison's girls and a couple of others that I guess she knows from daycare. Also, how in the world do a bunch of little kids know how to do the Cupid Shuffle? They were doing better than some adults I've seen at Short Creek."

I laugh. "That's all Madison. She takes music and movement time very seriously."

"I guess so." He says, shaking his head. "I'll send you all the pictures and videos I took when I get home. But seriously, we had so much fun."

"I'm so glad you did. And thank you again for taking her. You really didn't have to, but it means so much that you did."

Derek leans forward and kisses my lips gently. "I wanted to. She means the world to me, just like you do. Thank you for letting me."

"Want to come in for a bit?" I ask, motioning towards the house.

He frowns. "I wish I could, but I am beat. After working all day and dancing all night, I'm going to fall asleep when my head hits the pillow. Rain check?"

"I totally get it. You go home and get some rest."

He leans forward and kisses me gently once more. "It meant a lot to me that you let me take her. I know it's not the same as her dad being able to do it, but I love that kid and spending that time with her tonight is something I'll never forget. Thanks for letting me be a part of her life."

"Thanks for being a part of ours. We love you, too."

* * *

"Happy Birthday!" Tyler shouts across the restaurant as Derek, Juliet and I step inside. Today is my twenty-ninth birthday and one week since the Daddy Daughter Dance.

"Well, that's one way to ensure I'm going to be wearing a stupid sombrero with whipped cream all over my face by the end of the night." I mutter under my breath.

He laughs. "Have you met this group? There's no way they were letting you out of here without a heavy dose of embarrassment first. Might as well just embrace it. I'd be shocked if Tyler didn't bring her own whipped cream, just in case. Your friends love you and they want to celebrate you. We all do."

We make our way towards the table. I move around the table, greeting each of my friends with a hug and a thank you for coming. When I land in front of Madison, I find once again that Ben is missing.

She shakes her head. "Working." is all she offers.

It seems to me that something is definitely up with the two of them. But I'm not sure what.

I put Juliet in a high chair next to Kenzi and then take a seat across from Sierra and Cody. Suddenly, looking over my group of people, something settles deep inside of me. I've always been the person to have a multitude of friends. Bar friends, girl's trip friends, work friends, and so on. But something has shifted in the friendship department ever since Tyler moved back home and got married. Instead of a plethora of different friend groups for a variety of reasons, they've meshed together into a group of people that I truly do life with. And I love it.

"Happy birthday to our famous friend! Your drink is on me!" The owner of the restaurant calls out from the bar, causing everyone in the place to turn to look, and causing me to sink down into my seat.

"Thank you!" I call back to him before turning to Derek with a flushed face. "That was so embarrassing. I am not famous."

"You definitely are small town famous." Tyler argues. "There were some preteen girls fawning over the fact that I'm your best friend at the store the other day. I should have offered to sell tickets to a meet and greet."

I let out a heavy sigh. "Of all the things I wanted to accomplish before thirty, this one was not even on my radar." I admit.

Madison shrugs. "Hey, if it's helping you reach your goals, then that's all that matters. Besides, I think it's kind of exciting. You're known for something you are truly good at. When you get to do what you love for a career, it's very rewarding."

I nod. "That would be great if it was my only career. Who knows how long this will actually last? I can't expect it to be this way forever."

"You should really think about opening a boutique." Madison suggests. "The women of Fawn Creek need your help shopping."

I laugh. "I love that idea, but I don't want a storefront. Then I'll be stuck there all the time and I'll miss out on everything with Juliet."

"What about an online boutique?" Sierra suggests. "You could start small. Then, if you ever decide to expand, maybe you'll be making enough to afford hire help."

I pause. "That's actually a good idea. I'll have to look into that."

"Yes! You could do vendor events and you could even set up a little area in my store if you want." Tyler offers. "It would be a great place to start."

I nod. "I think you're right. I'm not ready yet, but when I am that may be the way to go."

Chapter 13

The ringing phone in the middle of the night causes me to jolt and sit up in bed. Even in my half asleep stupor, I can see Susan's name flash across the screen, causing me to panic. Juliet is with Susan tonight and it's currently three in the morning. A million thoughts immediately flood my brain and none of them are good.

"Please let my baby be okay." I pray as I fumble with hitting the answer button.

"Hello?" I answer quickly and out of breath, bracing myself for the worst.

"Avery, Juliet is okay." Susan immediately blurts out. "Cory got into a terrible wreck in Dallas. It's really, really bad. I have to go to him. I need to bring you Juliet right now." She rattles off with a shaking voice.

"Of course." I say, clutching the phone to my ear. I climb from my bed in the darkness and move towards the closet to get some clothes. "Do you want me to come there? Or.."

She cuts me off quickly. "Nope, it's fine. I'm stopping at your house and then driving straight to the hospital. I'll be there in about five minutes to drop her off." She pauses, almost as though she's catching her breath. "Thank you, Avery. I know I probably sound like a crazy old woman right now, but Cory is and always will be my baby. I just need to get there. No matter how old your kids get, when they are hurt, you just want to be with them."

I nod in the darkness as though she can see me. "You don't sound crazy at all." I assure her. "I'll be waiting downstairs for you. See you soon." I add, before we both say goodbye and disconnect the call.

Just as I finish dressing, I step out of the closet and find Derek propped up on one elbow in bed, squinting in the light spilling out from behind me.

"Hey." I whisper. "You can go back to sleep. Cory got in a wreck and his mom is going to see him. I guess it's pretty bad. She's bringing Juliet home right now."

Derek doesn't even hesitate. He sits right up and begins to gather his clothes. "I'll get up with you." He says. "I'm sure you'll be up for a while trying to get Juliet down."

I shake my head. "No, it's okay. I know you have to work tomorrow. I can handle it. She and I can sleep on the couch."

"I'll be fine." He says, already wearing his jeans. He closes the space between us and pulls me close to him. "I want to be where you are, not in this empty bed without you."

* * *

Headlights flash across the living room wall as Susan pulls into the driveway. I rush to open the front door, just as Susan is making her way towards me, with Juliet in her arms.

"Thank you, Avery. I'm so sorry I woke you." She says, handing Juliet's diaper bag to me.

"Nonsense." I say, tossing it on the floor next to me. "Don't

115

worry about me. You just worry about getting to the hospital safely."

Susan transfers Juliet into my arms, and I use my spare arm to wrap her in a hug. "Be careful, okay? And let me know if there is anything I can do."

"Thank you, Avery. For just being who you are. You really mean the world to me," Susan says, squeezing my hand. "Goodbye Juliet. Grandma loves you." She adds before turning and making her way back down the driveway.

I close the door and turn around to face Derek, while Juliet clutches me. "Mama, I sleep with you." Juliet mumbles, rubbing her face into my hair.

Derek smiles softly. "Go on up to bed. I'll sleep on the couch."

I frown. This is not how our night alone was supposed to go. "I'm sorry, Derek. I know you stayed the night to stay with me, not to sleep on my uncomfortable sofa."

"Go. It's only a few hours. I'll wake you up before I leave for work." He says, leaning in to kiss my lips. "Love you."

I want to argue with him, but I'm so tired. And Juliet is so heavy already half asleep in my arms. "Love you, too." I groggily reply, as I turn to make my way up the stairs and back to my room.

It's not long before Juliet cuddles against me in bed, peacefully snoozing away in the safety of my bed. This may not have been the night I wanted, but it turned out to be exactly what she needed.

* * *

The smell of bacon tickles my nose and wakes me from a deep slumber. Slowly, I sit up in my bed and look around, trying to make sense of the fact that my house smells like food. It never smells like food unless... Derek's here.

Quickly, it all comes rushing back to me. The house smells like breakfast because Derek spent the night. On my sofa because Juliet slept with me. I feel around next to me for my sleeping toddler and she's not there.

My heart races as I spring from my bed, looking for my missing toddler. "Juliet, where are you?" I ask, peeking my head into my closet. No sign of her there. My bedroom door is closed, just like it was when I came to bed last night, and she's not tall enough to turn the knob herself. Where could she be?

I fling the bedroom door open and rush downstairs in search of her, praying that Derek has her. I'm met with the sound of Juliet's giggles and red dirt music playing on my Alexa. Relief washes over me. I quietly creep into the kitchen and take in the scene.

Derek is standing at the stove, removing the last of the bacon from the frying pan and adding it to a plate rested on the counter. Across the room, Juliet is sitting in her high chair wearing her princess footie pajamas from last night, while munching away on a plate of scrambled eggs with toast. Derek sings along to "Pearl Snap Shirts" by Jason Boland & The Stragglers while rocking his hips from side to side. Juliet dances along in her highchair while she eats.

I pause and rest against the door frame, just enjoying the show. Until Derek turns around and catches me.

"Hey, beautiful." He says, his face immediately turning a dark shade of red. "Breakfast is almost ready. You hungry?"

"Starving, but please, don't stop dancing on my behalf." I

say with a laugh before making my way towards Juliet.

She grins up at me happily and says "Mommy!" before I kiss the top of her head.

"Hi, baby. Did Derek make you some yummy breakfast?"

"Mmmmm Hmmm." She hums in agreement before shoving another handful of scrambled eggs into her mouth.

I move towards Derek and kiss his cheek. "Thanks for all this, and for letting me sleep in. You could have woken me up when she got up."

He moves towards me and wraps his arms around my waist, pulling me in close to him. "I was up early. Your couch sucks." He says with a laugh. "After seeing that you have no actual food in this house, I ran to my place and ransacked my fridge. I figured you girls could use a decent breakfast after last night. When I got back, I checked on you. You were still out cold, but she was stirring. I figured I'd get her started on breakfast so you could sleep in a little longer."

I frown. "I have food in my fridge."

He laughs. "You have three eggs, four pieces of cheese, and a cup of milk."

"Well, I was planning to go to the store at some point today. That would have been plenty of food for Juliet and me for this morning."

"Which is why I ransacked my own house. I eat three eggs myself every morning." He says, handing me a plate of food and then turning to make his own.

I break off a piece of bacon and toss it in my mouth. "Man. With as many eggs as you eat, you should try to convince the city to allow people in town to have chickens."

Derek laughs. "There's a lady just outside of the city limits that has something like fifty chickens. I buy all of my eggs from her."

I chuckle. "I'm pretty sure that's where Tyler's rooster went to live. His name is Fernandez."

Derek laughs. "Do I want to even know how Tyler got a rooster?"

I shrug. "He just showed up one day and kind of adopted her after she moved into Hazel's house. No one knows where he came from. He just showed up and became her alarm clock."

Derek laughs. "Well, that's weird, but sounds exactly like something that would happen to Tyler." He says, shaking his head. "Hey, have you heard anything from Susan this morning?"

"I haven't even thought to check my phone. After I woke up and found Juliet missing, I panicked and ran down the stairs to find her." I admit. "Be right back."

I hurry back upstairs to retrieve my phone from the charger. The first message on the screen is from Susan.

Susan: Hi Avery. I hope this doesn't wake you. Cory's accident is worse than I could have ever imagined, I'm afraid. He's in the ICU with a lot of broken bones and a brain bleed. They are keeping him under right now to speed up the healing process, but honestly, the doctor is not sure he is going to make it.

I read the words once and then once more, trying to make sense of them. Suddenly, my mind is racing in a million different directions. How did this happen? What if he doesn't make it? How do I help a toddler understand if her dad dies? How I raise a kid for her entire life without her father? What am I supposed to do next?

I stand from the bed and quickly rush back down the stairs to Derek. I enter the kitchen to find him washing the breakfast dishes in the sink. Gently, I slide the phone onto the counter so he can read the message. As he reads, the words echo in my mind.

Cory. ICU. Brain Bleed. He might not make it.

I look back towards my daughter, happily chewing on her toast, completely oblivious to the fact that her father is almost six hours away fighting for his life right now.

My heart shatters for her, and for the unknown future that lies ahead for the both of us. It's all hanging in the balance, just waiting for Cory to open his eyes. No matter how much I despise that man, or what he's done to me, I'd never want something like this to happen to him. Or to Juliet.

Suddenly, I can no longer fight it. Before I can stop it from happening, the tears race down my face. Quickly, I turn to and throw myself into Derek's arms.

Derek hugs me tightly and kisses the top of my head. I know it probably makes no sense to him and I don't know if I can explain how incredibly complex this whole situation is to me. But he doesn't ask. He just holds me and allows me to cry.

"Mama?" Juliet's voice calls out from across the room, bringing me back to the current moment.

I step back from Derek and quickly wipe the tears from my face before turning to face my baby.

She reaches egg covered hands towards me and makes the grabbing motion. "Hold you?" She asks, sadly.

I've always thought it was so cute that she said it this way instead of asking me to hold her. Today I especially love it. I need it, even.

I force my best smile and remove the highchair tray before

unbuckling her and lifting her from her seat. I carry Juliet to the sink and seat her on the counter before using a dish towel to clean her hands and face. She, of course, fights me the entire time because nothing else is on her mind other than being held. After I finish, I scoop her into my arms and hold her close to my body. Quickly, she melts into me, rubbing her face into my hair that's pooling around my shoulder.

I turn to face Derek, my eyes searching his for answers that I know neither of us has.

"I don't know what to do." I whisper.

"Whatever you need to do, we will make it happen." He promises.

Chapter 14

"Are you sure you want to do this?" I ask as I buckle Juliet into her car seat, and Derek takes his place in the driver's seat of my car.

"For the twelfth time, yes, I'm sure." Derek reassures me. "There's no way I'm going to make you drive to downtown Dallas all by yourself. You don't even like driving in towns with stop lights. Of course I'm coming with you."

I take my place in the passenger seat and turn towards him. "You might get stuck sitting in the waiting room for a while."

"I can watch Tiktok for hours." He reassures me. "I do it all the time by accident."

When I don't reply to his joke, he turns towards me and picks up my hand before looking into my eyes. "I will be fine. I am merely here as a driver and a bodyguard at sketchy gas stations when you need to pee. You just worry about taking care of you and Juliet." He says before turning back towards the steering wheel.

It's been three days since Cory's accident. Last night, Susan called and told me he does not seem to be making much progress. The doctor suggested that if anyone wants to see him, now might be the time. I called Derek and told him I was going to have to make the drive to Dallas to take Juliet to see her dad.

I don't have any other option. Juliet needs to see her father and if I were the one laying in that bed, I would want him to do anything possible to get her to me one last time.

Derek immediately offered to drive us, and I reluctantly accepted. My reluctance wasn't because I wanted to do this alone by any means, but because I didn't want him to feel obligated to drive me.

Of course, he refused to listen to any kind of push back. He found someone to cover his shifts at work and told me to be ready by seven this morning. We have a long day and a long drive ahead of us.

I would never admit it to him, but I do find myself worrying that I am becoming too much work for him. I don't want him to regret his decision to be with me because of all of this drama in my life.

The hours stretch on as we make our way out of Kansas and across the entire state of Oklahoma. As expected, Derek is patient with his carload of inexperienced road trippers. He doesn't roll his eyes or lose his cool when Juliet poops in her diaper, twenty minutes after we stop for gas. He doesn't even laugh when I beg him to stop at Buc-ee's after we get into Texas and leave with an iced coffee, a taco and a stuffed beaver for Juliet.

To the naked eye, we just look like a family headed out for a vacation. Maybe we're headed to Galveston to get a weekend of sun. Or maybe just to Dallas to go to Great Wolf Lodge and the aquarium. The last thing that anyone would guess is that we are taking my toddler to possibly see her father alive for one last time. The reality of the situation hits me like a ton of bricks. This really could be it.

I watch Derek as he drives along, quietly singing along to the radio while Juliet sleeps in the backseat. Slowly, I reach my hand across the center console and place my hand on his thigh. He looks at me and smiles softly.

"Thank you for this." I say, just above a whisper.

He shakes his head. "No need to thank me. I would have been worried sick about you the entire time you were gone. It's better for all of us that I'm here."

I shake my head. "Not just for coming with me today. I'm so thankful for who you are, Derek. Even when we were just friends, you always came to my rescue. No matter how busy you already were or how tired you were from working all night. It didn't matter if I wanted you to drive by my house to make sure Cory wasn't lurking around outside after we got into a fight, or if I asked you to come kill a spider for me. You have just always been there for me. You've always been my knight in shining armor, and I don't know what I would do without you." I take a deep breath. "I just love you so much."

Derek smiles and squeezes my hand. "Avery, I love you, too. You make it easy for me to want to rescue you. The both of you. You two are my girls and I will do anything to make your life better. Even if it means driving through downtown Dallas to sit in a hospital with your ex future mother-in-law."

I grin. "You're really one of a kind, you know that? We're so lucky to have you."

Derek just shakes his head. "I'm the lucky one."

* * *

We park in the covered lot and take a second to get our bearings before heading inside.

"You ready for this?" Derek asks, turning towards me.

"I... have no idea." I admit. "Hospitals honestly freak me out. I'm not good with tubes and blood and all that. My mom used to beg me to go into nursing when I was in high school, so I'd have a stable job. I considered it until a kid at school cut his finger during home economics and bled all over the place. I fainted at the sight of his blood. That was easily the most embarrassing day of my life." I shake my head, the memory itself causing me to shiver. "I just don't do blood. Just like the night with Cory."

Derek nods. "Oh. I remember that night. It felt like a nightmare coming true. I have a buddy that works for the Owen police department. As soon as the two of you started dating, I talked to him about you both. You just moved to Owen and disappeared off the face of the Earth, and I was concerned. While Cory hadn't been in trouble before, he knew who the guy was and told me he'd watch out for you. Anyway, he called that night to tell me Cory had been booked and told me everything that had happened. I was working and I swear time had never moved as slowly as it did while I waited for my shift to end so I could come check on you." He frowns. "I thought I was doing the right thing by giving you space. So, I had to convince myself that you didn't feel for me like I did for you. I thought stepping back and letting you live your life was the right choice. That morning, I found out how wrong I was to just let you go. And I promised myself that if I ever was lucky enough to have you, I'd never let you go again."

I let out a haggard breath and quickly wipe away the tears streaming down my face. "I wish I hadn't been so blind. It sure would have saved me a lot of headaches."

He nods. "Yeah, you were kind of blind." He agrees. "But I wouldn't change it for the world. Because without all of those headaches, Juliet wouldn't be here. And I wouldn't get to fall in love with you, as a mom. And that's why I can never hate Cory as much as I really want to. Because at least he was a part of my favorite kid in the world. And for that, I'll always be grateful."

* * *

As we approach the sliding doors of the hospital from the parking garage, I spot Susan standing inside, waiting for us. I had texted her when we arrived so she could meet us at the door. The last thing I need is to get lost in this big hospital.

The anxiety and stress that she's endured for the last few days is already apparent on her face and body. Her eyes are swollen and they look as though she's done nothing but cry since she got the call. She was already a tiny woman, but she looks like she's lost ten pounds in the past few days. I wish I knew what to do to help her feel better. While Cory wasn't the dad I would have chosen for my baby, I couldn't have chosen a better grandmother myself.

As soon as she spots us, she rushes towards me. She pulls me into an embrace as though I'm an old friend, not the ex-fiancé of her son. I stand and let her continue to hug me for as long as she needs, which turns out to be quite a while.

"Thank you for coming." She whispers into my ear.

"Of course. You do so much for us. We had no problem doing this for you." I reply when I finally step back from her embrace and squeeze her hand.

We follow her down the halls of the cold hospital. I push

the stroller while I follow Susan, with Derek trailing behind carrying the diaper bag. Once we get into the waiting room, I take Juliet to the bathroom to change her diaper. She's in a good mood, despite being stuck in her car seat all day. Luckily for us, she did a good job of napping and quietly snacking on cheerios and goldfish crackers for most of the way here. Hopefully, that means she will continue to be in a good mood for her visit with her dad.

We step back into the waiting room to find Derek and Susan waiting for us. Susan's eyes light up just a little when she sees us enter the space. She moves towards me and takes Juliet into her arms.

"Are you ready to go see Daddy?" Susan asks.

Juliet answers "Yes!" excitedly before hugging her grandma.

I can't help but frown. My poor baby. She's so excited to go somewhere with her beloved grandma, but what's waiting for her down the hall is surely not what she's expecting.

I watch the two of them make their way down the hall. I wish I knew what Juliet was walking into. Is he covered in bandages? Will she even recognize him? Will she be afraid to see her dad lying in that bed? I trust Susan and her judgment, but I also can't help but pray that my baby will be okay. This is a lot for a toddler.

After a few moments, I finally feel as though I can let out a sigh of relief. I don't hear Juliet crying. Susan hasn't rushed to bring her back to me. This must mean that they are okay. At least that's what I tell myself to calm my nerves.

I turn to Derek and our eyes meet. I send him a gentle smile and he reaches across to squeeze my hand. "You doing okay?" He asks.

I nod. "I guess so. This just all feels super weird." I admit.

"You're doing the right thing for her. You're a wonderful mom and she's lucky to have you." He tells me softly.

"Thank you." I reply. The feeling of anxiousness still refuses to leave my body. I just want my daughter to come back and to be okay. And as much as I dislike Cory, I want him to be okay, too. For the sake of Juliet and Susan.

Derek and I sit quietly, scrolling through our phones, but I can't keep my eyes from moving to the hall every few minutes or so. After what feels like an eternity, but is really only just about twenty minutes, Susan and Juliet return. Juliet is still all smiles, snuggled against her grandma and clutching her stuffed beaver from the gas station.

I open my arms wide and welcome my toddler back into my lap. She happily accepts my offer.

"Hi Sweet Girl." I greet her as I hug her close, kissing the side of her head.

"That probably felt like a really long drive for such a brief visit." Susan says with a frown. "I'm sorry."

I shake my head as I stand from my seat. "No, don't be sorry. It's okay." I assure her. "What matters is that Juliet got to be here, even if just for a little bit." I glance over at Derek before speaking again. "We are actually planning to stay at the Hilton around the corner for the night. We can stop back by in the morning before we leave if you'd like us to."

Susan's eyes fill with tears. "I would love that." She says, quickly pulling me into a hug once again. "If it's not too much trouble." She adds, this time addressing Derek.

"Nope, none at all." He assures her.

I let my hand meet his at my side and squeeze it tightly, thankful for this selfless man that has been brought into my life.

Chapter 15

It's the morning after our visit with Cory and we are getting ready to make our way back towards the hospital. But first, we decide to take advantage of the free breakfast at the hotel. As Juliet is munching away on a biscuit, an older woman stops by our table and pauses.

"I just have to say that the three of you make a beautiful family. And she." The woman adds, pointing to Juliet. "Looks just like her daddy."

I grin at Derek as he graciously thanks the woman for her kind words. We pause and watch her make her way out of the front door of the hotel before speaking. When the coast is clear, I turn and face Derek with an embarrassed smile. "Well, that was slightly awkward." I say with a chuckle.

Derek laughs. "Meh. She's a cute kid, so it was quite the compliment. I'll claim her. I guess I'll claim both of you, actually."

"Oh, that's kind of you." I joke.

"What can I say? I'm a giver." Derek says with a smile before getting up to throw away his trash. "You ladies about ready to get this show on the road?"

"We might as well." I agree, cleaning up Juliet's biscuit mess.

I text Susan as we leave the hotel and again when we arrive in the parking garage to let her know we've made it. Once again, she's waiting for us at the door, but today she has a look of hope spread across her face.

"Cory woke up last night." She tells me, excitedly, as I make my way towards her. "And he spoke. He asked to see you and Juliet this morning."

I try to hide the scowl on my face when she mentions he asked to see me. Juliet? Sure. But why me? I don't want to see him. We came for her and her alone. I'd rather he not even know that I'm here at this point.

All the way to the waiting room, I wrestle with myself in my head, trying to decide how I should handle this. Do I go in and risk there being a big dramatic moment in the hospital? Every time we see each other, Cory can't help but to start a fight. And the last time we saw each other, there was drama over Derek. I don't want to deal with that again today.

Do I refuse to see him and cause an even bigger problem? I don't want to upset his mom. She's been nothing but a blessing to me since day one. I feel like no matter what I do, I can't possibly win. Either way, it's going to be a total shit show.

I park the stroller in the waiting room and look at Derek for guidance. He smiles softly and pulls me into a hug. "It'll be okay." He whispers. "Maybe he wants to thank you for bringing her. Just get it over with. I'll be right here waiting for you. Besides, he's injured, so you can definitely outrun him."

I nod. Of course. There is no reason for me to assume that he wants to see me so he can start a fight. He's hurt. He nearly died. Surely, he has bigger things to worry about than who I'm sleeping with.

I clutch Juliet in my arms, and slowly follow his mother down the hall to his room. Cory is sitting up in bed waiting for us, with a groggy expression on his face. He looks rough. You can tell that he's been through a lot in the last several days. He's bruised and covered in bandages, but nothing I would worry about scaring Juliet. She probably just thinks he looks silly, to be honest.

I turn to look at Susan, waiting for her to lead the way. Instead, she points to a sign on the door instructing that there can only be two visitors in an ICU room at one time.

I nod and take a deep breath. I wish I had known I was going into this alone. A bit of a warning would have been nice. I look back at Cory. While he looks better than I pictured, the pain he's in is obvious. His eyes look tired. He seems to have lost a lot of his muscle structure since the last time I saw him. I admit, I feel awful for him. He's not a great person, but no one deserves this much pain.

He smiles weakly, but his eyes light up as we enter the room. I reassure myself that his delight is over Juliet, not me. I am merely a vessel for bringing his daughter to see him.

"Avery." He croaks out, with a rough scratchy voice.

I smile politely and step closer, holding Juliet in front of my body like a shield. "Hi, Cory." I offer in response. "How are you feeling?"

He lifts his hand with an obvious look of pain on his face and slides a finger across Juliet's arm as she sits on my hip. She turns to look at him momentarily, before turning her attention back to the stuffed animal from the gas station.

"Avery." He speaks again, as he attempts to push his hand against the bed to sit himself up higher. He winces in pain and immediately falls back to his original position. "I just wanted to tell you I'm sorry. I know I was a jerk, and you didn't deserve the way I treated you."

It takes every ounce of strength in my body to keep from rolling my eyes. Why is it that near-death experiences make people finally want to become a better person? Why can't they just choose not to be assholes to begin with?

"I know you're sorry." I tell him, skirting around accepting his apology. "Juliet, can you say hi to your dad?" I ask the toddler in my arms, trying to take the attention off of me. She looks at him and back at me. This time, she quickly buries her face in my chest.

"No." She declares.

Of course, she wouldn't be in the mood to speak to him either. She hardly knows who he is.

I offer him a frown. "Sorry, she's probably just tired. I imagine it's been a weird couple of days for her coming to a strange place and seeing her dad hurting."

As if on cue, Juliet begins to cry.

He nods and pauses for a beat, like he's going to say something, but then changes his mind. "It's okay. I just wanted to tell you I was sorry. I better let you guys head back home. You have a long drive." He says, finally. "Thank you for bringing her to come see me. Bye, Juliet. I love you." He adds that last part, almost as an afterthought.

"Of course." I say with a nod. "Get better." I add, before turning and leaving the room.

We meet Susan and Derek in the waiting room. Derek is staring at his phone and Susan is quietly reading a newspaper. I stop to take in the scene. At the end of the day, they really are just two strangers. Two people only tied together by me, and my daughter. But, they are two strangers that love us both so much. Life is weird.

"Okay." I say, breaking the silence and causing both of them to look up at me. "I guess we're ready to go."

Susan frowns, just slightly. "That wasn't very long." She says.

I shake my head. "Juliet wasn't really having it this morning, I'm afraid. We're going to let Cory get some rest and head back home." I say, bending down and buckling Juliet into her stroller once again for the walk to the parking garage. For some reason, I can't shake the feeling of being in that room with him. I need air.

Susan smiles warmly. "I get it. I don't enjoy hanging out in germy hospitals, either." She tells Juliet, before turning to look at me. "Thank you so much for making the trip up here. I know it meant a lot to Cory, and it means a lot to me as well."

"Of course." I reply. "If it were me, I would have wanted the same thing. Do you need anything before we go? Or anything I can do for you at home? I don't mind watering plants or gathering your mail if you need me to."

She shakes her head softly. "No, thank you, but I have it all covered. I will let you know when I'm back and when Cory is better, too."

"Okay." I say with a soft smile. "Get a hold of me if you change your mind about needing anything done at your house. I'm happy to help."

"I will." She says as she bends down to tell Juliet goodbye before turning to Derek. "And thank you for driving them and getting them here safely." She says to him, sincerely. "It makes me feel so much better knowing they aren't alone."

Derek waves her off. "No problem at all." He says with a smile, as he reaches out his hand and rests it in the middle of my back. "I was happy to do it."

With that, we say our goodbyes and make our way back to

the covered parking garage. Leaving Dallas in our dust.

* * *

We stop once more at Buc-ee's on our way out of Texas and then settle in for our long drive home. I sip my iced coffee and stare out the window, watching the world fly by.

It's crazy to me that it's only been a week since my birthday dinner. If Cory hadn't been so lucky, we could be at his funeral instead of driving home from seeing him in the hospital.

"What are you thinking about over there?" Derek asks, as he reaches across the center console and squeezes my knee.

I shake my head. "Everything and nothing." I confess, before turning to see if Juliet is sleeping. Her reflection in the over the seat mirror in front of her backwards facing car seat tells me she is out like a light.

I turn to Derek. "I feel like a total jerk."

He furrows his brow. "Why?"

"Do you know how many times I've joked about wanting something to happen to that guy? Like, I've seriously said to people that if he would just die, my life would be so much easier." I shake my head. "That's a terrible thing to say. Especially about my child's dad. And now he really did almost die."

Derek shakes his head and turns to steal a glance at me. "Avery. Everyone says crap like that sometimes."

I don't reply, I just look down at my lap.

"Avery. You went through hell and back with that guy. He had you convinced that you two were made for each other. Then, he moved you out of town and then he quickly got to work on breaking your spirit. He took the most beautiful, fun, friendly girl I've ever met and turned her into someone that quit leaving the house and quit having friends just to make him happy. That guy guilt tripped you and lied to you and turned your life upside down. You have every right to have felt those things about him. It doesn't make you a bad person, it makes you human."

I nod. "I would just feel awful if he had died. We could have easily been at his funeral today instead of visiting him in the hospital. And then my kid would have lost her chance at ever really getting to know her dad."

Derek squeezes my hand. "I love you, Avery. You have a bigger heart than you give yourself credit for."

Chapter 16

Four Weeks Later

"Hey, I'm here!" Derek calls up the wooden staircase to me. "Hungry?"

"Starving! I'll be right down." I shout back to him, leaning over the bathroom counter to apply a layer of mascara.

It's Tuesday and Juliet is with Susan and Cory tonight. Cory is back home after a brief rehab stay and wanted to spend some extra time with her. Since Derek's off work we decided to have an impromptu movie night. He even cooked us some homemade hibachi and brought it over for dinner.

We may not be going anywhere fancy, but I still want to look nice for my date, so I'm quickly finishing up my hair and makeup. I toss my mascara into my makeup bag and fluff my hair once more. Then, I pull out my phone to take a quick mirror selfie to post on my social media. Of course, I need a cute picture of myself in the lounge wear I'm sporting, so I can use it as content later. But, I get distracted by a text.

Cory: Hey. I was wondering if we can get together sometime. To talk.

I frown down at my phone. What could he possibly want to talk about now?

Cory: I know you're dating Derek and he's probably a nice guy but Avery, we belong together. Me, you and Juliet are a family. I'd really like to make things work between us. I want our family under one roof, how kids are meant to be raised. I love you, Avery. And I think deep down, you still love me.

I read the final text before locking the phone and sliding it into my pocket. I don't know how to even begin responding to something like that. But, I will not be letting it ruin my date night with my boyfriend. Besides, Cory should be spending time with his daughter instead of texting me.

After everything he put me through, what makes him think I'm going to go back to him now? Even if Derek wasn't in the picture, I would never put myself through all of that trauma again. And I refuse to raise my daughter in a toxic environment like that. She will not grow up to see me married to anyone that doesn't treat me like an equal. It's what I deserve and what I want her to demand in her own relationships as she grows up.

Besides, Derek IS in the picture, and things are going well for us. We get along great and really enjoy spending time together. There is no one in the world that I'd rather be with. Nothing and no one is going to change that.

I make my way down the stairs and find Derek waiting on the couch for me.

As I enter the room, he grins. "I swear, woman. You can't even get to your living room on time. One of these days I'll teach you to be punctual."

"If anyone can do it, I'm sure you'll be the one to pull it off." I say with a laugh. "Just don't be surprised if not even you change me."

He grins. "It's a challenge I'm willing to take, even if I have to work at it for the rest of our lives." He says, before pulling me in for a kiss.

The rest of our lives? I don't hate the sound of that.

* * *

"Well, that was... something." I say with a laugh, as Derek uses the remote to turn off the movie.

"I still can't believe that's the first time you've ever watched *Stepbrothers*. It's a classic." He says, shaking his head.

"Where would I be without you exposing me to all this culture?" I laugh, as I stand up in front of Derek before lowering myself down onto this lap. This time, straddling his legs so that I'm facing him.

"You'd be lost, really." He says into my hair, as his hands grip my sides. "Hey, Avery. I have a question. What do you think about us moving in together?"

Out of everything I could have possibly expected for him to ask me, this was the last thing I expected. I pause, trying to formulate a response. "Well. I don't know. I guess I hadn't really thought much about it yet. My house is super little. Where will we put your gym equipment? And Diesel? He needs a fenced-in yard." My mind begins to race with everything that needs to be taken care of before we could move forward. Immediately, I feel overwhelmed.

Derek laughs. "Actually, I was thinking that we could move into my house. My gym equipment can go in the garage and I already have a fence. There's plenty of room."

I frown. "Your house? But you live on the outside of town. You can't walk anywhere from your house and it's just a rental."

He shrugs. "Sure, but we could work on saving up to buy something else. If we live together, we can split the bills and save up just as quickly, and we could buy our dream house in no time."

My thoughts begin to race.

Dream house? I don't want a dream house. I want my house. If I move out of my house and in with him, what happens when we break up? I'll be homeless again and I'll have to move in with my mom and I'll have to start from scratch for the second time. And what about my plan? I was going to pay my house off early and have no debt. How could I do that if we buy a dream house?

Derek reaches over and grabs my hand, pulling it towards his mouth to lightly kiss it. "You still in there, Avery?" He asks with a kind smile. "Talk to me."

His words break through the reel running through my mind, as I contemplate every possible worst case scenario I can think of for this. "Sorry." I apologize sheepishly. "Can we maybe talk about this later? Give me some time to think about it? I'm just tired."

"Sure. We don't have to talk about it until you're ready." The sadness in his voice causes my heart to ache. This is not how I meant for this night to turn out.

"Okay, I'm sorry." I apologize again. "Can we just go to bed?"

"Sure." He says, helping me stand from his lap and then taking my hand. "Let's go to bed."

And for the first time in our relationship, we lay in bed and go right to sleep.

Chapter 17

"Good morning!" I call out to Madison as Juliet and I make our way across the park towards her. It's Saturday and today is Fawn Creek's annual Easter Egg Hunt.

Madison is standing on the sidewalk watching her two girls play on the equipment while she talks to Ava and her daughter, Piper. I approach the women and bend down to release an excited Juliet. Immediately, she dashes off to play with her daycare friends.

"Mommy." Ava's daughter, Piper, whines. "This dress is itchy and the dumb sweater makes me look like a grandma. Can I please go to the car and put my normal clothes back on? I can't even play anything fun when I'm wearing this."

Ava crouches down to speak to her child. "Piper, I told you. You can change as soon as you take a picture with the Easter Bunny."

"I don't want a picture with that dumb bunny." Piper pouts, crossing her arms. "I just want chocolate." She adds with a sigh.

"Piper, that's enough." Ava says, with a raised brow, almost as a warning. "We had a deal. You smile cute for a picture for your grandma and then you get to do the egg hunt and keep all the candy for yourself. If I hear another complaint from you, we are going home and skipping the hunt. You got it?"

Piper sighs loudly. "Fine." She reluctantly agrees before turning on her heel and stomping towards the Easter Bunny.

Ava lets out a sigh of her own. "Sorry girls. You know, my mom used to say she hoped I'd end up with a kid just like me one day." She shakes her head and looks back at her daughter, who is standing in line with a scowl. "I grossly underestimated how bad that would be. I gotta go."

We watch Ava join her daughter in line and I can't help but laugh. "That's what I have to look forward to, isn't it?" I ask, eyeing Juliet, who is on the toddler sized play equipment, playing hide and seek with Kenzi.

Madison shrugs. "Well, if it helps any, Piper is kind of a rare breed. She's just..." Madison thinks for a moment, choosing her words carefully. "Piper's a great kid. She's just a little spicy." She says with a soft chuckle.

"I kind of got that vibe from her." I say with a laugh. "Honestly, I like girls that are a little spunky. She will probably be a great leader one day."

"Yeah, well. Let's hope she runs a cooperation, and not a prison gang." Madison adds. "Anyway. Juliet's first egg hunt. That's very exciting. Are you ready for this?"

I shake my head. "Not really. I can't believe she's already big enough to take part in this." I say, looking over at my daughter. "I'm a little worried that she will trampled by the big kids. But, I guess as long as she gets one egg, she will be happy. I honestly just want to get a picture of her with the Easter Bunny."

"She'll be fine." Madison promises. "Mostly, the toddler section is pretty calm. Only the kids that are up to two years old are allowed in there, so it is actually pretty tame."

"Good. I wasn't ready to have to fight a ten-year-old over

a plastic egg." I say with a laugh before checking my watch. "Okay, I think we have just enough time for our picture. I'm going to go take care of that while we can." We say our goodbyes and I go to get Juliet so we can join the photo line.

What I'm not expecting is to see my favorite on-duty officer making his way towards me across the park as we reach our destination.

"Hey you." I say, as Derek approaches us.

It's been a three days since Derek brought up the two of us living together, and just as long that I've been avoiding having the conversation. I'm still not sure how to approach the idea, but luckily he hasn't brought it back up yet.

Derek leans forward to lightly kiss my lips before bending down to say hi to Juliet.

"Are you ready to hunt for some eggs, pretty girl?" He asks.

Juliet nods excitedly in response. "Yes!" She announces. "I got a bucket!" Quickly, she takes her bright pink Easter pail from me and presents it to Derek.

"Oh, it's so pretty. Do you like pink?" He asks, examining the pail as though it's the most interesting thing he's ever seen.

"Yes!" she confirms with an excited nod. "I love it!"

"She's been very excited all morning." I tell him as we move forward in the line.

"I bet she has been." He says with a laugh. "Think she will actually get any of them?"

I shake my head. "Honestly, I'm not sure. I can't wait to see how she reacts."

Finally, it's our turn for a photo. I walk over to the bunny, who is sitting in an old wicker chair. "Hi Mr. Rabbit," I say, placing Juliet in his lap before stepping back to take a series of photos with my phone.

Juliet says "Cheese" and smiles widely, with no fear. I'm not sure this child has ever met a stranger, which may be a good or very terrible thing.

"Mom, you want to hop in here, too?" The rabbit asks.

"Oh, no it's okay." I wave him off, but Derek interrupts.

"Yes. She does." He says with a smirk. "Give me your phone." He commands with his hand out. "Everything is content, remember?"

I sigh loudly and make my way over to the rabbit. I stand next to the chair, behind where he is holding Juliet.

"Say cheese!" Derek shouts, taking the photo.

"Cheese!" the three of us repeat.

"Thanks, Mr. Rabbit." I say with a smile, as I remove Juliet from his lap and place her feet on the ground. She immediately bolts back to Derek.

He turns to me, trying to not break character by maintaining his attempted cartoon rabbit's voice. "You know, your mom probably has a photo somewhere of me and you when you were that age." He says, pointing to Juliet, who is now hugging Derek's leg as though she hasn't seen him in years.

The local Lions Club puts the egg hunt on every year and the rabbit is one of Fawn Creek's retired police officers. He takes hiding his true identity very seriously, however when your mom knows everything about everyone in town, you also get insider information such as this.

"I didn't know you've been a rabbit for all that time." I say, shaking my head.

"I guess when you're great at something, the town lets you do it forever." He chuckles. "I wouldn't have it any other way."

"I see that." I say with a laugh. "Well, it was good seeing you. I better go get her lined up for her first egg hunt." We say our goodbyes and I make my way back towards Derek and Juliet.

Just as we turn to find where Juliet needs to be, I see the last person I was expecting today. Cory is making his way across the park towards us. We lock eyes and he instantly lights up, giving me a wave. I feel my stomach turn.

I exchange a look with Derek and sigh. "What do you think he's doing here?" I mutter quietly enough for Juliet not to hear.

Derek shrugs. "Maybe he just wants to see Juliet do her hunt. It's nice that he wants to be involved while he's home." He reminds me.

"I guess." I agree, just as Cory finishes crossing the park towards us, meeting us on the sidewalk.

"Hi Baby Girl." He greets Juliet. "Are you going to hunt for some eggs?"

She nods her head excitedly. "Yes!" She replies. "My basket!" She adds, showing him her pail.

"Oh, nice." He says before standing up to look at us. "Hey Avery. Derek." He nods at us both. "Why didn't you tell me about the egg hunt? I would have been here sooner. I just saw on Facebook that it was today."

My jaw drops momentarily, and I immediately feel defensive. How was I supposed to know that he suddenly wants to be an involved parent?

"I'm sorry. I didn't know that you'd want to come."

He rolls his eyes. "Of course, I wanted to come. She's my daughter."

My eyes flick over to meet Derek's and we exchange a knowing glance. Oh, brother.

Not one time since this baby was born has this guy wanted to be involved in anything. Now suddenly he wants to know why I didn't invite him? Now it's on me to see if he wants to be an active father?

"Welp, she's getting ready to start." I say, picking up Juliet and turning on my heel before making my way towards the patch of grass where Juliet's age group is meeting. Derek and Cory follow close behind, wordlessly. Juliet and I stand along the edge of the marked area where the hunt will take place and I bend down to coach her on what to do. The men stop, too. Allowing several feet between the two of them.

"When I say go, you run and pick up as many eggs as you can, okay?"

She nods, her eyes landing on one hot pink egg in particular. "Eggs." She repeats, with a determined look on her face.

The whistle sounds, alerting all the children of Fawn Creek to get started and off they go. Juliet takes off running and makes a dive for the pink egg she was watching so intently. Once she has it safely in her hand, she drops to the ground and gets to work on trying to pry it open.

"Juliet!" I call out. "Put the egg in your bucket and get some more."

However, she ignores me. She's content with her one pink egg. Instead, she abandons her bucket and then stands back up before toddling back to me. By the time she reaches me, the hunt is over.

"Did you get one?" I ask my very excited toddler. "Want to see what's inside?"

Juliet nods and hands me her prized possession. I open it and pull out a small bag of M&M's.

"Candy!" she cheers, jumping up and down. "I love candy!"

I quickly open the bag for her and hand her a piece of chocolate, while Derek goes to pick up the empty bucket still sitting in the grass.

Derek makes his way back to me and places it on the ground next to me.

"Good job, kiddo." He tells her, stooping down to her level to offer her a high five. She quickly reciprocates just as Derek's radio sounds. The dispatcher rattles off something I can't quite understand, but I know what it means.

"Crap. I have to go," He says, looking at me, darting his eyes back to Cory, who is standing nearby watching our interaction. "You good here?"

I frown slightly and nod. "Yep. I'll see you tonight. Love you."

"Love you, too. Bye Juliet." He adds before sprinting towards his car.

I watch as he disappears, and then I stand to pick up Juliet for our trek back to the car. I look up just in time to see Cory walking towards me.

"You didn't text me back." He says in an accusing tone.

I should have known he wouldn't just let this go.

"Cory, I don't want to do this right now. Thanks for coming to see her do her hunt, but I can't do this with you."

He frowns. "Avery. I'm better now. Being in that wreck changed me. I want to marry you and raise our daughter together. We could even have another baby and we can do it right this time. I want to be the husband and father that you guys deserve." He says, reaching out to touch me, but I jump back.

"Cory, I hear what you're saying. However, it's not happening. I'm in a healthy and happy relationship. I do not want to be with you. So, drop it. Thanks so much for coming today, but we are done here." I say, turning to continue my walk through the park.

"Wait. You're making a mistake." Cory calls back to me as he hobbles in my direction.

Against my better judgment, I pause and wait for him to catch up so he's not yelling at me across the park in front of the entire town.

Once he closes the distance, he continues. "Avery, I love you. Both of you. You are my family and I want to take care of you. Derek is going to get tired of dealing with a kid that isn't his, and he will leave. Then you'll wish you had taken me back. You just need to open your eyes and see it before it's too late."

Anger courses through my veins, and I respond to him through gritted teeth. "Believe me, Cory. I've seen more than enough when it comes to you. I'd rather raise Juliet alone than with you. From now on, unless it has to do with our daughter, don't contact me again." I say before turning on my heel and storming away.

I should have known it wouldn't stop there.

* * *

It's the evening after the egg hunt and I'm upstairs tucking Juliet into bed when the doorbell rings. "Come in!" I yell down the staircase before I lay Juliet down in her bed. "That silly Derek. He knows not to ring the doorbell after eight o'clock." I tell her. "He knows it's past your bedtime."

Juliet gives me a sleepy smile and cuddles into her stuffed beaver we picked up from the gas station during our Texas trip. For some reason, this is the stuffy that she insists on sleeping with every night. She is such a weird child, but I honestly love it.

"I love you. Get some sleep and I'll see you in the morning."

"Love you." Juliet echoes as I turn on her sound machine and shut off the overhead light.

"Hey, you know better than to ring the bell…" I say as I make my way down the stairs, expecting to find Derek waiting for me on the couch. Instead, I find Cory waiting for me. The sight of him standing in my entryway causes me to startle.

"What are you doing here?" I ask defensively. Kicking myself for not having access to the pepper spray that's hanging from my purse.

"You yelled for me to come in. So I came in." He replies. "I figured you looked at the doorbell camera and knew who it was."

I frown. The one time I didn't check the app on my phone to see who is at my door would, of course, be the one time he is standing outside my door. "Well, I was expecting someone else."

He snickers. "The cop, right?"

I cross my arms over my chest. "He has a name. It's Derek, and he's my boyfriend. He's going to be here any minute." I add, hoping to deter him from doing anything stupid.

Cory rolls his eyes. "Avery, when are you going to give up? You know that you and I belong together."

Instantly, I feel heat race through my body. "No, Cory, we don't. We don't even belong on the same planet." I shake my head. "When are you going to get that? Why can't you just co-parent with me and stay out of my personal life?"

"Because, Avery, I know you, and I know what you want." He says, taking a step towards me.

I throw my hands up to motion for him to stop. "Cory, all I want is for you to leave and to leave me alone. Do not come any closer to me."

"That's bullshit and you know it," Cory replies, motioning around my living room that's currently lined wall to wall with mine and Juliet's belongings. "Avery, you don't want to live like this in some tiny ass house because it's all you can afford. The last thing you want is to be the mom that has to work 24/7 to keep a roof over your head and food on your table. I know you want to give Juliet a better life than you had growing up. You want to be involved in her life. You want to spend time with her and actually raise her instead of letting daycare do it. He can't give you any of that."

I shake my head. "You don't know what you're talking about."

"Yes, I do!" Cory says, raising his voice. "As soon as you found out you were pregnant with Juliet, you told me you want to be more involved than your mom was! I know that hasn't changed. You and I both know Derek can't support you all on a small town cops' salary. Let me make it possible for you! I'll buy you a house. Hell, I'll even buy one in Fawn Creek so you can be close to your mom. I'm going back to work soon where I'm going to make great money. You can quit your job and you can be a stay at home mom." Cory almost sounds like he's begging at this point. "You don't have to do anything you don't want to do. Stop being so damn stubborn and let me take care of you for you."

I shake my head. "I don't need you to take care of me. I'm with Derek and I'm happy. There's no changing that. We're through."

Cory's face grows red and the vein on his forehead pokes out, a clear indicator that I made him angry. "Avery, we're a family. Me, you and Juliet. It doesn't matter how hard you try to force it with him, because I will always be the one that's meant to be with you. You've known him for years. Why didn't you two get together before me? Because you don't really want him. You're just settling. Why can't you see that?"

"Cory leave." I command, pointing at the door. "It doesn't matter how good of a speech you give me. Nothing is going to change how I feel about you. The chance of us being together went out the door a long time ago. Do you remember when you sent me to the hospital? Because I do."

"Avery..." He huffs. "That was just an accident. I didn't mean to hurt you. It wasn't even that bad."

No, the wound sure wasn't. It healed, but the mental abuse, and the manipulation is something I'll never forget. And I'll never forgive him for it, either.

"Leave! Now!" I scream at the top of my lungs. "Go or I'll call the police!" As soon as the words leave my mouth, I hear Juliet scream. The sound of her voice breaks my heart. I woke her up fighting with her dad. This is the exact life I never wanted for her.

Cory furrows his brow and turns back towards the door. He places his hand on the knob and then turns back to face me. I set my mouth in a straight line and try my best to make myself appear as tough as possible while I tremble inside.

Please don't hurt me.

He shakes his head and flings the door open, to find Derek waiting on the other side with wide eyes.

For a second, I brace myself, wondering what will happen next. Will he hit Derek? Will Derek hit him?

Thankfully, Cory simply pushes past Derek and barrels down the stairs. Derek and I watch in silence as he climbs into his car and drives away.

Chapter 18

"Okay, I think I finally have her settled back down." I say, as I make my way back down the stairs and into the living room. My screaming match with Cory woke up Juliet, and she had a hard time getting back to sleep afterwards.

"It's okay." Derek says, shaking his head. "What was all that about? Are you okay?" He asks, reaching over to squeeze my hand.

"I'm fine. Just shaken up a bit." I admit.

"What was he even doing here?"

"To talk I guess. I was upstairs putting Juliet down for bed when he rang the doorbell. I thought it was you, so I yelled down for you to come in. But when I came downstairs, he was standing in my entryway."

"Man. I'm glad he didn't hurt you, and I'm glad I came when I did." Derek frowns. "We need to get you a gun and maybe a self defense class."

I frown. "A gun? I don't even know how to shoot a gun."

"You should probably learn. You really need to be able to defend yourself. Next time, you may not be so lucky."

"Derek, you're acting like Cory is out to kill me." I say, shaking my head.

His face hardens. "Avery, he sent you to the ER when you

were pregnant with Juliet. The guy isn't exactly innocent. Besides, if he's just going to show up here with no warning, then you need a way to protect yourself."

"I mean, it wasn't really out of nowhere." I admit. "He texted me a few days ago, trying to convince me to take him back. I just ignored him. I was hoping if I didn't reply, he would leave me alone. But then, today after you left the park, he started in again. I told him no, and I left, but he came back tonight because apparently he wasn't willing to take no for an answer."

Derek pauses to look up at the ceiling. "Wait. You said he texted you a few days ago?"

I nod. "Yeah, why?"

"So was that before or after I asked if you wanted to move in together and you completely shut down?"

I narrow my eyes. I don't like where this is headed. Cory has nothing to do with what I'm feeling.

"He texted me the night of our movie date while I was getting ready. I just kind of swiped it away because I was trying to get down here to see you and I didn't want to mess with it. That has nothing to do with us moving in together, though." I say, shaking my head.

"Then why didn't you say anything to me about it?" He asks.

I stand from the couch and cross my arms over my chest. "Because it didn't matter. I ignored him and he dropped it."

"Until today." Derek adds.

"Yes, until today." I agree. "What Derek? You don't really think I'd go back to him, do you? After all he put me through? I'm not an idiot."

Derek shakes his head. "No, of course not. I just don't know why you didn't tell me. Especially given your history with him and his temper. Plus, the fact that you wouldn't even entertain the idea of moving in with me is kind of perfect timing. You have to admit that." He runs his hands down his face. "Avery, you've been acting weird ever since the other night."

I let out a heavy sigh. "I never said I don't want to move in with you."

"You never said you did, either." He frowns. "You haven't said one word about it since I brought it up."

"It's more complicated than that."

"Then uncomplicate it, Avery."

I pause and try to find the right words, but I keep coming up blank. "This is not how tonight was supposed to go." I say, shaking my head.

"You can say that again." He mutters.

"What is that supposed to mean?" I ask.

Derek stands from the sofa and makes his way towards the door before turning back to look at me. "It means I think we aren't getting anywhere with this. I'm going to go home and give us both a chance to cool off. Then maybe you can figure out what you actually want."

"Derek, please don't leave." I beg him. "I'm sorry. For everything. I love you."

His face softens only just a little when the words leave my mouth. "Avery, I love you, too. That hasn't changed, but I mean it. If you don't see a future with me, then I want to know now instead of wasting both of our time. Lock the door behind me so no one can just walk in, okay?" With that, he closes the door and disappears into the darkness.

My tears fall before the sounds of his footsteps disappear.

What in the hell just happened?

* * *

"Bye Juliet! I'll see you tonight." I call out to my daughter as she and her grandma make their way down the driveway towards her car. It's Easter morning and since we have nothing going on today, Susan is taking Juliet with her to church and to celebrate Easter at her house with Cory. I'm just thankful she didn't bring Cory with her this morning.

I close the front door and turn to lean my back against it, before I slowly melt and find myself in a seated position on the floor. Today I wasn't supposed to wake up alone and spend the day in an empty house. I was supposed to spend the day alone with Derek while Juliet was gone. And now who knows if or when he will stay over here again?

I slept very little last night, instead I just laid in the dark, rethinking mine and Derek's conversation instead. Yet still, I don't know what to even think of the whole thing.

I stretch to reach for my phone from the entryway table next to the door, hoping that he would have sent a text by now. But there's nothing on my lock screen.

I frown and open my texts, scrolling to Tyler's name instead. I fire off a message to her.

Me: Hey. What are you doing this morning? Anything?

Tyler: Just getting ready to head up to TBR and do some inventory. What's up?

Me: Want some help? And maybe while you're at it, you can evaluate my life?

Tyler: That doesn't sound so good. Yes, meet me up there in half an hour?

Me: It's not. And I'll be there.

* * *

155

I plop down into the crushed green velvet chair at TBR. I just finished pacing the room and giving Tyler the lowdown on the last twenty-four hours of my life.

"I just... I don't know how all this happened." I say with a sigh.

Tyler moves towards me with a box of Kleenex and offers me one before taking a seat next to me.

"I just have so many emotions running through me right now. I'm pissed at Cory for showing up at my house and for having the audacity to think that I would ever take him back. Also, I'm confused as hell with the way Derek reacted to all of this. I'm mad at myself for making Derek mad and even more so for hurting his feelings." I take a sip of my coffee sitting on the side table and pout. "I just feel so lost right now."

Tyler frowns but simply just continues to listen.

"How is it possible that I messed up the best relationship I've ever had without even realizing I was doing something wrong?" I ask, mostly to myself. "Never has there been a guy that's treated me this well and loved me that hard. There's never been anyone that I truly saw myself marrying and spending the rest of my life with, until Derek." I pause. "And now, I might have not only screwed up our relationship, but our friendship, too."

Tyler frowns and reaches out to touch my arm. "Well, first off, I think you probably need to take it down a notch. Just because you and Derek had an argument doesn't mean that you two are going to break up."

I sigh and nod slowly. "Okay, but why did he just leave? What about that whole 'don't go to bed angry' crap that people are always going on about? I thought if you have a fight you are supposed to work it out, not just walk away? If it was worth working on, wouldn't he have stayed and worked on it? I feel like he's just prolonging the heartbreak at this point."

Tyler shakes her head. "That's not true, Avery." She leans towards me. "I think Derek is more sensitive than you realize. Sure, he's a cop. He has the tough guy persona down pretty well. However, I think underneath all of that, he's kind of a softy. You can see that in the way he takes care of you and how he handles Juliet." She takes a deep breath and continues. "Also, I think he's pretty laid back, which is the opposite of what you are used to with Cory. Derek doesn't want to yell or fight with you. He wants to sit down and have a rational conversation with you when you are both calm. That wasn't going to happen last night."

Tyler has a point. Derek is not much of a screamer. And he is a bit of a softy, he even released the mouse from my closet into the wild.

"I hope you're right." I say, letting out a heavy sigh.

"But the real question is." Tyler says, crossing her arms over her chest. "What's the deal with you not wanting to move in with him?"

I turn to look at her. "Tyler, don't you think it's too soon? We've only been together for four months."

She shrugs. "Sure. It's soon, but when will it be the right time? Six months? A year? He's already at your house most of the time, anyway. Maybe he would feel better if you could give him a time frame."

"There's another thing. I don't want to give up my house." I say with a frown. "Tyler, I love my house. I love the location. Not to mention all the work I've put into it. Plus, I got a great deal when I got it and I can have it paid off in less than ten years. He wants to buy a big house. I don't want that. I want financial stability. Something I know I can afford no matter who is in my life."

Tyler shakes her head. "Avery, this isn't about the house, is it?"

I frown. "Okay, not completely." I admit. "But, come on. The last time I moved in with a guy, it was a disaster. I lost my cute little house. I had to break my lease and put everything I owned in storage, and I had to start over from scratch after just a few months. Last time was a little easier because it was just me, but now I have Juliet. I can't just move a toddler in and out of places while I try out living arrangements. Kids need consistency."

Tyler moves towards me and puts her hands on my shoulders. "Listen to me. Derek is not Cory. Derek is not going to turn into a monster the second he moves in with you. He loves you."

Her words immediately bring tears to my eyes.

"Friend, I'm going to put this as delicately as possible, okay? You have got to stop living your life in fear that everyone you love is going to hurt you. Just because other men in your past have let you down doesn't mean Derek will. He is not your father, and he is not Cory. Derek has loved you and taken care of you for a long time. The only difference is now the two of you sleep together. He is not going to just screw you over. You have got to give him a chance to prove that. Stop fighting what is right."

"I don't know how to fix this."

"Yes, you do." Says Tyler. "But how badly do you want to?"

* * *

After my talk with Tyler, I spend the rest of my day working on creating content to keep my mind off of the mess that my life has become. No matter how many times I attempt to pick up my phone and text Derek, I don't. Not until I have handled the situation with Cory. I've lost track of time when a knock at the door interrupts me.

I pause my recording and make my way towards the front door to find Cory waiting for me, with Juliet in his arms. Immediately, she reaches for me. I take her into my arms and hug her tight while breathing her in. It seems crazy that after all this time; I miss her so much when she's gone, even when she's just across town. I still don't know that I'll ever get used to this.

I place Juliet down on the floor, and she takes off to play with her toys. I turn back towards Cory, who is still standing in my entryway.

"You know, you wouldn't have to have moments like this if you would just stop being stubborn." He says, raising an eyebrow at me. "You are the one making the choice for our family to be apart. We could get married tomorrow and become the family we were supposed to be if you would just let it happen."

I take in a deep breath and silently count to three, trying to keep myself calm. The last thing I need is for this conversation to turn into a fight, but I need Cory to know that my stance on us will not change.

"Cory, all of this has to stop right now. The chances of you and I being together went out the window a long time ago. It doesn't matter what you say to me, I will not come back to you. I'm happy for you that you have turned over a new leaf. Plus, I'm so glad that you want to be an active part of Juliet's life, but you will never be an active part of mine ever again." I cross my arms over my chest and stand firmly, looking him in the eyes.

He shakes his head. "Avery, you don't mean that."

"I do." I argue. "Cory, after the night you hurt me, something flipped a switch in my heart and that switch is never going back to where it once was. I'm never going to be able to look at you like I did before that night. Even if we tried again, that is always going to be in the back of my mind. We are not meant to be together. We can't even have a conversation without raising our voices. Our only job is to raise our daughter without killing each other. And we will be doing that job in our own separate homes. Either you can accept that and we can co-parent as a team, or we can start doing these trade-offs at the police station to ensure my safety. Those are your options."

Cory rolls his eyes. "Your safety? Whatever. Avery, you're going to regret this. I could have given you the best life possible. Instead, you are just going to end up like your mother. Broke and alone."

I shake my head. That one hurt, even though I'll never admit it to him. "If I end up like my mom, then that'll be my biggest accomplishment ever. Have a nice day." I say before stepping back and closing the front door. I stand on tiptoe and watch through the peephole as he makes his way back towards his car. Once he backs out of my driveway onto the street, I finally let loose of the tears I'm holding back. One conversation down, one more to go.

"Juliet. Wanna go for a ride?"

* * *

I pull my SUV to a stop in Derek's driveway and turn back to look at Juliet. She's sitting in her car seat, happily munching on a package of goldfish crackers and grinning back at me.

"Puppy?" she asks, pointing to Derek's house.

"Do you want to go say hi to the puppy?" I ask her with a smile. "And Derek too?"

"RICK!" she exclaims with a clap at the mention of Derek's name. "I want Rick!"

The excitement that my daughter feels over the sheer mention of Derek's name isn't lost on me. I also won't even pretend to notice that I have never seen her excited to see her own father.

I can only hope that Derek is just as excited to see us. I didn't tell him I was coming. Normally, I would have, but given the events that have transpired in the last twenty-four hours, I was too afraid to give him the chance to ignore me or leave the house.

I unbuckle Juliet from her seat and carry her to Derek's wooden porch, cautiously making my way up his steps. Immediately, the sound of claws running on the hardwood floor comes from inside the house. Diesel barks, alerting Derek of our arrival. There's no chance of being sneaky around here.

Derek opens the heavy interior front door and pauses when he catches sight of me. "Diesel, go lay down." He tells the dog, before sliding through the open screen door and meeting us on the porch.

Juliet immediately holds her arms out to him, and without hesitation, he pulls her into his arms. She melts into his embrace and my breath hitches when I feel something that I can only describe as jealousy over the fact that I can't do the same. Not yet anyway.

161

"Hi." I say carefully. It seemed as though all day I tried to imagine what I would say when I got here, but now, looking at him, I forget it all.

"Hi." He responds, with a soft smile, allowing me to continue. He continues to hold Juliet casually, as though she is his own child.

"I'm sorry I didn't call first." I say, just above a whisper. "I wasn't really sure if you wanted to see me."

Derek frowns. "Avery, of course I wanted to see you. I always want to see you. I just wanted to give you the space to figure out what you want."

I shake my head. "Space is the last thing I want." I admit.

"Then what do you want?" He asks, taking a seat on the top step of his porch.

Juliet stands from his lap and makes her way to the door, where Diesel is standing, staring at her through the screen.

I take a seat beside him. "You." I say, trying to blink back tears. "Us. All of us." I add, motioning towards Juliet and Diesel. "I'm sorry I didn't tell you about Cory texting me. I honestly didn't think it was an issue, especially after he said nothing else. I absolutely would have told you about him bothering me again last night if you hadn't shown up and heard it all yourself."

He nods. "And the moving in together conversation?"

I let out a heavy sigh. "You are going to think I'm stupid, but I'm going to say it, anyway."

Derek shakes his head and opens his mouth as though he's going to speak, but I stop him by holding up a finger.

"It's not that I don't want to move in with you. I love you and you're right, we are together most nights, anyway. It would just make sense. It's the next logical step." I say, gripping his hand. "However, I guess I have a little bit of unresolved trauma surrounding the whole thing. I moved in with Cory right off the bat. I gave up my house. My very cute little rental house I loved very much. I put all my stuff in storage and broke my lease. I trusted my gut and my gut was terribly wrong. Then, not six months later, I had to start all over again. I had to move all of my crap back home with my tail between my legs. Then, I had to live with my mother until I could afford a place of my own again. I'm scared to death, Derek."

Derek nods and looks down at the concrete step where his feet are resting.

"And that's nothing against you. It's not me saying that I don't think we will make it. I know you're not like Cory. I know you love me. I just need time."

"Avery." Derek succeeds at interrupting me this time. "I understand." He says, wrapping his arm around my shoulders. "I don't want you to do anything you aren't ready for yet."

"I promise, it won't be long."

Chapter 19

"Good morning, you two!" Cassidy calls out from behind the counter of Drip when Derek and I walk through the door, with Diesel in tow. "No baby today?" She asks sadly.

I shake my head. "No, she's with her grandma this weekend."

"Well, at least you brought this good boy with you." She says with a smile as she fills up a tiny cup with whipped cream for Diesel. She makes her way around the counter to feed Diesel his pup cup. "So, what do you two crazy kids have planned for the day?"

I shrug. "Not much, honestly. We thought it felt like the perfect day to grab a coffee and then head on down to the farmer's market. "

Cassidy pets Diesel and then stands to face us. "Well, you probably better plan to just turn around and get Derek's truck before you go. Today is the FFA plant sale. It's always such a good sale. That's usually where I get all the flowers for my flower bed. And veggies for my garden."

We give our coffee order to Devin and then turn back to Cassidy. "That plant sale sounds like fun." I say, looking at Derek. "We could spend the afternoon getting my flowerbed cleaned up and some new flowers planted."

"It sounds like we probably do need to go back to your house and get my truck, then." Derek teases. "I have a feeling we will not be able to carry home everything you decide to buy today."

I smirk. "Do you mind?"

"Sounds like a good way to spend the day together." Derek smiles and grabs my free hand, pulling it to his mouth to kiss it gently.

I practically melt on the spot.

"Oh, you two." Cassidy gushes. "I just love brand new love. You can tell you guys haven't been together for long because he didn't even flinch when you asked him to help with yard work." She observes. "I hope you stay that way for a long time." She adds softly.

I turn to Derek and smile.

Me too.

* * *

I stand from my stooped position at the edge of the flower bed and step back to the sidewalk to survey our work. Derek, now shirtless, is busy spreading the last bit of mulch around my freshly planted pink and purple pansies. The mulch we had to drive to the hardware store and pick up after our brief trip to the farmer's market.

"Juliet is going to love these when she gets home. That was a good call when you suggested pink and purple. Those are her favorite colors." I say to him.

"Oh I remember. She told me at the egg hunt." Derek turns just as he finishes spreading the mulch and finds me concentrating deeply on his biceps.

He raises an eyebrow. "Can I help you, ma'am? My eyes are up here." He says, pointing to his face.

I shake my head. "No, I'm just enjoying the show. Thanks anyway." I tease.

"Should I get you a drink? A chair?"

"Ooh yes." I agree. "And maybe a bowl of grapes that you can feed me? Oh, also one of those giant leaves to fan me with. It's getting a bit warm out here."

He laughs and shakes his head. "Come on. We better get you inside and into a shower. You're getting delirious."

I frown. "I might be too tired from all this hard work to be trusted in the shower alone."

"Well, luckily for you." He says, taking off his work gloves and tossing them onto the steps. "I took a vow to protect and serve. And I take that vow seriously." He says, walking towards me and lifting me up from the ground, practically throwing me over his shoulder. "Let's get you inside."

* * *

After a much needed shower for two and a quick nap, I wake up to catch Derek in the act of getting dressed.

"And where do you think you're going?" I ask, rolling over to my side.

Derek smirks before leaning over to kiss me. "I'm going to unload the grill from the back of my truck. Then, you are getting a lesson on how to use it. Are you ready for your first cooking class?"

I nod, sleepily. "Yes, I'll be right down."

After I get dressed, I make my way downstairs and onto the

back patio. I arrive just as Derek is wheeling his grill through the back gate.

I take a seat in my wooden rocking chair as he makes his way to me.

"I can't believe you brought your entire grill over to my house."

"I can't believe you don't own one already." He retorts. "It's not a big deal. With as much as I'm here, I bet we will get more use out of it at your house than mine. Besides, you need to learn how to use it." He shrugs. "Everyone needs to know how to grill."

"Why do I need to learn how to grill when I have you around?" I tease.

Derek laughs and attaches the propane tank to the side of the cooking device. "Because my job is unpredictable. There's nothing like marinating a steak all day and looking forward to it, only for me to be stuck at work until ten o'clock at night and you to be stuck eating cereal because you don't know how to grill."

I frown. "Okay, I guess that's a fair point. And I suppose it would be nice to know how to make more than boxed mac and cheese."

Over the course of the next half hour, we work side by side. We grill the steaks that we bought from a local rancher at the farmer's market. Then, we pair our meat with green beans, baked potatoes and lemon blueberry cookies that we also picked up from the farmer's market.

"That." I say, leaning back in my dining room chair after we finish our feast. "Was one of the best meals I've had in a long time. Good job."

"Hey, you helped, too. And it really was amazing." He turns

167

and smiles at me. "We make a pretty good team."

"Well, I must say, I do microwave a pretty great baked potato. But you're right. We really do make a good team."

"Hey, by the way, what are you doing next weekend?"

I shrug. "It's Mother's Day. I don't really have any plans. I figured Juliet and I would just hang out around the house."

"You aren't doing anything with your mom?" He asks.

I shake my head. "We don't really do a lot of gatherings in my family. Mom works a lot. Usually we just get together for Christmas and Thanksgiving. What about you?"

"My mom and dad are going out of town for the weekend. I will probably take her over some flowers and a card when she gets back. I'm off work until Sunday afternoon. Why don't you let me take you and Juliet somewhere on Saturday and then we can have a lazy Sunday morning before I go to work?"

"That sounds like a great idea to me." I nod, fighting back tears.

"Wait. Why are you crying?" Derek asks, scooting over closer to me.

I shake my head. "It's silly. I'm just being emotional."

"No, if it makes you cry, it's not that silly." He shakes his head. "What's wrong?"

"It's nothing bad." I assure him. "I just... I love that you are attempting to do something with me for Mother's Day. Last year just kind of sucked."

"What happened last year?"

I take a deep breath. "Well, it was my first Mother's Day, and I was so excited. I just felt like it was a much bigger deal than it actually was. It was technically Cory's weekend, and he threw this big fit over having her Friday and Saturday, instead of letting me keep her all weekend. Of course, in order to keep the peace, I folded. I compromised and offered to let him keep her until late Saturday night. When I went to pick her up, he was a total jerk about it still. Then, he didn't even tell me Happy Mother's Day. When his mom called him out on it, he just waved me off and said I wasn't his mom, so there was no reason for him to make a big deal out of it. Madison helped Juliet make a cute little gift for me at daycare, but otherwise Mother's Day was nothing more than just another typical Sunday. I sat at home taking care of a screaming baby while I cleaned my house and did the laundry. I know it sounds kinda stupid, but I just assumed that's the way Mother's Day would just be for me. At least until Juliet is old enough to know what's going on. I've been dreading it all Spring."

Derek reaches over to squeeze my hand. "You deserve for someone to make a big deal of this day for you. And that's just what I'm going to do."

* * *

"Are you ladies ready to go?" Derek calls up the stairs. He doesn't mention the fact that I was supposed to be ready five minutes ago. I guess at least on Mother's Day, no one will call me out for taking too long to get ready. Which is exceptionally helpful since I have to get Juliet ready as well.

"Yes! Be right down!" I call back. Juliet and I are in her bedroom, finishing fixing her hair. "You ready to go out for a fun day?" I ask her.

"Yes! Let's go!" She replies enthusiastically. She stands from the floor and grabs my hand, pulling me towards the doorway.

"Okay, okay!" I reply, climbing up into a standing position. "Wait for me." I scoop Juliet up and quickly we make our way downstairs to an awaiting Derek.

"I got the diaper bag filled with snacks and drinks." He says, holding up the black backpack. "I figured I'd make myself useful while I was waiting."

I smile back at him warmly. Derek is already so good at stepping up and taking care of what's needed. The more things like this that he does for the two of us, the more I know we are doing the right thing by being together.

"Sounds like we're ready, then." I smile, trying to stuff down all the emotions this man is making me feel today. "Except, you still haven't told me where we're going."

"It's a surprise." He says simply as he herds us out the door. "Let's get going."

I buckle Juliet into her seat and then climb into the passenger side of my car. "How comfy should I get?" I ask.

"I mean, I wouldn't take a nap." Derek laughs. "We will be there in just a few minutes."

The fact that we will be there in minutes causes me to be even more curious. Where could he possibly be taking us? Fawn Creek is a small town with a population of 1,200 people, right in the middle of Southeast Kansas. There aren't a lot of places we can go nearby.

"First stop!" Derek announces as he pulls into a spot in front of Drip. "Hang tight, I'll be back." Within minutes, he returns with two iced coffees in hand. "Iced Caramel Macchiato." He declares as he hands me my drink. "Ready for the next leg of our trip?"

Before I can answer, Derek pulls out of our parking spot and we make our way towards the city limits. Within minutes, we are pulling into the gravel parking lot at the Safari Zoological Park.

"Oh, the zoo!" I squeal, looking out the window. "I haven't been here in ages. Probably not since I was a kid." I admit.

He shakes his head. "Me neither. I thought it would be a great way for the three of us to spend the day together." He says with a smile. "Is this okay with you? I hope you didn't have something more exciting in mind."

"No!" I protest. "This is perfect. I've been meaning to get back to this place one day, but I've just never gotten around to it. I can't wait to see how much it's changed over the years."

We both climb out of the car and load Juliet into her stroller before making our way towards the entrance.

"Are you ready to see some animals?" I ask Juliet as we make our way towards the building. "They have lions and bears, and who knows what else? We are going to have so much fun." I turn to Derek and add. "And we can get back home in time for her afternoon nap."

"Bingo." Derek says with a laugh. "The perfect day for everyone."

We make our way inside and after Derek pays our entry fee we meet with our tour guide, Bryce.

"Perfect timing." He says with a smile. "I was just getting ready to start the next tour. Follow me, folks."

We step out of the gift shop, and suddenly we are transported to an incredible wild animal sanctuary. It's hard to believe that just minutes ago we were driving through Southeast Kansas, past hay fields and cows, on the way to get here.

We spend the morning strolling along, down the shade covered sidewalks, as we listen to Bryce introducing us to the animals by name and telling us facts about each one.

I gaze down at Juliet, sitting comfortably in her stroller and clapping with glee as a bear cub does a trick in anticipation of a treat. Her excitement makes my heart soar.

I shake my head and turn to Derek. "I've never seen this child stay interested in anything for this long. She's having the time of her life. And I am, too." I admit. "Thank you for bringing us here today."

Derek squeezes my hand. "Hey, I'm enjoying it, too. I've wanted to make my way back here for a while, but I didn't want to be the weird guy walking through the zoo alone."

I laugh. "So you just used us in order to come here?" I accuse him, shaking my head teasingly. "Where next? Legoland?"

He pauses. "Hey. That's actually a great idea for a weekend trip. I'll try to keep that one in mind." He says with a wink.

Juliet squeals in excitement, interrupting our conversation. "Kitty!" She repeats, holding her arms out wide as though she is trying to welcome a white tiger cub into her lap. "I want kitty!"

Derek laughs. "You're going to have to get her a pet."

"A pet lion has to be against city code." I laugh. "Besides, she already has Diesel. Maybe she just needs to spend more time with him." I say with a wink, hinting at the fact that I'm getting more comfortable with the idea of us moving in together.

"I bet we can arrange something." Derek replies, his face turning a light shade of pink.

Eventually, the tour is over and Derek informs me we have one more thing to do before we can leave. He leads me back over to the monkey exhibit and tells me to have a seat on a nearby bench.

"What's up? I thought we've seen it all." I ask, looking around.

"I might have signed you up for one of the animal experiences." Derek says with a smile.

Before he can explain any further, another tour guide steps out of the cage, carrying a small monkey who is practically draped around her neck.

"Are you Avery?" the guide asks as she approaches us.

"I am!"

"I'm Carissa and this is Grace." She says, motioning her chin towards the monkey she's holding. "Are you ready to hold her? She's super snuggly."

I look back and forth between Derek and Carissa. "Um, sure! Sorry, I didn't know we were doing this, so I'm caught a little off guard."

"No worries. She loves to be held." Carissa assures me. Slowly, she unravels the monkey's arms from around her neck and hands Grace to me, almost as though she's handing me a child.

Immediately, Grace wraps her arms around me and lays her head on my chest. "She's adorable." I whisper.

"If you think she likes you now, just wait until you give her these." Carissa says, offering me a handful of animal crackers.

I take the food from Carissa and hand one to the monkey.

Juliet watches intently as the monkey eats, smacking her own lips. "I want a snack." Juliet demands, stretching her hand out towards me.

Before I can even ask, Derek unzips the diaper bag and fishes a bag of animal crackers out for Juliet. "These are for you." He tells her as she opens the bag and hands it to her. "You can't have the monkey's treat."

I sit and simply enjoy the quiet as I soak up all the snuggles from Grace. Derek, again without me having to ask, takes several photos and videos. "And look at that, now you have content to use for this weekend." He says with a laugh. "Two birds, one stone."

"My followers won't even know what hit them." I say, shaking my head, as my time runs out and I hand the monkey back to the guide.

As Carissa walks away, I turn to Derek with a huge grin plastered on my face. "That was so cool. Thank you for buying me a ticket to do that." I say. "You didn't have to."

He kisses my forehead, just as Juliet fusses in her seat. "I knew you'd like it."

I look down at Juliet, moving her stroller lightly back and forth with my foot. "I think someone is ready for a nap. She's had a full morning."

"Agreed. I think we could use one, too." He says with a yawn of his own. He grabs the stroller and leads us back into the gift shop.

On our way out, Juliet turns her head and sees a stack of stuffed lion cubs. "Kitty!" She proclaims again, reaching her hands out towards the stuffed animals.

Before I can tell her no, Derek grabs one from the pile and takes it to the counter. "I know she won't remember our first zoo trip, but I just feel like I need to buy it for her. One more animal to add to her growing collection." He says, as he hands the lion and his debit card over to the guide running the cash register. He finishes paying and then hands Juliet the new toy.

"She already has you wrapped around her finger." I proclaim on our way out the door.

"That makes two of you." He adds with a smirk. "And I wouldn't have it any other way."

Chapter 20

One Month Later

I step onto my porch just in time to catch Derek pulling into the driveway. I wave my arms, trying to motion for him to not shut off the truck. Unfortunately, it doesn't work.

"What are you waving at?" He asks with a laugh as he steps out of his pickup.

"Well, I was trying and failing to get you to park in the street." I say, shaking my head. "Can you move?"

"Sure. But, why?"

Before I can say the words, Andrew's truck pulls to a stop in front of the house and he answers for me. "Hey, D. Move your truck," Andrew calls, motioning to the street where my SUV is parked. "I need in there."

Derek looks to Andrew and then at his bed full of lumber with a confused expression before looking back at me.

"I'll explain everything here in a few."

Once the men are done with their little vehicle rodeo in front of my house, Derek meets me in my living room.

"I didn't know you were having work done."

"Well, it was a surprise, actually. So, surprise!" I say, throwing my arms in the air.

Derek raises a brow at me. "Um, thanks, but what is it? Are

you building me a doghouse to sleep in?"

I roll my eyes at his terrible attempt at a joke. "No, I'm having Andrew and Cody put up a privacy fence." I say, rocking back on my heels. "So that Diesel can have a yard to play in."

Derek smirks. "You're building a fence for my dog?"

"Well, I figure we can all make use of it." I admit with a shrug. "But there's no way we can take the next step and move in together without first giving Diesel a safe play to play."

Derek's face softens. "What are you saying, Avery?"

I take a deep breath before moving closer and interlace my fingers in his. "What I'm saying is that I'd like to reopen the discussion about moving in together." I admit, biting my lip. "I'm saying that the past six months with you have been everything I've ever dreamed of and more. And I know it's only been a couple of months since we last discussed it, but that couple of months is what I needed. I've loved watching our lives intertwine and I am so tired of not waking up next to you every day. So, if you're ready. I'm ready."

A wide grin spreads across Derek's face. "Of course I'm ready. I've never been more ready for anything in my life." He says, pulling me into him and kissing me gently. "Are you sure you want to live here, though? My house has more room. I'm just renting, but it would give us some more space until we're ready to buy something bigger."

I lead Derek to the couch and sit down. "That's the thing. Derek, I love this house. It's full of character and charm that we are only going to find in an older house. Not only that, but it's close to downtown and my mom. This is the street I grew up on as a kid. I rode my bike on these wobbly brick roads and learned to skate on the cracked sidewalks. This just feels like home. I can't imagine raising Juliet and maybe another kid or two, anywhere else. So, when Andrew came to give me a quote on the fence, I had him quote me on something else, too." I get up from the couch and fetch a small pile of papers from the table by the entryway before handing it to him.

Derek takes the pages and looks them over. "What's this?"

"That's a quote for adding on a master suite to this house. Andrew says that since my lot is big, we have plenty of space to build on the side of the house. He said we can stretch the addition all the way to the backyard. We could have plenty of room for a bedroom, bathroom, and an enormous closet. That would give us another full bedroom upstairs to use in whatever way we choose." I say, blushing at the thought of adding another baby to the mix in a few years. "And my detached garage is huge. It'll need to be cleaned up, but I think we could set up your gym equipment there. That is, if you're willing to move in here. I'm not saying it would be ready for you to move in tomorrow, but maybe we could start making some progress?"

Derek places the papers on the coffee table before reaching over to squeeze my hand. "You really have been putting a lot of thought into this, haven't you?"

I nod. "Basically since the day you took me and Juliet out for Mother's Day." I admit. "And Andrew said that we can save some money on the addition by doing some things ourselves. Even with him doing it all, we could still pay for it in just a few months once we only have one set of bills between us."

Derek presses his hands against his knees and gets into a standing position. "Well, what are we waiting for, then? Sounds like we have a garage to empty."

* * *

One month later

I hear my front door creak open and close with a thud.

"Hey, it's just me," Derek calls up the stairs. "You about ready?"

"Just about! Give me like two minutes!" I call back down the stairs to him.

"I've heard that one before." He calls back with a chuckle.

It's the Fourth Of July weekend and Juliet is with Susan and Cory tonight. The city of Fawn Creek does an amazing job of putting on a large firework show on the fourth. While it can be seen from just about anywhere in town, Derek promised me he was taking me somewhere tonight for the best view of the fireworks I've ever seen. I can't even imagine what he's talking about, but my interest is definitely piqued.

I grab my oversized American Flag sweater that's laying on my bed and shimmy it on my over my tank top and holy jean shorts. Before heading downstairs, I pause for a second, attaching my phone to my ring light and taking a few photos to use later. I'm just checking over what I got when Derek calls up the stairs once again.

"Avery! We're going to miss the show if we don't get a move on!"

"Coming!" I reply. Quickly, I slip on my flip-flops and make my way down the stairs. Derek is waiting at the bottom of the staircase, and when his eyes meet mine, they light up. I love how this is one thing that has stayed consistent with him for our entire relationship. He always makes it clear that he is happy to see me.

"Hey. Sorry I took so long." I say, moving towards him to lightly kiss his lips.

He grins and pulls me in closer, gripping the sides of my

sweater while he kisses me again, but more deeply this time. "It's okay. It was worth the wait." He assures me. "But we really should get going. I swear I'm going to start telling you to be ready fifteen minutes earlier than I actually need you to be. Maybe then you'll be on time."

"I doubt it." I answer with a shrug, as I lead him out the door and towards his truck.

Within minutes, we are headed towards the outskirts of town. It's not long before he pulls off of the highway and onto a little gravel path leading to a gate. He places the truck in park and opens his door, just as I turn to him in confusion. "Where are we?"

"You'll see." He says with a wink before bounding out of the vehicle.

Within seconds, he's back in the truck and we are making our way into the pasture. Slowly, we follow a path that has been beaten down in the grass by what I can only assume is truck tires. After a few minutes, he brings the truck to a stop once again.

"Stay." He says, turning towards me with a mischievous grin. "I'll be right back to get you."

"What is this place?" I ask, looking around.

"Don't worry, we have permission to come out here." He says, leaning over the console to kiss my lips softly. "Stay here. I'll be back." He commands.

Before I can ask anything further, he climbs out of the vehicle and disappears into the darkness. I feel the vehicle sway as he climbs into the bed. I try to look back to see what he's doing, but between the darkness of the night and the tint on his back window, I can't make anything out.

After a few minutes of the truck swaying back and forth,

Derek appears at my door, opening it for me. "Now you can get out." He says with a grin, with his arm extended to help me climb from the cab.

My feet land in the grass with a thud. I eye him cautiously as he leads me around to the back of his truck. As we reach the bed, I see what he was working on while I was waiting. The cover on the bed of his truck has been rolled up to the back of the cab, exposing an actual bed in the bed of his truck. The entire surface is covered in what appears to be an air mattress, as well as pillows, sleeping bags, and blankets.

"What is this?" I whisper, looking around at his elaborate set up.

"Our date." He simply replies with a shrug. "Climb on up and get comfy." He commands gently.

I do as I'm told, resting my back against a pile of pillows that are propped against the back of the cab. He joins me, and then I snuggle close to him.

"How are you sure the view from here will be so good?" I ask. "Honestly, I'm not even sure where we are."

"This is the future site of your brother's new home and business." He says with a smirk. "As far as the view, I'm just hopeful, I guess." He chuckles. "But, if I'm right, we will have a clear view of them all, without the lights of town in our way. Plus, it sure is peaceful out here."

I raise a brow. "Does my brother know we're out here?"

Derek laughs. "Yes, it was his idea that we watch the fireworks from here. I suppose he wants us to scout out the view for him."

I shake my head. "He's weird, but that was nice of him."

Just then, the firework show starts. One by one, the light sky fills with bursts of color. Just as Derek hoped, our view is perfect. In fact, it almost looks as though the show is being put on just for us. I snuggle in close to Derek and enjoy the show for a couple of minutes before I steal a glance at him. He is looking back at me.

I smile softly. "What are you thinking about?" I ask.

He grins. "Just thinking about how lucky I am. And how much I love you." He pauses, and then reaches his hand under the blanket beside him, pulling out a small box. "And how badly I want you to be my wife." He adds, opening the lid.

My eyes dart quickly from Derek's face to the open box. The moon puts off just enough light for me to make out the gorgeous vintage engagement ring. My eyes quickly fill with tears as I try to steady my breathing. I can't believe this is happening.

"Avery. The day I met you, I knew that my life was forever changed. Since then, there hasn't been a day when you haven't crossed my mind. The first time we kissed, I knew that I never wanted to experience another day without your lips on mine. You just have something about you, some magnetic force that makes people want to be near you, and I can't imagine another day without you by my side. I love you. I love Juliet and I want nothing more than to be a family with the two of you." He pauses for a second and stares at me with a soft smile. "Avery, will you please marry me?"

Suddenly, it's almost as though I can't remember how to speak. All I can do is quickly nod my head, while the tears I was harboring are now streaming down my face.

Derek gently slides the ring on my finger and then gathers me into his arms, pulling me into his lap. "I love you, Avery." He breathes into my ear. "I promise I'm going to do everything I can to make you happy for the rest of your life. And I promise

181

we can wait for as long as you need before we have a wedding. Just knowing that you are mine is enough for me."

"I can't wait to be your wife, and honestly, I'd do it tomorrow if I could." I admit.

* * *

Tyler squeals and makes her way across her living room to pull me into a tight hug. "I can't believe you're engaged! What can I do to help you?"

I grin wide and take a seat on the couch. "Well, first off, let's try not running across the house when you're 97 weeks pregnant." I say in a teasing tone. "That baby needs to bake a bit longer and we don't need it falling out onto Grandma Hazel's vintage rug."

"I couldn't help it!" She exclaims. "You can't just drop a bomb like that on me when I'm across the room!"

I chuckle. "Noted, I won't do that again. The next engagement, I will make sure you're sitting down first."

She ignores me. "So, when are you going to do the wedding? We need to get the event center booked as soon as possible."

I send her a tight-lipped smile. "Well, that's just it. I was actually thinking about doing something a little different."

Tyler raises a brow. "Are we having a shotgun wedding? The women in town are going to have a heyday with you, Missy."

I groan. "No. I was just thinking that it might be fun to have a destination wedding over New Year's Eve. That will be exactly one year since we first said 'I love you', so the date holds a special place in my heart. What do you think about going to Mexico in December? I know the baby won't be very old yet, so if you're not comfortable traveling with her, or leaving her, I totally get it and I can think of something else..."

Tyler cuts me off. "No, you will not change your entire wedding plan for me. She'll be five months old by New Year's Eve. Surely, I'll be ready for a break by then and I'm sure my parents would be thrilled to keep her for me. I'm in. Where are you thinking of going in Mexico?" She asks.

"Well, I have an idea." I say with a grin.

Chapter 21

Ms. Thompson,

We have reviewed your social media platforms and because of your incredible knack for authentic storytelling, plus the impressive amount of followers that you maintain, we would be absolutely interested in collaborating with you for your destination wedding. We at the Hyatt Ziva Cancun would love to host you and your wedding party at our resort, free, in exchange for content filmed during your stay. This offer includes an onsite wedding ceremony. Please review the attached contract and let me know if you have questions.

Mia Martinez
Head of Marketing
Hyatt Ziva Cancun

I sit at my desk in my office at work and read over the email twice before I really can come to terms with what's happening. Quickly, I pick up my phone and call Tyler.

"Hey. What's up?" She asks when she answers on the second ring.

"Are you busy? I know you're working, but do you have a second to look over an email that I just got?" I ask as I squirm in my seat.

"Oh, is it about the wedding?" Tyler asks, sounding excited.

"It is." I confirm. "A resort is offering us a free stay in exchange for content. I just want someone else to look over the contract before I get too excited." I forward the email to her. "Sent! You should have it in your inbox any minute now."

The line goes quiet with only the sounds of her nails on the keyboard, telling me she's still on the other end of the line. "Got it. Just a second." Tyler murmurs to herself as she reads through the email and the attached contract. Finally, she finishes and returns to the call. "I mean, I'm no lawyer, but this looks legit to me. This is a place that you reached out to?"

"Yes." I confirm. "They were actually my first choice. Honestly, I assumed they were going to ignore me, but I took a chance and emailed them anyway."

Tyler scoffs. "Ignore you? You're the Fawn Creek Influencer. They would be crazy to let this chance slip through their fingers."

I laugh at the exchange. "Well, thanks. I can always count on you to hype me up. Okay, I think I'm going to see if my lawyer will look at it for me, just in case. But, if all works out, plan on heading to Cancun this winter!"

"I've already started shopping." Tyler confesses. "I'm so ready."

"Ready for the beach or ready for there to no longer be a human growing inside your body?" I ask.

"Both." Tyler groans. "Okay, get that sent over to her and let me know when I need to book a flight."

"Will do! Thanks for the help." I say before disconnecting the call.

Immediately, I draft an email to my lawyer, Jessica. She's the one that handled my custody case with Cory and she's a long-time friend of my mom's. Thankfully, she is always willing to answer any legal questions that I throw her way. I send the email off to her and quickly text Derek to give him an update. Then, I cross my fingers and try to concentrate on my actual job.

By the time I'm finishing up for the day, I have an email from Jessica waiting for me.

Avery,

Everything here looks good to me! So proud of you for making this a lucrative form of income for you and for your family.

I do suggest before signing anything with the hotel that you get the needed paperwork from Cory to get Juliet's passport. That is, if you are planning to take her along to be in the ceremony. Call me if you have any trouble or need help. Attached is the link for the needed paperwork when requesting a passport for a minor. You'll need his signature, a copy of his ID and a notary witness.

Jessica Harper,

Family Law Attorney

Fawn Creek Legal Services

I read over the email and my heart drops. There's no way Cory is going to go for this. Especially since it has to do with me marrying Derek. He wasn't exactly excited when he found out we were living together, but luckily there was nothing in our custody agreement saying we couldn't.

I can't believe I've been given this incredible opportunity and I might as well throw in the towel on the whole thing.

Still, I print the needed paperwork and then email Jessica to thank her for her time. Next, I fire off an email to the hotel marketing manager. I let her know I am interested and will reach out once I confirm I will be able to make this happen.

Then, I call Derek.

"Hey, Babe. What's up?" He answers immediately.

"Well, I have news. I heard from the resort I reached out to." I announce. "They are offering us the full wedding package in exchange for content."

"WHAT! Baby, this is amazing!" Derek says so loudly that I have to hold the phone away from my ear. "You know, when you said you were going to try this, I wasn't sure it would work, but wow. I'm impressed."

I let out a heavy sigh. "Well, don't get too impressed. There's a problem."

"What problem?"

"I emailed my lawyer to have her check it over. She said it looks good, but if I want to take Juliet, which I do, I am going to have to have Cory sign off on her passport paperwork. And I need it notarized."

"Well, is Cory still in town?" Derek asks.

"Yes. He's here until this weekend." I confirm.

"Ava is a notary. You might call and see if she can help. She does stuff for us at city hall all the time." He suggests. "That is, if Cory will sign off."

"Okay, I'll call her and then I'll shoot him a text and see if he's free. But I have a feeling it will not go well." I groan. "I might as well do all of this before I go get Juliet, just in case he freaks out on me."

"Let me know how it goes." Derek says. "Or if you need police backup. I'd be happy to make an appearance."

I wish I felt like he was joking.

* * *

Cory furrows his brows and looks at me from his seat on his mom's recliner. Susan, Ava and I are seated across the living room on the sofa.

"Mexico? Why do you want to take our kid to Mexico? She's not old enough to even remember a vacation." He says with a snarl. "Can't you just take her to Galveston like a normal person?"

I take a deep breath in an attempt to keep my cool. I need to handle this like an adult. "Well, it's actually for more than just a vacation." I confess, exchanging a look with Susan. "I am getting married on this trip and I would like Juliet to be there."

Cory's face turns red, and the vein on his forehead pokes out, showing his anger. "So, you're really doing it? You're marrying the cop. You really are giving up on us that easily, Avery?"

I gently bite my tongue. *Don't let him trigger you.* I remind myself.

"And what if I say no to signing off on her passport?" He asks, crossing his arms over his chest and glaring at me.

I feel my face redden, but I fight back the urge to scream at him. Of course, he couldn't allow this to be easy. I might as well give up my dream wedding. I should have known that he would always find a way to control me.

Before I can open my mouth to respond, Susan interjects. "Cory, shut your mouth and sign the papers." She says sternly.

The room falls silent, and we all turn to look at Susan, who is glaring at Cory.

She continues. "You have done enough to wreak havoc on Avery's life, and I will not stand by and watch you try to ruin her wedding day, too."

Cory turns to his mother. "So what? I just let her take my

baby to Mexico? What if something happens to her while she's in another country?"

Susan raises her voice another octave. "The last thing that Avery would ever do is allow anything to happen to that child. She is an incredible mother who loves that baby so much." Susan picks up the pile of papers and carries them to Cory, shoving them into his chest. "Do the right thing and be the man I raised you to be. Sign the papers, and let Avery have this special day. She does not want to be with you, and you need to accept that. Hell, I'd talk her out of dating you if she even acted interested."

Ava and I exchange a look and I have to hold my breath to keep from laughing at what Susan said.

"What if I don't sign them?" He challenges her, puffing out his chest as though he is trying to be intimidating. "What are you going to do?"

"Then you can forget about getting a damn dime when I die." She replies with a shrug of her shoulders. "I will leave every dollar I have to Juliet and her legal guardian. Do not test me, child."

Cory rolls his eyes, knowing he has been defeated. "Fine." He says, picking up the paper and a pen from the side table. He signs the places I've marked and tosses them back down on the table.

"I also need a copy of your driver's license." I add softly, not moving my eyes from the floor in front of me.

Cory huffs and removes his wallet from his pocket before holding his license in the air.

"I'll take that." Susan says, plucking the card from his fingers and making her way to the next room to scan and copy the card for me. "Be right back." She says to me with a smile.

"And I'll take those." Ava says, motioning towards the pile of papers that Cory has finished signing.

Cory hands her the papers, and she moves to the dining table to finish the notary work.

Cory and I sit in silence while the two of them are gone from the room. I move my eyes to look at him when I feel his gaze on me.

"Are you sure about this?" Cory asks when his eyes meet mine. "You really want to marry him?"

"I am and I do." I answer truthfully.

"He's good to you? And Juliet?" He asks, just above a whisper.

"Yes." I reply with a nod.

I want to tell him that Juliet loves Derek, and he feels the same about her. I want to tell him that the three of us are a family. But, I don't. The last thing I want to do is make him jealous. I don't want to take the chance of him tearing up the papers I so desperately need from him.

"Then I guess you know what you're doing." He replies, his face now pointed down to the floor. "I'm sorry I wasn't good enough for you." He pauses. "I'm sorry I wasn't good enough to you, either."

I nod. "Maybe you should just worry about being good enough for Juliet, now." I reply, as his mom reenters the room again. "You're her dad, and she still needs you. That's never going to change."

Ava reenters the room and smiles softly to let me know she's ready to leave this awkward moment. I thank them both and make my way towards the door, breathing a sign of relief.

Once outside, I pay Ava and thank her for her help.

"Hey, no problem." She says with a chuckle. "That was kind

of awkward." She adds. "Does his mom reprimand him in front of you often? That was almost like when I'd go to Sierra's house in high school and listen to her and her mother fight about chores."

I laugh. "That actually has never happened before. But I was impressed."

"Well, hopefully now she laid down the law enough that it never will again." Ava says, shaking her head.

"Hopefully you're right." I agree.

* * *

"I can't believe you were able to pull off this big of a birthday party for Juliet, while you're planning a destination wedding." Tyler says, as she carefully leans against a chair off to the side of the balloon arch at the back of the church basement.

"I can't believe you are still pregnant." I say with a chuckle. "To be honest, I thought for sure since this is your first baby, you would have had her at least two weeks ago. I can't believe the doctor let you go past your due date."

Tyler shrugs and rests her hand on her belly. "What can I say? She's comfy in there. I guess she will make her way out when she's good and ready."

I frown. "Hopefully, she will be ready soon. You look miserable."

She nods. "I feel miserable, too. And if one more person asks me how many babies I'm having, I am gonna slap...."

"Oh dear, Tyler. Look at you. You look like you're about to pop!" a voice calls out from the doorway. We turn to find my neighbor, Mrs. Johanson, shuffling into the room. "How many babies do you have in there?" She adds with a soft grin. "Has to be at least three."

I quickly spin around so my back is to Mrs. Johanson and I'm facing Tyler. "Don't slap her. She's just a sweet old lady." I mutter softly. "Violence isn't the answer."

Tyler plasters on a fake smile and responds to the woman. "Oh, I certainly am ready." She confirms. "I'm not sure how many are in there, though. I asked the doctor not to tell me so we can be surprised." She adds while somehow keeping a straight face. "I'm hoping for at least a half dozen."

The woman's eyes widen in disbelief. It's clear to see that she's trying to decide how to respond when my mom enters the room and saves us. "Margaret! Thank you so much for coming. Can I take that gift for you?"

Mom gets the bewildered woman seated and returns to us, shooting Tyler a warning glare.

Tyler frowns at the silent reprimand. "She was asking for it." She argues, defending herself.

Mom just shakes her head and turns to me. "You better get this party started before Tyler gets into a fight."

"Good idea." I agree with a laugh before turning towards the crowd. "Hey, everyone, thank you so much for coming to help celebrate Juliet's second birthday! Please help yourself to some snacks and we will start opening gifts in just a few minutes."

I turn back towards Tyler as she turns to face me. "Hey, do you mind taking photos while I help Juliet open her presents?" I ask. "Or would you rather write down what she opens so I can send out thank you cards later?"

Suddenly, Tyler's face turns ghost white, and she looks down to the ground. I watch as a small wet stain appears on the thin grey carpet beneath her feet.

I look back up at Tyler's face just as her eyes meet mine. "Um.. did your water just break?" I ask, just above a whisper.

"Either that or I peed my pants." She says, biting her lip. "Pretty sure pee would have stopped by now."

My eyes widen as I spin in a circle in search of Andrew. I spot him talking to Cody and Derek in the back of the room. The alarmed look on my face tells the men something is wrong. Quickly, they make their way over to us.

"What's up?" Derek asks as they approach me.

I turn to Andrew and motion my head towards Tyler. "Hey Dad? It's baby time."

* * *

"Knock, knock." I say, just as I enter Tyler's hospital room. "How's it going in here?"

Tyler looks up from her bed. "Better now, that's for sure." She replies with a tired smile as she glances down at the bundle in her arms.

I lean over the bed and peer down at the sleeping newborn, swaddled in a thin pink blanket. The sight of the sleeping baby takes my breath away. "Oh friend. She is perfect." I gush, fighting tears in my eyes. "Besides Juliet, she might be the cutest baby I've ever seen."

Tyler gives me a tired smile. "You're supposed to think that. She's practically your niece."

I furrow my brows. "No, I mean it. She has the cutest little nose I've ever seen in my life and the poutiest lips ever. She looks like a porcelain doll. I love her so much already."

"Yeah, we did a pretty good job." Andrew agrees, as he makes his way back into the room carrying an iced coffee and a large paper to go bag.

"Oh, what'd you bring me?" I ask.

Andrew shakes his head as he hands the coffee to Tyler. He sets the bag down on the bedside table. "You'll have to fight her for this. This is the first thing she's had to eat since breakfast before Juliet's party yesterday." He rolls the table towards Tyler and then moves to the sink to wash his hands.

"Cluck and Squeal Mac and Cheese from Painted Horse." Tyler says, bouncing her eyebrows at me as though she's talking about something dirty, rather than macaroni and cheese covered in chicken and bacon bits. "As soon as they wheeled me into this room, I sent him out to get me some real food. I deserve it after twenty hours of labor."

"Yes, you certainly do." I agree before turning to Andrew. "Are you eating too?"

He smirks. "Not that I deserve it, but yes. I won't ever turn down a chance to eat."

"Well, let me wash my hands then and I'll hold Molly so you guys can eat." I say, making my way to the sink.

After a few minutes, we are all settled around the room and the new parents are enjoying their feast while I enjoy the newborn cuddles.

"Sorry for leaking all over the floor of your party." Tyler says, squishing her face as though the memory of the previous day is paining her.

I wave her off. "It's fine."

"I feel bad for leaving a mess and hightailing it out of there." She confesses.

I scoff. "Girl, I can only imagine that you're not the first one to leak amniotic fluid all over the carpet in that church basement. That carpet had to have been installed in 1957 and there have been many birthday parties and baby showers hosted in that place. Not to mention that it's the town tornado shelter."

She shrugs as she swallows her mouth full of food. "I still feel bad about stealing the spotlight during Juliet's party."

"It's fine, I promise. Besides, did you realize that now our girls share a birthday?"

Tyler's eyes light up. "I totally forgot that today is Juliet's actual birthday." She confesses.

I nod. "Yep, the church is kind of a busy place on Sunday's so if I wanted a space to throw the party, we had to do it on a Saturday. You timed it just right. I guess if we couldn't be pregnant and have babies together, then at least they can celebrate together in the years to come."

Andrew smirks. "Maybe we can time the next one a little better."

Chapter 22

Two Months Later

"I can't believe it's Juliet's first Halloween parade." Mom says, as she steps back onto my sidewalk to take a photo of Juliet and me together in our costumes. "I also can't quite get over this ensemble you've chosen." She adds with a laugh.

I scoff and look down at my black dress. "What's wrong with our costumes?" I ask, pulling my white faux fur coat tighter around my body. "Cruella and a baby dalmatian are the perfect pair for this weather. We will both stay nice and warm." I insist. "Besides, I think we look pretty cute."

Juliet is dressed in a white sweatsuit that I painted with dalmatian spots, complete with little floppy ears that I glued to the hood.

"You are just a lot more crafty than I realized." Mom observes, lightly tracing Juliet's dalmatian spots.

"I enjoyed doing it." I confess. "It's been fun to flex my creative muscles."

"Well, you should do it more often. Juliet, do you like being a puppy?"

"Woof-Woof!" she replies. "I'm a puppy!"

"You are the cutest puppy ever." Mom tells her, lightly booping her on the nose before turning to me. "Enjoy matching with her, and picking out her costume, for as long as she will let you. Before you know it, she will be insistent on dressing up as her favorite princess and you'll just be in charge of carrying her candy bag."

I fake a sniffle. "I don't want to think about it."

Mom gives me a hug and pats my back. "I know. All of us older moms drive you guys crazy by telling you how fast it goes. I used to get so annoyed when people said it to me and now I'm just as bad." She says, shaking her head. "We only say it because it's true, though."

"It's okay." I shrug, hugging Juliet close. "I think it's good to have a reminder not to take these days for granted. Her first two years have already gone by so quickly. I swear I get whiplash every time I look at her anymore."

Mom smiles softly. "I'd love to tell you it gets easier, but it really doesn't. Over time, you get used to it, or at least you think you're used to it. Then, suddenly you wake up one day and your kid is standing in front of her very own house, holding your grandchild, and you question the passage of time again." She gives me a soft smile. "But it's so fun to watch them grow up and become the people they were meant to be."

I look down at Juliet and back to my mom. I can only imagine how hard it is.

"What time is the parade?" Mom asks, looking at her watch. "I need to make sure I'm there in time to get a good spot."

The grade school has a tradition of putting on a Halloween parade every year. The kids get dressed at school in their costumes and then make their way downtown. They walk through the business district, showing off their costumes to all the parents and citizens of Fawn Creek, and then they go back to the school for their classroom parties. The daycare centers in town join in on the fun, too. The Halloween parade is one of my best memories of grade school, so when Madison asked if I would come help with her daycare kids, I knew I couldn't say no.

"2:45," I answer, checking my watch. "Juliet and I are going to make our way down there so we can help Madison get lined up." I announce. "We'll see you in a little bit."

"I'll get lots of pictures." Mom promises, and I can't help but grin.

Ever since my social media career has taken off, my mom has been one of my biggest cheerleaders. Anytime she sees me wearing a cute outfit or just out spending time with Juliet, she makes sure to get plenty of pictures and videos to send to me for use later. She even bought herself a new iPhone so she could have a better quality camera.

I buckle Juliet into her wagon and we wave goodbye to Grandma as we make our way downtown to the parade line up. I fire off a text to Madison, confirming our meeting place, and within a few minutes, I'm wheeling the wagon up to Madison's minivan parked at the fire station.

"Thank you so much for helping me with this." She says, climbing out of her van. Madison's dressed in a pink shirt with blue overalls and a headband. She even put on a brown wig to complete her look. "Can you tell who I am?"

"Duh, you're Miss Rachel." I say with a laugh. "Did the kids freak out when you walked out dressed like that?"

She laughs. "Yes. I was in costume when they got to daycare today. I've only sung "The Wheels on the Bus" nine hundred and sixty-five times today."

"I bet you loved every second of it, too." I say with a wink. "You early childhood people are a different breed. I could never do it."

She works on getting her four-seater stroller out of the back of her van and one by one; we get the kids settled in. As we get the last child in place, she turns back to me with a smile. "Avery, this is honestly my dream job. I wouldn't change it for anything."

"Thank goodness, too." I tell her. "The world needs people like you. The world being me, mostly." I joke. "If I can't be with Juliet every day, you're the only other one I can picture her with."

Madison and I make our way down the street and fall in line in front of the elementary school kids. In my wagon, I have my dalmatian and a very spooky witch. Madison leads the way, pushing her giant stroller. She has a princess, a tiny Hulk, a firefighter, and Piper, dressed as Spiderman.

The parade begins with a police officer leading the way with full lights and sirens, just like the Christmas parade. Class by class, starting with the daycare centers and leading up to sixth grade, the children are led through downtown. As we make our way through the business district, Juliet gets a kick out of waving to all the people lining the street.

"Juliet! Hi Puppy!" I hear a voice call out and we make our way past Tyler's shop. I turn to see my mother and Cory's mom standing together in front of TBR. Two proud grandmas with their phones out, documenting the momentous occasion. I almost wish I could pull out my own camera and snap a photo of the two of them. I may not have been able to make it work with Cory, but his mother has been such an incredible grandma. Seeing his mom and my mom together makes my heart melt.

"Juliet, wave to your grandmas!" I tell her.

Juliet reaches her arms over the side of the wagon and grins as she waves. "Woof, woof!" She replies.

The pair of ladies gush over the sweet toddler as we complete our walk and circle back towards the fire station.

As we make our way back to the van, Madison and I make plans to meet back up this evening. "It'll just be me and the girls tonight, if you want to tag along with us." She leans over to mutter to me. "Ben's working, as usual."

"I'd love to." I say. "Derek's working tonight, too. I can't imagine I'll be able to keep her out too late, though."

"We probably won't stay out super long." Madison promises. "I don't care if it's Halloween. My kids have got to be in bed no later than 8:30 or they are going to make my life hell tomorrow."

I chuckle and shake my head. "Sounds good then. I'll meet you downtown for Trunk or Treat at 6:30 then?"

"Perfect!"

* * *

"Wanna go see the police officer?" I ask Madison's girls as we are making our way through the downtown trunk of treat. We've walked through half of the cars set up for trunk or treat so far, and I have to admit I am in just as much of a hurry to see the officer that's on duty as they are.

"Yes!" they cry out in unison, causing Juliet to clap and squeal along too.

"Well, let's go then. I bet he's got some cool stuff in the trunk of his car."

Our group makes our way towards Derek as he stands next to the open trunk of his police cruiser. I stand on tiptoe to see what he has inside. The entire trunk, which he and I decorated to look like the open mouth of a monster, is full of badge stickers and an assortment of candy. The girls take turns fishing out their loot as we wait for Derek to finish having his photo taken with a little boy also dressed as a police officer.

"Hey, you." He finally says, turning towards me. He quickly steals a kiss before bending down to talk to the girls. "Did you guys get plenty of candy?" He asks, inspecting their bags. "Nope, you need more than that." He decides, before burying his hands into his trunk and putting a handful of candy into each girl's bag. "I might have gone a little overboard on the candy buying this year."

I shake my head. "Welp, you should be good for the Christmas parade."

"And the next year at this rate." He says with a laugh. "But the year after that I'll know that I don't need to buy fifty pounds of candy for trunk or treat."

My eyes widen. "Fifty? I don't think Tyler even bought that much for the Christmas parade last year and she had some left over." I say, shaking my head. "The chief is going to be pissed."

"He'll get over it. At least he didn't have to brave the store, so he will be more than happy to know we have plenty to save for later." He says with a chuckle. "So, where are you guys headed to next? More trick or treating?"

I nod. "Oh yes. We have a very detailed plan. When we get done here, we are hitting up the library, the cotton candy house, and then the Nightmare on Bradley for a funnel cake." I grin. "Then, it's back to the house to put this puppy to bed and watch a scary movie while I hand out candy to the more dedicated trick-or-treaters."

"Sounds like a great night. I should be home by eleven." He says, as the line behind us forms, urging us to move forward.

"Okay, I'll see you then." I promise.

* * *

"I'll never be too old for the cotton candy house." I say, as I pull off a piece of the sugary substance and let it melt in my mouth.

"Me neither." Tyler agrees as she walks along beside us, with Molly strapped to her chest in a baby carrier. "I just can't believe these people are still making cotton candy on Halloween night for trick or treaters after all these years."

"Funny story about that." Begins Madison. "It's not the same people. The people that used to live here moved. When the house was on the market, they wanted it to be known to the new owners that they would either have to pick up the tradition or have a yard full of people looking for cotton candy every Halloween." She throws a piece of cotton candy in her mouth. "Luckily, they agreed to take it on. The old owners left their machines and everything to go with the house."

"Well, I'm glad they did. I love being able to take Juliet to the things I enjoyed as a kid." I say, holding a tiny bit of the pink sugar up to Juliet's mouth. She takes a bite and her eyes immediately light up.

"Yummmm" she proclaims. "More."

Tyler laughs. "I bet after all these years, my mom is still complaining about this place."

Madison raises a brow. "Does she have something against cotton candy?"

"No. She has something against the stick that the cotton candy is spun on to. They live about a block that way." She points toward their house. "And for some reason, her yard is a magnet for kids to throw the trash from their cotton candy in her yard. It got so bad she started leaving a trash can in her yard with a sign telling them to throw their sticks away. That might be my fondest Halloween memory, actually. My mom in her windbreaker every November first, cussing to herself while picking up cotton candy stick trash."

"I guess if you can't be the cotton candy house, you can be the cotton candy stick house." I say with a laugh. "Your poor mom."

Tyler laughs. "Back then, I thought she was being way to anal about the whole thing. Now that I'm older though, I get it. I'd be pissed, too." She shakes her head and finishes her snack, throwing the stick in a nearby trash can. "So, where to next?" She asks, pausing quickly to glance down at her sleeping baby.

"The only place left on my list is the Nightmare on Bradley." I reply.

"Is that new?" asks Tyler. "I haven't heard of that one."

"Fairly. It's been around for a few years, but it started after you left." I shrug.

"Oh, it's so cool," Madison chimes in. "The people that own that house spend the entire week before Halloween decorating their yard. They have it all. Fake spiderwebs, inflatable decorations, spooky statues, black lights... you name it. They make this spooky, but totally kid friendly, path through their yard. You travel through all the decor and when you get to the end, you are rewarded with your own individual sized funnel cake."

"Um, that sounds amazing." Tyler says, her eyes already

glowing with excitement.

"It's seriously the coolest thing ever, and it's so cool after dark." I confirm. "I don't know how, but it just keeps getting better year after year. The woman that owns the house is an artist and I wish I could be anywhere near as creative as she is. It's easily my favorite thing about Halloween." I shrug. "And I love a lot about Halloween, so that is saying something."

"Well, what are we waiting for? Let's go." Tyler proclaims.

*　*　*

Tyler, Madison and I, with all our kids in tow, make our way towards the entrance of The Nightmare on Bradley.

"Dude. You weren't kidding." Tyler says, as she keeps her head on swivel, taking in the scene all around us. "This is the coolest Halloween setup I've ever seen." She confirms, walking through the giant inflatable tunnel at the entrance.

"It really is." I agree, as I snap a couple of pictures with Tyler and her snuggly baby, and then Madison with her kids.

"Avery, I love that you are so good at getting pictures of all of us," Madison says. "I swear I have a million pictures of my kids over the years with Ben. The only ones I have of them with me are selfies or professional photos, though. Of course, except for when you're with me. I don't know what I'd do without friends like you."

I shrug. "No worries. You can always count on me to take too many pictures." I say with a wink. "Mom's have to look out for each other, after all. Tyler, can you get a couple of me and Juliet, too?" I ask, handing her my phone.

Tyler takes several pictures of Juliet and me at the entrance before handing the phone back to me.

I watch as Ava and Piper make their way into the yard. Piper is still dressed in her Spiderman costume from earlier today. "Hey, how's the wedding planning going?" Ava calls over to me.

"So good." I reply. "Thank you again for all of your help."

"It was nothing at all. I can't wait to see pictures of your big day. I love Mexico." She confesses. "It's one of my favorite places. I'll be watching your socials and living vicariously through you."

"There will be plenty of pictures, don't worry." I say with a laugh.

Our group continues our journey through the Halloween wonderland. As we inch closer to the funnel cake table, the scent of the sugary treat reaches my nose. It nearly causes me to drool.

"Is that weird?" Tyler asks in a whisper as soon as Ava is out of earshot.

"Is what weird?"

"Knowing that everyone in town has all this access to your life? Like everyone always knows what you're up to because you get paid to post about it online."

"Honestly, no," I say, shaking my head. "Fawn Creek is small enough that if I do anything worth knowing, everyone will hear about it, anyway. And if they don't know, they'll just make something up. So, I might as well just live my life and make some money from it."

Madison shakes her head. "I am so jealous of your success with this. I knew you'd do good, but I never dreamed it would go as far as it has."

"It is a lot of fun." I agree. "But, listen, this content creation thing is not all puppies and rainbows, though. The locals have been great and so supportive, but there are a lot of jerks on the internet. People seem to forget, or maybe just not care, that there is a real person on the other side of the screen."

"So, I take it your peanut butter and jelly sandwich video is still gaining traction." Tyler chuckles.

"The last I checked, it was nearing four million views, and the people seeing it now are NOT my target audience. Instead, it's a bunch of angry trolls."

"Wait. What video?" Madison asks, looking confused. "I'm missing something here."

I shake my head. "It's so dumb. I made a video that Derek used the rim of a glass to cut Juliet's PBJ into a circle the other day. Now Juliet is refusing to eat a regular sandwich. She demands for it to be a circle."

"Ugh. Be the fun guy one time and then you're stuck doing it forever." Madison groans.

"Exactly. Anyway, the internet is pissed about the whole thing. Either I'm a jerk for being annoyed with him about it, because at least he made her a sandwich. Or I'm a terrible person for not forcing her to eat crust. And don't get me started on how lazy I am. People are crazy."

"That's fine. The more engagement, the more money you'll make." Tyler reminds me. "She's already made close to four thousand dollars off that video." She tells Madison.

Madison's eyes widen. "Are you serious?"

"It's crazy, isn't it? I just have to keep my notifications turned off for the time being. The amount of alerts from my phone because of all the comments is kind of overwhelming."

"It'll be worth it." Tyler reminds me. "Then this will die down and something else will go viral instead."

"Hopefully, my sanity will make it that long."

"If not, you'll have the money for therapy." Madison jokes, and we finally reach the table at the end of the Halloween maze.

Each of us receives our individual sized funnel cakes. We thank the homeowners and compliment them on their hard work before making our way back towards our cars.

I shrug. "Who needs therapy when you have powdered sugar?"

Chapter 23

Two Weeks later

Madison: Hey, can I come over? I need to talk to you.
Me: Sure! I'm home, come on over. You okay?
Madison: Yes and no. Be right there.

"Hey. Sorry." Madison says, as I open the door to let her into my house.

"Don't be sorry. Come sit down and talk to me." I say, motioning towards the living room.

Madison takes a seat on my sofa and, from the look on her face, it's clear that she's been crying.

"What's wrong?"

Madison lets out a heavy sigh. "Ben is not coming to Mexico for your wedding."

I raise a brow. Honestly, I could have called this one. Ben hasn't shown up to anything in months. I've almost forgotten the guy exists at this point. "That's fine. Are you still coming?"

She nods, still wiping tears from her face. "Yes. I'll be there. I wouldn't miss it for the world."

"That's all that matters. We will still have plenty of fun without him."

"Avery, he's not coming because we're getting a divorce." Madison finally says, just above a whisper.

"A divorce? Madison, are you sure? What happened?" I reach over and squeeze my friend's hand. Madison and Ben have been married since high school. If they can't make it, what does that say for the rest of us?

Madison pauses for a beat and takes another deep breath before she speaks again. "Ben had an affair. With some woman at work named Amber."

I feel all the air empty from my lungs. "Madi, oh no. I'm so sorry."

"There's more." She confesses. "The woman is pregnant and due any day now. She's having a boy."

"What?!" The sadness I was feeling towards Madi, only seconds ago, has now turned into a white fiery rage against Ben.

"Can you believe that? A boy. I tried to give him a boy twice. And he was so disappointed when they were both girls. Just another way I couldn't measure up."

"Um, you measured up just fine. Ben is a moron and you deserve better. When did you find out about this? Today?"

Madison shakes her head.

"How long ago?"

"Months." She admits. "June, actually. When Amber found out she was having a boy, she reached out to me on Facebook and told me the news. She said she had been trying to get Ben to tell me, but he hadn't, so she took matters into her own hands."

I count the months on my fingers and the look at her with wide eyes. "Madison, it's November. You've known about this for five months? And you've kept it to yourself? Why?"

She shakes her head. "I don't know. At first, I was probably in denial. Ben just kept saying that the woman was crazy, and she was trying to get him fired from his job. He would just not admit it. I wanted to believe him, but I did some detective work and caught him red-handed. All those nights he said he was working, all the events he missed. He was with her. I knew something was going on. It's been going on for over a year. I just thought we were growing apart."

"What an asshole." I say, shaking my head. "So, what did he say when you caught him?"

"Well, I didn't tell him I knew. Not until a few weeks ago. Instead, I just worked on getting my ducks in a row. First, I took on a couple more kids at daycare so I could increase my income. Then, I started putting away money. I made sure I can make it on my own. Then I told him I knew."

She stares down at her lap. "I'm sorry, Avery. I wanted to tell you he wouldn't be coming to Mexico, but I couldn't yet. Truthfully, I couldn't chance him knowing that he was caught until I was ready. So, I just never bought him a plane ticket. I filed for divorce the day before Halloween. He moved out. It's official."

I reach over and pull my friend into a hug. "I am so proud of you. You did what you had to do in order to take care of your family. Not everyone is strong enough to do that. You are going to be just fine. I promise."

She lets out a heavy sigh. "I hope you're right."

* * *

Six Weeks Later

"Margarita, anyone?" Tyler calls out from Madison's

kitchen.

"Yes!" Madison, Ava and Sierra reply.

"You pour. I'll deliver." I tell Tyler with a laugh.

Tonight is Madison's Divorce Party. Yesterday was court and her divorce from Ben is officially finalized, so we decided to celebrate her new life. The men are currently outside grilling burgers while we sip on Tyler's very strong margaritas.

I pass out the drinks and we all sit on Madison's living room floor and wait for dinner.

Madison looks up from her cup and smiles at us softly.

"Thank you guys for doing this for me." She says. "When Sierra said she wanted to throw me this party, I wasn't so sure it was a great idea. It kind of felt weird to celebrate the fact that my marriage failed. But, I'm so glad we did this. There's no one else I would rather be surrounded by while I restart my life."

I reach out my hand and squeeze hers. "We love you and we hate that this happened to you. Your marriage didn't fail. Ben failed." I say with a sigh. "What he did to you was unimaginable. We are celebrating you rising from the ashes and starting over fresh. We are so proud of you for standing your ground and kicking him to the curb. You deserve to celebrate."

Tyler nods. "She's right. This is the best possible excuse for a party and we are here for you. He's a dirtbag." She takes a sip of her drink. "I didn't even know him, but I hate him." She adds.

"It feels so weird to be single after all this time. I haven't been single since junior high." Madison admits with a frown.

"Better to be single than married to a cheater." Sierra says. "When you find the next guy, it'll be the right one."

Madison sighs. "That will be a long time from now. I am in no hurry to do that again."

"Just be prepared. It always seems to happen when you least expect it. Just like Tyler and me." I warn, shooting a look at my best friend.

"Honestly, it was about damn time." Madison says with a grin. "Everyone in this town knew you two were going to end up together. I'm just glad it finally happened."

"Food's ready!" Andrew calls out to us around the kitchen doorway, interrupting our conversation. "Better come get it."

With that, we file into the kitchen to make our plates and then meet back in the living room.

I sit down and take a bite of my burger. Instantly, my mouth waters for more. "Andrew, these are amazing. Like seriously, one of the best burgers I've ever had." I announce. "Who knew you could cook like this?"

Cody chimes in. "He makes a damn good burger, but it wouldn't be nearly as good if it wasn't from our own cows."

Tyler frowns. "I don't want to talk about it." She says, putting her burger back on her plate. "Now my appetite is ruined."

Andrew shakes his head. "Babe, you have to get over it. This is all part of raising cattle. It's the circle of life."

"I know." She says with a sigh. "But do they have to be so cute before you take them off to be butchered?"

The rest of the room stares at her.

"What? I'm doing my best to be a country girl, but it's still taking some getting used to, okay?"

"Anyway." Sierra interrupts, changing the subject. "Madison, I forgot to show you the cheesecake I had the bakery make for us." She says, standing from her seat on the floor and moving to her insulated tote near the front door. She holds up the tin so we can read the writing in chocolate frosting on the white cheesecake background.

"Congrats. We hated him anyway." Derek reads out loud with a chuckle. "That's pretty good."

Madison laughs politely, but I can tell she is also fighting back tears. "Thank you, Sierra." She says and then she pauses. "You guys didn't, though, right?"

Andrew shakes his head. "We do now. That's all that matters."

Derek nods in agreement. "I gotta admit. He had me fooled. All this time, I thought he was a good guy. I never would have pictured him cheating on you." He turns to look directly at Madison with kind eyes. "I swear Madison, I didn't know or I would have told you."

She shakes her head and then looks down at her plate. "It's okay. He had many people fooled. Including me. I'm better off, or I guess I will be."

"I'll toast to that." I say, holding up my glass. "To new beginnings."

"Cheers." Our friends echo once again.

Chapter 24

"What time are you planning to leave work today?" Tyler asks over my office speaker phone. Tomorrow we are leaving for the airport to make our way towards Mexico for my wedding.

"Probably around three. I have just a couple of reports to finish and then I'll be ready to step away from this place for a week. And I can not wait." I respond. "I still need to pack when I get home."

"You mean you need to finish packing, right?" Tyler asks, sounding stressed.

"Yes." I agree. "And also I need to start."

"You're going to give me an aneurysm." Tyler huffs into the phone. "I've been packed for two weeks now. Did you even look at the packing list I sent you? Do you need help?"

"If you want to come help me, you can. Yes, I've been going over your list, but I've had a hard time actually getting around to putting any of it together. I'll get it done, eventually." I say, trying to calm her. It doesn't work.

"You'll get it done when you get home from work." Tyler sighs. "Text me when you leave and I'll meet you at your house. I'm not going to be able to sleep tonight unless I know you are packed and ready to go."

"Sounds good. I need to stop at the store on the way home for some travel toiletry bottles. And maybe some sunscreen. I can't remember if I have any." I say more to myself than to her.

"Okay, I'm going to hang up now before you give me a nervous breakdown. Let me know when you're home and I'll come help you knock it out."

"Okay, I'll let you know when I head home." I say, before disconnecting the call and turning back to my computer.

As soon as I disconnect my call with her, my cell phone rings. The caller ID states UNKNOWN CALLER.

I frown and hesitate to press the answer button. Most of the time, I would just ignore it in case it's a spam caller. However, with our wedding this week, I don't want to miss a call from the resort to go over last-minute details.

"Hello?"

A male voice on the other end startles me when he speaks.

"Avery. Hi. It's... Dad."

The vague familiarity of his voice causes my breath to hitch. Quickly, I try to do the math to figure out how long it's been since I talked to him last. Perhaps eleven years? Not since my high school graduation when he brought his wife and kids, whom I had never met, to the ceremony. Afterwards, he was more concerned about getting a photo of all of us together than anything else. Never once did he congratulate me. He didn't even bother with coming to my party. He simply posed for his photo and then loaded his family back up in his wife's Tahoe and drove away, disappearing just as quickly as he had when I was a kid. It was pretty par for the course for this guy.

"Avery, you there?" He asks, interrupting my thinking.

"Yes... I..." I stutter, stumbling over my words. "I'm here.

215

How can I help you?" I ask, trying to sound as professional as possible. Not the kind of tone one would usually use with their dad. But of course, he's not exactly dad material. He lost the right for me to call him that years ago.

"Hey kiddo. Your sister, Katherine, was showing me a video on that Tiktok app a little while ago. Something about a sandwich. I just couldn't believe my eyes when I realized you were the woman on the screen. So, I looked around on your profile and found you advertising for a clothing company, too."

I let out a heavy sigh and move across the room to close my office door for privacy.

"Yeah. That's me. If you want to place an order, you can just shop directly from my page." I reply. "I can't get you a discount or whatever, if that's what you're looking for."

"Oh, no. That's not what I was reaching out for." He answers quickly. "I was actually calling about something else, though."

"Um, okay. What then?" I ask. I want to tell him to cut to the chase. Or to lose my number and never to call me again. I've been all these years without speaking to him and this is the last thing I need today. I need to focus on my wedding and my vacation.

"Well I happened to notice that you're getting married soon."

I pause, waiting for him to explain what this has to do with him calling me.

Sensing that I won't be speaking, he continues. "Avery, I know we haven't had the best relationship, but I have to admit that I was surprised not to get an invitation in the mail. Your step-mom and siblings and I would love to be there for you if it's not too late. And of course, I'd love to be the one to give you away."

I grit my teeth. "You're kidding me, right?"

"Well, I just thought." He attempts to explain, but I interrupt.

"You thought what? That you could just disappear from my life before I was five years old and run off to create a new life with a new family, only popping in to give a shit about us every ten years? Yes, Gary. It's too late for you to come to my wedding. It's too late for you to meet your granddaughter. You will not choose to have something to do with me only when it's convenient for you."

Silence fills the line, and for a moment, I assume he disconnected the call. Finally, he speaks up. "Avery, I'm sorry. I know I haven't always done a great job of being your dad, but I'd really like it if you would give me another chance."

I shake my head, fighting back the tears welling in my eyes. The last thing I will let him do is find out that his words hurt me. I have cried too many tears over this man for my entire life, and I will not let him know he's gotten to me today. I take a deep breath.

"Well, it sounds to me like you should have made that decision a long time ago, then. Maybe you can be a better dad for your other kids than you bothered to be for me." I pause, with my finger hovering over the disconnect button. "And don't worry. You already gave me away years ago when you left our family to make a new one. I'm not yours to give away. Goodbye."

I smash my finger down to the disconnect button and once I know the call is hung up, I finally let the tears free. I bury my head in my hands and try to soften the sound of my cries. How is this happening right before the happiest day of my life?

I quickly finish up my workday and lock up my office as I leave for my first real vacation in years. The entire way home,

I can't shake the anger I'm feeling after the conversation with my dad. Where did that man get the audacity to reach out to me like that?

I let out a heavy sigh and call the one person who I know will understand how I feel.

"Hey Sis, what's up?" Bryan answers the phone. I hear the sounds of metal clanging around in the background. I can only imagine that he's still at work for the day.

"Hey. Are you busy?"

"Nah. What's up? Wait. Don't tell me you're bailing on the wedding."

I sigh. "Everything is fine with the wedding, but I did just get an unexpected phone call. From our father."

Bryan lets out a disgusted chuckle. "What did that joker want?"

"Oh, he just saw me on Tiktok. After he stalked me for a while, he realized that my life is fantastic and I'm thriving without him, so he had to call and try to ruin that." I huff. "He wanted to know if he and the rest of his family were invited to my wedding. You know, so he could give me away."

"You have to be kidding me. Did you tell him to go to hell?"

"Basically. I told him that if he wanted anything to do with me, he should have stepped up a long time ago. Then I told him he can't give me away, because he already did that when I was four." I recall shaking my head. "Where does he get the nerve to reach out to me like that?"

"I don't know. He tried it with me a couple of years ago and I just blew him off, too. He must have realized you're some famous Tiktoker, and he wants to ride your coattails."

"I'm not even famous. I have a hundred thousand followers. That's nothing compared to some people."

"It's a lot compared to other people." Bryan reminds me. "And cut yourself some slack. You are having a wedding for free in Mexico in just a few days because of your silly little following. You are a big deal, and I'm proud of you."

Suddenly, a feeling of calm washes over me, bringing me down to reality after my father got me into such a tailspin. Bryan has a way of doing this sort of thing, or at least he did when we were kids. I forgot how good he was at it.

"Thank you, Bryan. I needed that."

"I know you did," He answers, almost sounding arrogant. "I'm sorry that you don't hear that enough."

"Bryan?" I ask as I pull into my parking spot at the store. "I was going to walk down the aisle on my own, but suddenly that doesn't seem right anymore. Would you be willing to give me away? You can totally say no if you want to. I was just thinking that you were really the closest to a male role model I ever had and...."

Bryan interrupts my rambling. "Avery, I'd be honored to give you away at your wedding." He answers. "I've been trying to get rid of you for ages. I'm happy to do it." He adds, changing the tone of our conversation before it gets too sappy.

I sigh loudly. "Okay, jerk. I'll see you tomorrow in Houston when our connecting flight arrives. Now, I need to get off here and grab some last-minute things from the store so I can start packing."

"You haven't started packing yet? For your own wedding?" Bryan sounds worried. "I've been done for days."

"It'll be fine. It'll take no time at all. Everything is fine."

* * *

"This is not fine." I say, plopping down on my bed next to my suitcase and a pile of clothes. "Maybe I should have started this a long time ago." I frown.

Tyler shakes her head and places Molly in the bouncer on the floor next to my bed. "Come on, we don't have time for should haves. We need to get to work." She says, taking control of the situation. She places the printed packing list on my bed and fires off commands to me.

"Okay, underwear. We are going to be there for five days. My rule is two pairs of underwear per day plus two extra."

I raise a brow and cross my arms. "That seems excessive."

"I didn't ask for your input," Tyler smirks. "Never in my life have I been on a trip and thought 'Wow, I wish I hadn't packed so much underwear.' It takes up basically no room and it won't hurt to have too many. Just do what I say, please." She commands.

I nod and follow Tyler's lead. There's no point in arguing with her now. If I wanted to do things my way, I should have worked on it long before tonight.

She lists off each needed item and I run around my room, gathering what she asks for. Before long, we find a decent rhythm. I pile everything on the bed and she packs it all away in my suitcase. In no time, everything is packed and zipped into my bag, with only a little bit spilling over into Juliet's suitcase.

We lug the suitcases across the house and park them in the entryway for tomorrow's early flight. As I park them, I turn around and pull Tyler into a half hug while she holds Molly on one side of her body. "Thank you for your help. I probably couldn't have ever got this done without you." I admit.

She shakes her head. "You're wrong. You definitely couldn't have gotten it done without me. But it's okay. I'm glad I could be helpful, and I can't wait to see you get married in just a few days." She turns towards the front door and looks back at me and smiles. "I'll see you bright and early tomorrow. Set more than one alarm, okay?"

"I will." I promise. "See you in the morning."

Chapter 25

I stretch my neck and wave to Tyler as she and Andrew make their way through the airport towards our gate. Madison, Derek, his parents, my mother, Juliet and I drove to the airport in a convoy while Tyler and Andrew planned to meet us here. My brother will catch up with us in Houston.

Tyler makes a big show of looking at her watch as she plops down next to me dramatically. "Dang it. I lost my bet." She says, frowning at Andrew. When she sees the puzzled look on my face, she continues. "I was sure we were going to beat you here and you would run through the gate at the last minute."

I scoff and attempt to defend myself when Derek grins and raises a hand. "Sorry, I ruined that one for you. I refuse to be at the airport any later than two hours before a flight. I'm not taking the chance of missing my wedding. Avery got a rude awakening this morning when I woke her up at four."

Tyler smirks. "Oh Derek, you are exactly who Avery needs in her life. Just don't let her change you, okay?"

I look back and forth between the two of them. "Um, I'm right here." I say, rolling my eyes.

"Yep, and you know exactly who you are. Chronically late." Tyler shrugs.

"She's always been that way." My mother adds, shaking her

head. "The only time in her life that she's ever been in a hurry was the day she was born."

I look down at Juliet, who is sitting on my lap facing me. "Can you believe they are making fun of me like this? How rude."

"How rude." Juliet repeats, crossing her arms over her chest and pouting out her bottom lip.

Tyler pats my leg. "Oh, don't worry, Avery. We love you and we know you have plenty of outstanding character traits. Being on time just isn't one of them. That's why you and Derek are perfect for each other. Where you're low, he's high. I'm sure in time, you'll find the same for his quirks and your strengths too. It's what makes a relationship work." She adds. I watch as Andrew reaches over and squeezes her hand, causing her to blush.

It's hard to believe that just over a year ago, the two of them were the ones getting married. Now here they are getting ready to be at our wedding and offering us relationship advice. It's absolutely wild how things can change in the course of a year.

Madison turns to me. "Hey, let's go get some photos and video snippets of you in front of the Tulsa backdrop." She motions to the photo backdrop positioned against the wall near our gate. "Since we have all this time to kill." She adds, smirking at Derek.

"Hey now." Derek argues. "You wouldn't be complaining if the line at the gate had been out of control."

"We're just teasing." I say, kissing the top of his head. "Tyler's right. I'm lucky to have you. Otherwise, I would have absolutely been running through the gate at the last second, frazzled and stressed. Let's go get a few pictures in our matching shirts."

For Christmas last year, Derek bought me a vinyl cutting

machine to use for crafting. This year, he bought me a heat press so that I can make my own shirts for myself and the business I will finally start after we get back home from this trip.

He wasn't nearly as excited as I was, however, when I showed him the matching bride and groom shirts I made for us to wear while traveling. Derek apparently isn't a big fan of being the center of attention.

Derek's face turns a little pink with embarrassment, but reluctantly he stands up to follow me.

"Don't worry, buddy." Andrew says, patting him on the back. "This is only the beginning."

* * *

"What took y'all so long?" Bryan asks teasingly as we enter the gate to find him waiting for us.

Andrew shrugs. "We tried to get them to fly the plane a little faster, but they didn't seem to want our advice." He reaches out and shakes Bryan's hand. "How's it going?" He asks.

"Oh ya know, just ready for bottomless margaritas and senoritas on the beach." He smiles and then looks back at me. "And I guess a wedding, too."

"Thanks, bro. So glad to have your support." I say, rolling my eyes.

Bryan winks at me and then reaches out for Juliet, who quickly goes to him. "How's my favorite girl?" He asks her. "Did you like your first plane ride?"

"She did so good." I report to him. "She never even made a peep. I was sure she was going to be one of those annoying kids on the plane that cried nonstop and drove everyone nuts. She surprised me, though."

"Well, of course she was great." Bryan says, reaching a hand to her belly to tickle her. "She's a brave girl." He adds before making his way through the crowd to say hello to everyone else. He puts an arm around my mom and hugs her close. "Hi, Mama. How was your first flight?"

My mom shakes her head. "Terrifying and exciting. I can't believe I almost made it my entire life without ever getting on a plane."

Bryan chuckles and shakes his head. "Well, it sounds like we need to get you on a few more of them, then."

Derek's mom, Joyce, smiles softly and rests a hand on Mom's shoulder. "You need to try a cruise one day, Julie. We go all the time and have so much fun."

Derek's father, Robert, nods in agreement. "You know, I never thought I'd be a cruising kind of person, but I went on one to make her happy." He says, motioning towards his wife. "Now I think I might even like them more than she does. We go on at least one a year."

My mom smiles. "Well, maybe one day we can plan a family cruise." She says, looking at Bryan and then me.

Joyce's eyes light up. "Oh, that would be so fun. You guys just give me the word and I'll start planning it." She says, before looking at me. "I mean, I guess we are all family now, right?"

I beam. "Of course we are. A family vacation sounds like fun." I offer.

Derek laughs and places a hand on Joyce's shoulder. "Maybe we should get through this trip before we book another one."

"Oh, sorry, I just can't help it. Someone starts talking about planning a trip and I'm mentally packing my bag and waiting at the door to leave. Even if I'm on vacation already." Joyce says with a laugh.

I smile at Joyce and shake my head. "I think I want to be you when I grow up."

Robert just laughs. "Me too, kid. Me too."

* * *

The hotel shuttle stops abruptly in front of The Hyatt Ziva in Cancun. I hug Juliet to my body tightly and smile down at her. It's been a long five months of planning and counting down for this trip and I still feel like I need to pinch myself to make sure this is real life.

"Are you ready to see the beach?" I ask Juliet.

"Beach!" she repeats, bobbing her head back and forth. "I want to play in the sand."

"You got it. As soon as we get checked in, we will put on our swimsuits and make our way to the beach, okay?"

"Yay! Beach!" She squeals in response, clapping her hands.

Once we get the bags unloaded and tip our driver, we make our way into the resort to check in. As soon as I step inside onto the marble flooring, my breath is taken away by the sheer beauty of it all. Immediately, I whip out my phone and begin taking photos. Without a pause, I post them on my story to alert my followers of my arrival.

"Ms. Thompson?" The hotel clerk calls out to me. "We can get you all checked in right here."

With a grin, I reach over and squeeze Derek's hand. "I can't believe that in just two days, I'll no longer answer to that name. I can't wait to be Mrs. Miller."

"I can't wait for you to be either." Derek says, pulling my hand towards his mouth and kissing it before following me to the check-in desk.

Within fifteen minutes, we are all checked into our rooms, and Juliet is more than ready to hit the beach.

"Okay, I have to get her swimsuit on her and take her down to the water." I tell my mother, as we make our way towards our block of rooms. "You are more than welcome to join us, or you can have some time to yourself if you'd rather."

Mom pauses and looks around. "You know, I'm not sure I even know what to do with myself."

I laugh. "That's because you are always all work and no play." I say with a smirk. "Mom, I think you should put on your swimsuit, grab a book and go lay out by the pool with a plate of nachos." I say. "At least that sounds dreamy to me."

"Well, I can take Juliet to the water so you can do that." Mom offers.

I shake my head. "Nope. You will have plenty of time later during this trip when I'll need your help. For now, your only job is to relax and see what a real vacation feels like. You deserve this more than anyone else here. Go enjoy it. We love you and will message you if we need anything, but for now, just consider yourself off duty."

Mom chews on her bottom lip, indicating that she's thinking. "Okay, if you're sure."

"More than sure." I assure her. "We will see you at dinner, okay?"

Mom nods and steps into her room, closing the door behind her, and I turn to Derek. "The poor woman doesn't know what to do with herself. She's been in hustle mode for so long she doesn't know how to relax." I tell him.

"Don't worry, my mom will influence her to catch the travel bug before this trip is over." He says with a grin as he opens the door to our room and ushers us inside.

"I hope you're right." I confess, as I put my backpack on the bed and dig for our swimsuits. Thankfully, I packed them in my carry on so I don't have to wait for the bellboy to drop off our suitcases. "She needs to learn how to relax before she works herself to death."

Juliet, in the meantime, is already out on the balcony looking through the slats in the concrete wall. "Beach, mommy! Beach!" She says, pointing towards the water we are over-looking. "I want to see the beach!"

"Okay girl, I hear you." I tell her with a smile. "Let's go put on our swimsuits and get some sun."

* * *

"Another margarita, senorita?" A waiter from the resort asks as he makes his way past our beach chairs. Juliet is sitting in the sand between mine and Derek's chairs, happily digging in the sand.

"Please." I reply with a smile, and then I turn to Derek. "This doesn't even feel real, you know that?"

"What do you mean?" He asks, overlooking the waves in front of us.

"I don't know. After everything, I went through with Cory. There was a point when I felt like my life was over." I sigh. "I was afraid to let myself truly live once I had Juliet. It didn't matter if he and I were over, he just still managed to be in charge of me. I truly wasn't sure I'd ever find myself again.

And if I hadn't found me, I wouldn't have found this with you."

Derek reaches over and grabs my hand before looking back at me. "Avery, I knew you were still in there. I knew you hadn't completely lost that fun, gorgeous, sexy woman that I fell for all those years ago. But, you know what?"

"What?" I ask with a soft smile.

"Watching you find yourself again was one of the most incredible transformations I've ever seen." He says with a smile. "And, if it's even possible, I think it made me fall in love with you even deeper than I was before. You're incredible, Avery, and you sure are a wonderful role model for Juliet. I'm just glad you let me come along on this journey."

I reach over and squeeze his hand. "Thank you, Derek. That means more to me than you know."

Just then, my phone alerts me to a Snapchat notification. It's Tyler messaging our group chat.

Tyler: "Hey everyone. Just a reminder that we have a table reserved for dinner at 6:30 at the beachside restaurant. See you soon."
  Madison: Bring on the tacos and margaritas!
  Julie: See you then. 💜

"Well, it looks like Tyler is taking her Maid of Honor duties seriously." Derek says with a smile as he finishes reading the message thread on his own phone.

I laugh. "You know, she has always been a bit of a leader, but ever since having the baby, she has really stepped into this role of taking charge. It's like she became the mom of the friend group. It honestly suits her well. I think it gives her a sense of purpose."

Derek nods. "I can imagine getting married, opening a business and having a baby all within a year could do that to a person."

I sigh. "I imagine so. Besides, I need all the organized people in my life I can get to help manage my hot mess self."

Derek stands and dusts the sand off his legs. "It's a tough job, but between several of us, I think we can manage." He teases. "Speaking of which. It's probably time for us to head upstairs to get ready for dinner. I have a feeling Tyler will not tolerate our tardiness."

Chapter 26

Derek, Juliet and I make our way to the outdoor restaurant for our dinner reservation. As we are led to our table, we find the rest of our group waiting for us.

"Mom, you look refreshed." I say, as I take a seat next to her. "What did you do this afternoon?"

"I filled up that giant tub in my room and laid in it while I watched a movie and ate some nachos from room service." She says with a laugh. "Then, I took a nap in the hammock on my balcony. It was incredible."

"See? I knew you had it in you." I joke, elbowing her lightly.

"Looks like you guys got some sun." She says as she lifts her glass and takes a sip.

I look down at my arms, which are noticeably darker than when we arrived today. "Yes, Juliet had the best time playing in the sand. And we missed her nap, so I'm sure she will be out early tonight."

"Well, I want to keep her tonight so that you can go out and enjoy the resort with your friends. I've had all the relaxation I need for one day. Anymore than that, I'm going to go stir crazy." Mom says with a chuckle.

I furrow my brows. "Are you sure? I don't want you to feel like a full-time babysitter on this trip."

"Yes, I'm sure. Don't worry about me. Juliet and I will have a great time and get to bed at a decent time tonight. In fact, why don't you let her stay with me for the rest of the trip? You and Derek deserve to spend time alone while you're here."

I start to argue, but she stops me.

"Please. Let me do this, okay?" She reaches over and squeezes my hand. "It's important to me. I may not be available to you as much as I'd like to be when we're at home. Let me at least do it while we're here."

I nod. "Okay, but as soon as you are ready for a break, you tell me. I'm more than happy to take over."

"Deal." she says with a grin.

"So." Sierra asks across the table. "Have you gotten a lot of good content so far?"

I finish sipping my margarita and nod, setting my glass back on the table. "Yes! Actually, I've already gotten a few messages from the marketing department thanking me for what I've posted so far. They have reposted several things already." I lower my voice. "And my following has grown by five thousand people since I got here."

Madison's eyes widen. "That's so exciting! Ugh, this is such a dream, Avery. Thanks for bringing us along for it."

I smile softly. "I wouldn't want to do this with anyone else."

Madison isn't kidding. This entire trip has felt like a dream. It's still so hard to believe that in just two more days we will be married, and then two days after that, we will head back to Fawn Creek and start our new life as husband and wife.

We finish our meal and thank the servers as we gather up and leave the restaurant, just as the sun is setting over the gulf of Mexico.

"Tell Mommy and Derek goodnight." My mom instructs

Juliet, handing her off to me for a series of hugs and kisses. After we finish, I had her back over, as well as hand Mom my room key so she can get Juliet's things.

"Just bring her over in the morning if you need a break." I tell my mom. "And I mean it."

She shakes her head. "We are going to be just fine. You guys enjoy yourselves and we will catch up with you tomorrow." Without another word, Mom and Juliet turn and make their way back towards the rooms.

Tyler steps next to me and rests her head on my shoulder. "I love watching your mom be a grandma. She was made for this role, you know?"

"I think so too. I'm sure naming Juliet after her helped the situation, too."

Bryan laughs. "You could have named that child Dumpster Fire and mom would still be just as in love with her as she is now."

I turn to him and grin. "You better hurry and get in on that, too. I'm sure she has room for a few more grandbabies in her heart." I say with a wink.

Bryan's face immediately turns beat red, and he changes the subject. "Um, so, what do you guys think about taking a sunset walk on the beach?"

"That sounds great." Sierra interjects. "All this baby talk makes me need a drink." She says with a nervous laugh as she pushes past us, towards the beachside bar.

I turn and raise an eyebrow at Tyler, but she just shakes her head and laces her arm in with mine. "A drink and a sunset walk sounds perfect." She agrees.

We get our drinks and wander along down the beach. Tyler and I walk together, with Andrew and Derek following behind.

Immediately behind them are Bryan and Madison, strolling along wordlessly. Cody and Sierra bring up the rear.

Tyler hooks her arm in mine and rests her head on my shoulder momentarily. "Avery, this place is amazing. Thank you so much for making this happen. Andrew and I haven't had alone time like this since before Molly was born and I didn't realize how much we needed it." She admits.

"Thank you for coming." I say, tightening my grip on her arm. "I know it wasn't easy leaving Molly with your parents, but I'm so glad you could be here with me. This wouldn't have been worth doing without you guys here." I admit. "I can't think of a better group of people to get married with."

"I miss her so much." Tyler admits. "But I know she's in capable hands. Plus, I needed an excuse to get away so I could sleep through the night for once. Too bad I had to leave the country to make it happen. Maybe Andrew and I will have to make a solo trip an annual thing. I needed this so badly." She says, shaking her head.

Tyler looks behind her at Andrew, and then quickly turns back to me. "By the way. Is there something going on between Madison and your brother?" She asks in a low voice.

I raise a brow and turn to look back at them. Somehow, they have fallen to the rear of our group and they are strolling along, lost in conversation. "I'm not sure I've ever seen my brother smile as big as he is smiling right now. I don't know that they have something going on, but I definitely get the feeling they like each other."

Tyler bites her lip. "What do you think about that? Is your friend and your brother a recipe for disaster?"

I shrug. "Truthfully, I don't hate the idea. Maybe she would be good for him. I wouldn't be sad if that turned into something."

"Holy crap, what is that?" I hear Derek's voice boom out from behind us, breaking our stride.

Tyler and I stop in our tracks to get a better look at the obstruction fifty feet in front of us.

I turn my head to the side, as though to get a better look. "Is that... a sea turtle?" I ask, as the rest of the group makes their way up to join Tyler and I.

The turtle, who doesn't seem to mind at all that she has gathered quite an audience, is laying in the sand, quickly kicking her arms and legs back and forth creating a dust storm all around her.

Just then, a man wearing a white polo shirt, bearing the hotel's logo on it, makes his way towards us. "Hi." I greet him as he approaches us. "What is that turtle doing?" I ask, hopeful that he can speak English.

The employee looks at her and then back at us, almost as though this is something he sees every day. "That's a mama sea turtle." He explains. "She's digging a nest so she can lay eggs."

"Oh! That's amazing." Tyler says, pulling her phone from her pocket to take a photo.

The employee raises his hand. "You can watch and you can take photos, but do not use flash or any bright lights. Also, don't approach her. You might scare her and make her run back to the ocean before her eggs are laid. Sea turtles are endangered and must be protected."

Tyler nods and checks her phone to make sure the flash is off before taking a photo. I check my phone as well before following suit.

Just then, another group of tourists approach the nesting

mother and the employee makes his way over to them to repeat his instructions. We stand back and watch in awe for several minutes until the crowd grows.

I turn to Derek. "Well, I guess we should move on and give someone else a chance to witness this." I say with a sigh. "That was probably the coolest thing I've ever seen in my life. This trip has been such a dream." I add.

Derek pulls my hand towards his lips and lightly kisses my knuckles. "Yeah it has. I love you. I can't wait to see how much better it gets from here."

* * *

"Well, you wanna grab some lunch?" I ask Derek, turning my head towards him in our covered poolside bungalow. "Derek?" I frown at his lack of a response until I hear just the tiniest snore escape his mouth.

Lightly, I elbow him. He shakes his head and turns to look at me sheepishly. "Did you say something?"

I laugh. "Yes, sleeping beauty. I was wondering if you want to go grab some lunch."

"Sure, whatever you want to do." He says, with a long stretch over his head. "Have you heard from your mom lately?"

I nod. "I texted her just a little bit ago and checked in. She told me she and Juliet are just fine and to enjoy our day. I bet they are napping away in her room, watching Bluey on her tablet."

Derek and I make our way into the resort, past the ice cream parlor, on the way towards the sushi restaurant. Suddenly, Derek laughs. "Check this out." He says, grabbing my elbow and motioning his head towards the window of the shop. I peek inside and immediately see what he's talking about. There on the leather sofa sits my spoiled daughter, wearing her swim cover and a pair of hot pink sunglasses while eating a giant ice cream cone.

I laugh at the sight of my toddler and her chocolate ice cream beard. "Well, that's freaking adorable." I say. "I better go say hi."

"I'm going to grab us a couple of coffees and I'll meet you back over there." He says, motioning towards the coffee shop next door.

I nod and watch him make his way towards the cafe before I turn to go visit my daughter. I make my way around the corner and stick my head into the room, expecting to find my mother sitting nearby. Instead, I find Bryan.

"Ope. There's Mommy. We've been busted." Bryan says with a laugh as I make my way towards them.

I shake my head and take a seat next to Juliet, kissing the top of her head. "Hi, baby. Are you having fun with Uncle Bryan?"

"Mmmmhmmm. I got ice cream!" Juliet responds proudly, holding the cone up to show me.

"I see that. It looks yummy." I say, before turning to Bryan. "Where's mom? If I knew she needed a break, I would have come to get her."

Bryan shakes his head. "I kidnapped her and forced mom to rest for a little bit. I got bored with sitting by the pool."

I furrow my brows and lower my voice. "You aren't using your niece to pick up girls, are you?"

Bryan chuckles. "Who do you think I am? I have no problem getting women. I don't need to use a two-year-old to help me."

"I'm sure." I say with a laugh. "Well, want me to take her for a while? I haven't seen her since breakfast this morning and that's only because I tracked mom down."

Bryan waves me off. "Nope, go enjoy your last day as a single woman. We are going to finish up here and then I have strict orders to take her back to mom for her afternoon nap. Do you need help with anything for tomorrow?"

I shake my head. "No, the resort has taken care of everything for us. Today is just a day to relax and hang out."

Bryan nods, looking down at the ground.

"Looks like you inherited mom's inability to relax on vacation." I say with a laugh.

"Absolutely I have." He agrees. "Even when I've traveled in the past, I've always been more of an adventurer than a vacationer."

"I never realized there's a difference before." I say, as Derek walks up next to me and hands me an iced coffee.

"Oh, there definitely is." Derek agrees. "Vacationers like to sit and relax by the pool all day, for days in a row. Adventurers can only do that for maybe one day before they are itching to explore."

"I only made it half a day before I got bored." Bryan admits. "But I probably won't go wandering around Mexico since we have an event tomorrow. I'd hate to miss your wedding because I'm locked in a Mexican prison."

"Thanks for taking one for the team." I say with a laugh. "Maybe Madison is free." I add, wiggling my eyebrows at him.

Bryan's face turns a bright shade of red. "Welp, Juliet. Time to go," He says, turning back towards his niece. Carefully, he picks up the ice cream covered toddler.

"Was it something I said?" I tease.

"Bye, Avery. Go enjoy your day and we will see you at dinner." Bryan says, as he makes his way towards the door. "Tell Mommy, bye." He instructs Juliet.

"Bye sissy. See you at dinner." I call out, waving to Juliet as they leave the shop.

I turn to Derek as they disappear. "Did I take it too far?"

Derek chuckles. "Nah, but I think you might be onto something."

* * *

"Have you heard anything from your parents lately?" I ask, turning to Derek.

Everyone in our crew had agreed that we would meet for dinner tonight. Well, everyone but Robert and Joyce. Instead, they simply said that they would "Play it by ear and maybe catch up with us later."

Derek shakes his head. "No, not since breakfast." He says with a concerned look on his face. Just as he pulls his phone from his pocket to check in with them, I watch the missing couple breeze on into the restaurant.

"So sorry we're late." Joyce says, removing the giant floppy beach hat from her head. "We got so busy today we just lost track of time."

"Oh! That's fine." I say, waving her off. "What did you guys do today? Anything fun?"

Robert settles into his seat and sighs heavily. "What didn't we do? We ate breakfast and then immediately headed out on an excursion. We went on a jungle tour on an ATV, then we rode a zip line and stopped to swim at the Cenotes. After that,

239

we had lunch and did some shopping."

My eyes widen, looking back and forth between the two of them. "You two went zip lining?"

"Oh, that's nothing." Joyce says, waving me off. "I wanted to go parasailing too, but it was all sold out." She adds with a frown.

"Derek, you didn't tell me your parents were so fearless." I say, turning to him. "I thought our day of laying by the pool and playing in the gulf was exciting."

Bryan shakes his head. "And here I was afraid to go exploring around Mexico."

Robert shrugs. "You just have to get a good cab driver and tip him well to make sure he comes back for you. It's nothing."

I shake my head. "Now, I really want to be Joyce when I grow up."

Chapter 27

A knock at the door on Saturday morning awakens both Derek and me from our slumber. I squint my eyes and stare at the door, trying to will whoever it is to go away, before realizing they won't. Because it's our wedding day, and we overslept.

The knock at the door begins again, this time with more force. I quickly throw on my robe and gently shake Derek awake. Then, I rush towards the door to see who is waiting on the other side. I fling it open and find myself face to face with Tyler, Sierra, and Madison.

"It's about time you answer. I thought we were going to have to get the staff to break in for us." Madison shakes her head.

Without a pause, the three women make their way into the room with their dresses in hand and two rolling suitcases behind them.

"Oh no. He's gotta get out of here." Tyler says, pointing to Derek, who is half awake and still laying in my bed.

He scrambles to sit up in bed, pulling the comforter tight across his naked lap. "Good morning to you too, Tyler." He grumbles nervously.

"You two weren't supposed to see each other on your wedding day." Sierra chimes in shaking her head. "It's bad luck."

"And you definitely weren't supposed to be sleeping naked

next to each other on the morning of your wedding," Madison adds.

I groan in response. "You all know that I am the least superstitious person in the world." I look over at Derek. "If our marriage fails, it's because one of us failed, not because we saw each other today before getting married. Besides, I'm in paradise. I will not miss a chance for a night here with the love of my life." I say with a shrug before plopping down next to him on the bed, hugging my robe tightly against my body.

I look at Derek for a nod of agreement, but instead, he pipes up nervously. "Any chance you guys could leave so I can put some pants on?"

"Fine." Tyler huffs. "But hurry, please. We have a lot to do to get ready."

"Can you go get me a coffee?" I ask the girls. "By the time you get back, I'll be ready for hair and makeup. I promise."

My wedding party groans in annoyance, but shuffles back out of the room to make their way towards the cafe. Once the coast is clear, Derek makes his move from his spot on the bed and begins to get dressed. I watch intently, studying every muscle on his body until he catches me.

Derek chuckles. "Ma'am, shouldn't you be getting in the shower or something?"

I shake my head. "No, I'm fine here watching this show. It's my favorite."

He grins mischievously and makes his way towards me. Before I know what's happening, he wraps his arms around my waist and pulls me close. His lips crash into mine and for a few seconds, he and I get lost in one another's embrace. Eventually, he pulls his head away and rests his head against my forehead. "You better stop looking at me like that. Otherwise, you are going to have three angry bridesmaids when they come back in a few minutes and find me on top of you."

I bite my lip and smirk back at him. "That sounds like a challenge." I say, as I slide my hands under the back of his shirt.

Derek laughs and leans in to kiss me again when the knock on the door returns.

"Busted." I mutter into his open mouth. "Just a second!" I call out to the bridal party in the hallway.

Quickly, he leans to kiss me once more and then pulls back from me. "Save it for the honeymoon, you horn dog." He says with a laugh, before softening his face towards me. "I'll see you in a little bit, okay? Have fun getting ready with your girls. I can't wait to see you as my wife. I love you."

"I love you, too." I repeat as the knock on the door returns. "Sorry! On my way!"

I quickly make my way towards the door, with Derek on my heels. I fling the door open and find a frowning Tyler standing in the doorway waiting for me with two iced coffees in hand.

"Out." she says to Derek, motioning her head behind her.

Derek, trying to contain his smile, lowers his gaze to the ground in front of him and exits the room quickly.

Sierra shakes her head at me. "Hussy." She says in a teasing tone.

"Alright girls." Tyler says with a shake of her head as she hands me my coffee. "We have some work to do."

* * *

Sierra is just putting the finishing touches on my lipstick when

Tyler's phone alarm goes off, signaling that it's time to head downstairs. Mom and Juliet have since joined in on the fun. Juliet is sitting happily on the bed, in her white flower girl dress, eating a package of fruit snacks.

"Okay, one more behind-the-scenes photo and then I promise I'm ready." I respond, checking myself over in the mirror one last time and then attaching my phone to my ring light stand.

"I can't believe you brought your ring light to Mexico." Sierra says with a laugh.

"Look at you, and your suitcase full of makeup." I point out. "I'm not the only ridiculous one."

"Hey, did you want free wedding hair and makeup?" She raises a brow at me, teasingly. "Then you gotta deal with all this." She says, pointing towards her arsenal.

"I'm not complaining." Tyler says, looking in the mirror. "I haven't looked this good since my own wedding." She checks the time again. "Okay, I am going to start complaining if we don't get a move on, though."

The girls gather around me, wearing their blush pink brides-maids' dresses, while I'm in my lace mermaid cut gown. We snap a few photos of our group. Then we get one photo of our matching sea turtle ankle bracelets I found in the gift shop yesterday morning. I felt as though they were the perfect touch after our turtle encounter.

"Okay. I think I'm ready." I say with a grin. "Let's do this."

One by one, we take turns dropping our phones into a leather bag that Tyler brought for the occasion. Once they are secured, she turns to hand them to Sierra to hold during the ceremony.

Madison turns to Tyler with a grin. "Tyler, you really have thought of everything for this wedding. Maybe if I ever get married again, I'll have you coordinate mine, too."

Tyler quickly shakes her head. "You couldn't pay me a million dollars to do this again." She says with a laugh before turning to me. "Avery, I love you and for you I'd do anything, but trying to organize your wedding was almost more stressful than planning my own."

I frown. "Oh, Tyler. I tried to make it as easy on you as possible. I mean, we let the hotel handle all the major details."

"And you did a great job. I have just been so worried that I would forget something important, and ruin your big day. If I ruined my own wedding, I could blame myself and get over it. If I messed up yours, I'd carry that guilt until the day I die." She confesses.

I shake my head. "Nothing could have ruined today. All that matters is that in just a little bit I'll be married to the love of my life and my favorite people are here to witness it. Everything else is just details."

We enter the lobby, with the girls walking in front of me to shield me in case we run into Derek. Suddenly, Mom falls in line next to me, squeezing my hand.

I turn to look at her with a soft smile as I see the tears brimming in her eyes. "You okay?" I ask.

"You just look so beautiful." She replies, just above a whisper, before turning to hug me. "I'm so proud of you, kid. You worked hard, and you have created a life for yourself better than I ever could have dreamed of for you. Both you and your brother have."

I turn towards her and squeeze her hands. "Do you know why we could do it, Mom? Because of you. You took care of us and loved us fiercely. You taught us to be resilient. Neither of our lives would have been possible if not for you building a firm foundation. You did exactly what you could and gave us exactly what we needed. Thank you for everything you do for us."

Mom blinks back her tears. "Oh Avery, I love you and I'm so proud of you. Okay, I have to go find my seat. I can't be a blubbering mess until you start down that aisle." She pulls me into a tight hug. "I'll see you soon, baby girl."

Just then, Marisol, the hotel wedding coordinator, approaches us with a bright, excited smile on her face. "Everyone ready?" She says.

We nod in unison, and Marisol leads us out the side of the hotel. We step into a small waiting area hidden behind a large white divider to protect me from being seen by my groom.

Bryan meets us as we line up. He hugs Juliet and then steps towards me to get into position. He quickly wraps his free arm around my shoulder and pulls me close to him.

"Hi Sis. You look beautiful." He says with a smile. "Are you ready for this? If not, I can create a diversion and get you out of here." He jokes.

I raise a brow. "I thought you liked Derek?"

"I do. I think he's perfect for you. But I want you to know you always have the option to run if needed." He says with a soft chuckle. "You always have options."

"Thankfully, I don't see myself needing a place to run. Not this time."

"Good. I'm glad to hear that. You deserve to be happy, and I'm glad I could be here to see it happen."

I nod and look down at our bare feet in the sand before looking back at him. "Thank you for being here to give me away." I say with a smile. "And thank you for always being ready to pick up the slack for our dad. I would have never made it without you. Neither would Mom. I'm glad we are finally getting to spend more time together."

He smiles down at me. "Anything for you, kiddo. Besides, not too much longer and I'll be living back in Fawn Creek." He reminds me. "You'll be so sick of me hanging around all the time, you'll be wishing I was back in Texas."

"Honestly, I doubt that. I bet other people in Fawn Creek will be happy to have you around, too." I add with a wink as I let my eyes motion towards Madison.

Bryan's face turns red again just as Marisol turns back towards us and makes her announcement that it's time to begin.

One by one, our wedding party makes their way down the short path towards Derek. Then, it's mine and Bryan's turn.

We begin our stride down the aisle and I feel Bryan's hand tighten over mine. Slowly, I turn my head to look at him, only to see one single tear running down his cheek. Our eyes meet, just as the tear drops from his cheek, landing on his shoulder.

"You okay over there, tough guy?" I whisper, teasing him.

"Allergies." He mumbles, without breaking his stride.

Just then, I look up and see Derek looking back at me. Even though I was the one to pick out his pale blue tux, and I've seen him in it more than once, my heart feels like it could explode. I want nothing more than to run the rest of the way down the aisle and throw myself into his arms. But, somehow I resist.

As we reach Derek, Bryan unravels his arm from mine, and I place my hands into Derek's.

"Hi." I whisper with a smile, only now seeing a line of tears brimming in his eyes.

"Hi." He repeats. "My gosh, you're beautiful." He says with a smile. "I just can't believe you're mine."

247

"Forever and ever." I promise.

Chapter 28

I'm upstairs in Juliet's room, working on putting away laundry from our trip, when I hear Derek's voice call for me from downstairs. "Hey, Avery! Can you come down here for a second?"

"Be right there!" I reply, scooping Juliet into my arms and making my way downstairs. "What's up?"

"Come outside for a second. I got you a little something." He says, motioning towards the front door.

"A gift?" I ask, but before he can answer, I'm on the porch, seeing my present parked at the curb in front of our house.

"Ta Da!" Derek shouts proudly, throwing his arms open to show me the janky travel trailer parked in front of our house.

I attempt to feign enthusiasm. "You bought me camper... " I finally state, with a raised brow. "Is that Andrew's old camper?"

"It is." He says with a nod, proudly.

"Oh. Well, thank you." I respond, trying by best to sound polite. "I've never been camping before. But I suppose we could try it out."

He shakes his head before wrapping his arms around me, and pulling my body in close to his. "Avery, I appreciate you trying to be polite, but I promise I know you better than it. This camper is not for camping."

I let out a giant sigh of relief. "Oh, thank goodness." I say, before I can stop myself. "But what is it for, exactly?" I ask, raising a brow.

He laughs out loud and shakes his head. "I was actually thinking you could use it as a mobile boutique."

I cock my head to the side and look at him with what I'm sure is a confused expression. "A what now?"

"A mobile boutique." He says again. "Remember when your friends suggested that you start an online boutique and travel around to vendor events? We can fix up the camper and turn it into a mobile store. If you want to go do a vendor event, we can hook the camper up to the back of my truck and pull it to wherever you want to go. Then, you can just open the door and throw out a welcome mat, and people can come shop inside. You'll have shade, and air conditioning. Then when you're done, you just close up shop and drive it on home."

I consider Derek's plan. "Actually, this might be a great idea. I would love to have a place to allow people to come shop, where I don't have to sit all day long every day. And I could do this around Juliet's schedule."

Derek nods. "You wouldn't have the overhead of a building, causing you to be open all day. Then, you can be free to keep working at your job if you want to, or work around Juliet's schedule... and maybe the schedules of any other kids we add to the mix." He adds with a wink.

I feel my face blush when Derek mentions adding more kids to our family. Derek has been such an incredible father figure to Juliet since we started dating. I honestly can't wait to see him as a father from the very beginning.

"Come check it out." He says, motioning towards the trailer.

I follow his lead, with a toddler and dog in tow. "It's kinda.... brown." I say, inspecting the old tin exterior that looks to have been taken apart and pieced back together over the years.

"That's all cosmetic." He assures me. "It's solid and there are no leaks. We can paint it whatever color you want, and add some signs and some decorations. I'm sure you could make this thing look really cool."

"Is there somewhere I could park it to sell things other than during vendor events?" I ask. "Fawn Creek hosts lots of festivals, but that still leaves plenty of months when I'll need to make sales. Some people will be happy to shop online but the locals will probably want to shop in person."

"I was actually thinking we could put it in the backyard. We could add some garden pavers leading up to it for a walkway. Then, when you want to have a sale, you can advertise and throw open the gate for customers." He suggests. "Plus, when there isn't a festival happening in Fawn Creek, there may be one in a surrounding town. I think you could stay pretty busy if you'd like to."

I turn to Derek, and can't help the excitement building through my body. "When can we get started?"

Epilogue

It's Mayfest weekend and the first time I've taken my mobile boutique out for a spin. Derek just unhitched the trailer and I'm busy getting everything set up while he parks the truck.

The last few months have been nothing short of busy as we've worked away on my business. Derek and I, with Andrew's help, have worked countless hours whipping the dated brown camper into shape. We stripped the interior by removing the old furniture and appliances. In place of those, we added shelving, clothing racks, and skinny display tables. We painted the exterior white with black trim. Under the window, we even added a removable window box full of succulents.

Inside, every surface is covered in new inventory; clothing, jewelry, purses and home decor. Some that I purchased wholesale, some vintage pieces and some I have learned to make on my own. Turns out, my Christmas crafting gifts really have paid off. While I officially launched my online store months ago, I'm excited to allow people to shop in person.

"Ready for opening day?" Tyler asks, peering around the side of the camper while she wheels Molly's stroller around to the front. Molly, who is just a few months shy of her first birthday, claps excitedly.

"I guess so. Who knew opening a business could be so

stressful?" I joke.

"Oof. Not me." Tyler declares. "This thing is so freaking cute. I can't get it over it. It's hard to believe it used to be that ugly old thing my husband drug to town."

"Thanks to our husbands, it has a whole new lease on life." I agree. "It's so homey and cute. I'm obsessed with it."

"You should be. You worked really hard, and it's paid off." Tyler agrees, as I throw a welcome mat outside the new metal steps.

Just as I'm about to switch on the open sign, I spot Derek walking towards me across the park. "Wait." He calls out. "I need to get some video of you opening for business for the very first time." He smirks. "Everything is content, after all." He reminds me, as he takes my phone and gets in position to record.

I shake my head, although I have to admit, I'm grateful for this man and his constant support of my dreams. When he's ready, I make a show of lighting up the neon Open sign and proclaiming that Prairie Chic Boutique is officially open for business.

Derek wraps me in a hug and holds me close. "I'm so proud of you, baby. I can't wait to see where this takes you."

"I can't wait to see what's next for all of us." I agree.

Bonus Chapter

This was the scene that changed everything for me. It didn't make it into the final book, but I thought about it often. Here, Avery finally sees herself clearly and makes the choice to leave. I hope you enjoy this extra look at her journey.

Mom pulls me into a tight hug, the best she can anyway around my growing belly. "I'm so glad you came to see me today." She whispers into the back of my head while smoothing out my hair. "I've missed you."

"I miss you too. And all of Fawn Creek. I never realized how noisy it is in Owen with all the sirens and traffic," I admit. "Honestly, I miss the calm and quiet that is this little town. And believe it or not, I even miss randomly running into people I know at the Dollar Store. Life is so much different in the city. I can't believe how much I took for granted."

Mom raises a brow and seizes the opportunity in front of her. "You know. There's a house for rent just two blocks from here. Right down the street from Tyler's Grandma Hazel. It's small, but it would be just enough room for a family that's getting started."

I smile, but just on one side of my face. "Mom, I'd love

nothing more than to move back to town," I confess. "I just don't know if I can convince Cory to go along with it. He's pretty hell bent on not living here."

"Maybe you should remind him that both of Juliet's grandma's live here in town. That means you'll have two eager babysitters at your disposal at all times. And speaking from experience, you'll be thankful to have us once the baby gets here."

"It's worth a shot, I suppose."

Within minutes, I find myself in front of a little white craftsman style house, with a beautifully manicured lawn. I put the car in park and pull out my phone to take a photo of the number on the FOR RENT sign. What I don't expect is for the owner to walk outside and catch me in the act.

"You wanna look around?" he asks, "I've got time."

I pause and glance towards the house. It's a tiny place, and life would be quite cramped, but it would do for now. Besides, mom's right, we are going to want our family close by when our baby girl gets here. "Why not?" I say, unbuckling my seat belt and following the old man towards the property.

I take my time walking through the house making note of things that Cory might like. If I'm going to convince him to move here, I need all of the help I can get. While he may not want to live in my hometown, perhaps a garage and a fenced in yard will sway him a bit. I'm elated. This house is exactly what we need.

All I can think of is cuddling our sweet baby on the front porch swing of this house, when my phone rings.

It's Cory.

"Hey," I answer, "you won't believe what I just found."

"Where the hell are you?" He interrupts, his voice dripping

with anger.

"Oh, I was just at my mom's and...."

He cuts me off, "Stop lying to me, Avery."

"I'm not lying!" I argue. "Mom told me about this..."

"You know what? I'm not doing this with you right now. Come home now or don't come home at all."

This is the first time in my life I've ever been afraid to go home.

* * *

With a deep breath, I slowly step into the apartment, bracing for the worst. Cory is sitting on the sofa waiting for me, with a beer in his hand. I pause in the entryway, and wait for him to speak first.

"Avery, what the hell is wrong with you?" He mumbles with slurred words.

My eyes shift to the table by the couch, and count four bottles sitting next to him. Has he drunk all of those since I left Fawn Creek? Or did he get started sooner?

"I asked you a question." He commands, this time raising his voice when I don't answer. "Why do you keep screwing up what we have?"

I furrow my brows. "Cory, I'm confused. I didn't do anything wrong."

He stands from the sofa and moves towards me, still clutching his beer in his hand. "Oh really. You were just at some random house in Fawn Creek when you were supposed to be visiting your mom? Don't act like you were at your mom's house. I put a tracker on your car and I saw where you were. Who were you screwing, Avery? Is it the cop?"

My stomach turns. "You were tracking me?"

"Of course I was tracking you. Obviously you can't be trusted. That's who it was, isn't it? I knew it."

I shake my head. "No, I wasn't screwing anyone. And especially not Derek. Derek and I are just friends." I search Cory's eyes with my own, trying with everything I can to deescalate the situation. "When I was at my mom's, she told me about a rental house a couple of blocks away from her. I drove by to look at it. When I stopped to get the number, the owner came out to meet me. It was a sweet old couple, and they gave me a quick tour. That's all."

His face reddens, and the vein in his forehead pokes out just a little. "Why in the hell are you looking at houses, Avery? Do you think you're just going to pack up and leave?" He clinches his fist tightly, and I watch his hand.

Cory's never gotten physical with me before, but the mix of anger and alcohol is a combination I don't want to test.

He points a finger at me, inches from my nose. "You better think twice about that one. If you leave, I'll make sure you never see that baby again," he points to my stomach. "She won't even know who you are. My mom has more money than you could ever dream of, and she will make sure I win full custody."

He steps back on one foot and I take the opportunity to try to move away from him. I just want to get away, to breathe without feeling my chest cave in.

As soon as I side step him, he lunges forward to stop me. Except, it doesn't stop me at all. He grabs my shoulder and jerks me towards him, causing me to lose my footing. I fall backwards and my head hits a sharp edge on the trim around the living room door. I moan out in pain, just as someone beats on the door from the other side.

257

"Owen Police Department. Open the door!" the voice commands.

Cory's eyes widen, and so do mine.

"Did you call the police?"

I shake my head. "No. How could I have called the police?" I ask. "I've been standing here being yelled at by you." Quickly, I turn and open the door to find two officers waiting on the other side.

As I make eye contact with the officers, I feel a warm sensation on the back of my head. I reach behind me and try to determine whats causing this feeling. Slowly, I bring my hand back into view, and immediately find it covered in blood. My heart races and I clutch my belly...

That is when the world goes dark.

* * *

Knock, knock.

The sound of knuckles connecting to the wooden door frame causes me to stir. I open my eyes and look towards the hall expecting to see Tyler or my mom, but instead, it's Derek.

"Shit. I'm sorry. I didn't mean to wake you." He says, moving towards the windowsill to deposit the vase of flowers he brought me. "I brought you some flowers and I just wanted to check on you. How do you feel?"

"My head hurts," I confess. "Otherwise I'm okay. Just shaken up. It wasn't a deep cut, they just had to glue it shut."

"So, you're hurting? Do you need me to get the nurse?" He asks, turning towards the hallway ready to put himself into motion at my command.

I shake my head, gently. "No, it's okay. They were in not too long ago to give me some Tylenol. It just hasn't kicked in yet, I guess. How did you know I'm here?"

"I know people," He shrugs, before moving towards me. "What the hell happened?"

I take a deep breath and settle into the hospital bed. "We got into an argument and he accidentally pushed me into the door frame. I cut my head on the trim, and seeing my own blood made me faint. EMS made me come in to get checked out. I'm just waiting for the doctor to release me now."

Derek nods. "They arrested him. He won't be out til Monday at the earliest."

I nod, unsure how to respond. All of this is too much at one time.

"Has he hit you before?"

I shake my head. "No. We do argue a lot, but it's never gotten physical."

"What was he mad about?"

I look down at my hands, resting on my pregnant belly. "I had gone to Fawn Creek tonight to visit my mom and while I was there I went to see about a rental house. Apparently, Cory had a tracker on me so when he saw that I wasn't at my moms he thought..."

Derek furrows his brows. "Thought what?"

"I... I don't know." I answer. "I guess he thought I was cheating on him." I throw my hands in the air. "I don't get it. I have never given him a reason to think I'm going to cheat on him." I say rubbing my stomach. "I'm not sure why he thinks that anyone would want me like this."

Derek starts to open his mouth and then pauses, as though

he is rethinking what he is going to say. "Avery, you could do better. There's no reason for him not to trust you, and definitely no reason for him to be controlling your every move."

He pauses for me to respond, but I have nothing to say. I have thought about this over and over for the last few months. I thought this was merely him being protective over me and the baby. I was sure it would get better in time, but honestly it's only gotten worse.

Derek frowns. "Avery, putting up with shit like this isn't like you. But honestly, I'm not sure anything about you is the same anymore. Not since he came along." He adds. "What happened to the Avery I used to know? The one that was independent and strong and stubborn as hell. I miss her."

I stare down at my hands. "I... I don't know, Derek. It started out so good. He was so good to me and he promised to take care of me and I thought that maybe I had finally found the one." I pause. "Then, we found out I was pregnant. Suddenly everything changed and he has something to say about everything I do and everything I wear and everyone I speak to."

"He's controlling you." Derek says with a frown. "Avery, he has taken away so much of who you are and squashed it down so that he could lord over you." Derek takes a seat on the side of the hospital bed. "You need to be with someone that will love you for who you are, not for who they can mold you into. This guy is not the answer."

I look down at my belly again and gently run my hand across it. I'm just about to speak when Tyler steps into the room. She and Derek look at one another briefly before she glides over to the other side of the hospital bed. At first she acts as though she's going to hug me, but then she steps back, almost as through she's afraid of hurting me.

"I'm not glass." I smile softly.

"It's all the wires." She says, motioning to the monitors that I'm hooked up to. She opts to squeeze my hand instead. "Are you okay? What did the doctor say?" She asks, eyes darting between Derek and myself.

"I'm okay," I assure her. "The nurses say the baby is fine. When the doctor gets here, they will release me."

"Thank God. I was scared to death." Tyler sighs with relief, as Derek stands from his seat on the side of my bed.

"Hey. I'm going to get out of here and let you two talk," he says. "Call me in you need me. I mean it."

"I will. Thank you for coming and for the flowers."

Tyler pauses to watch Derek leave before turning back towards me. "You're not going back there are you?" She asks with a raised brow.

The silence of the room is deafening, while I try to formulate a response.

"Avery." Tyler says sternly, almost as a warning.

I push myself up on the bed, to sit up a little straighter. Her eyes burn through me waiting for my response. I can't help but tear up. "I don't want to, but what about the baby?" I ask. "If he and I were just dating, leaving would be so easy. I probably would have done it a long time ago. But this," I say rubbing my belly again, "makes it so freaking complicated."

Tyler's face softens as she reaches over and gently grabs my hand. "Oh Avery. Yes, the baby absolutely does make things more complicated," she agrees, "but it's not impossible. If anyone is strong enough to handle this, it's you. You can't go back and take the risk of this happening again, or something worse happening next time."

"What about the baby? Cory will fight me for custody. What if he wins and I lose my baby?"

She shakes her head. "That's not going to happen. That guy is an idiot. No judge is going to look at his track record and take your baby from you."

"You really think so?"

She nods. "I know so. Honey, you and this baby are going to be just fine without him. I know you watched your mom raise you and Bryan on her own and you swore you would never put a kid through that kind of struggle."

I nod in agreement. "It's literally my biggest fear."

Tyler continues. "A baby is better off growing up with a single mom than with two parents that don't love each other. And that baby does not need to grow up thinking that it's normal for a man to mentally or physically abuse his wife."

Of course, Tyler is right though. I don't want to raise my baby in a home where her parents don't get along and where her mother is afraid to be strong and independent. I want her to be proud of me, for everything that I do. Even if that means I have to be less available than I would like to be.

"Avery," Tyler's voice breaks through my thoughts, "I am begging you, don't go back to him. If something happens to you or to that baby, I don't know what I'll do."

Those are the words I needed to hear. Forgot about me, what about the baby? What if he loses his patience with me again, and I lose her? I can't go back.

I let out a heavy breath and make my decision. "You're right. I'm not going to go back. I'll move in with my mom and make it work."

Tyler's eyes soften, and she squeezes my hand again. "That's my girl. You're brave, Avery. Stronger than you even know."

I smile through the tears and rub my belly gently. "I just want to do right by her. I want her to know she can be safe, loved, and proud of her mom."

Tyler leans back slightly, a small smile tugging at her lips. "She's going to know that, Avery. And she'll have the best mom in the world."

For the first time in what feels like forever, a sense of calm washes over me. I can do this. I will do this. Not for Cory, not for anyone else—but for me and for my baby.

I glance around the hospital room, at the monitors and the sterile walls, and then back at Tyler. "Thank you," I whisper. "For being here. For helping me see what I needed to see."

She nods, tears glinting in her eyes. "Always. Now let's get you home and start fresh."

I squeeze her hand one last time, feeling a spark of hope ignite in my chest. It's going to be hard, yes. But I finally know this: I'm not just surviving. I'm starting to live—on my terms, for my baby, and for me.

And that's exactly what I'm going to do.

About the Author

Michelle Lynn Ross is the author of humorous and heart-warming small-town romances set in Kansas, in the fictional town of Fawn Creek. When she's not writing, she enjoys traveling, reading, and spending time with her husband and three daughters.

You can connect with me on:

🌐 https://michellelynnross.com

f https://www.facebook.com/ThatsWhatShellSaid

🔗 https://www.instagram.com/michellelynnrosswrites

🔗 https://www.tiktok.com/@michellelynnrossauthor

Also by Michelle Lynn Ross

There's No Place Like Home

Book One in the Fawn Creek Series.

When Tyler Burris turned eighteen and left her hometown of Fawn Creek, Kansas, she insisted she would never be back for anything more than a short visit; and for ten years, she held true to that promise.

That is until her long-term boyfriend drops a bomb on their relationship, leaving her blindsided, as well as homeless. With no other choice, Tyler returns home to Fawn Creek with one goal in mind: to get her life back in order and to get back to the city as quickly as possible. Thanks to a pet snake, a displaced rooster, gossipy townsfolk and a run in with a grumpy neighbor, it seems that she would have no problem getting back out of town without looking back. That is, until she finds out that the grumpy neighbor isn't so bad after all... or is he?

There's No Place Like Home is a story about realizing your dreams, learning to not settle for less than you deserve, and a reminder that it's never too late to go back home.

Single In A Small Town

After a messy divorce, Madison King is determined to start fresh—new hair, new walls, new life. The only rule? Absolutely no more Bryan Thompson. But in Fawn Creek, where dating options are scarce and secrets don't stay hidden, resisting temptation might be the hardest rule she's ever tried to keep.